THE GUILD CODEX: WARPED / TWO

HELLBOUND GUILDS
& OTHER MISDIRECTIONS

ANNETTE MARIE
ROB JACOBSEN

dark owl
fantasy

Hellbound Guilds & Other Misdirections
The Guild Codex: Warped / Book Two
By Annette Marie & Rob Jacobsen

Dark Owl Fantasy Inc.
PO Box 88106, Rabbit Hill Post Office
Edmonton, AB, Canada T6R 0M5
www.darkowlfantasy.com

Cover Copyright © 2021 by Annette Ahner
Cover and Book Interior by Midnight Whimsy Designs
www.midnightwhimsydesigns.com

Editing by Elizabeth Darkley
arrowheadediting.wordpress.com

ISBN 978-1-988153-57-5

BOOKS IN THE GUILD CODEX

WARPED

Warping Minds & Other Misdemeanors
Hellbound Guilds & Other Misdirections
Rogue Ghosts & Other Miscreants

SPELLBOUND

Three Mages and a Margarita
Dark Arts and a Daiquiri
Two Witches and a Whiskey
Demon Magic and a Martini
The Alchemist and an Amaretto
Druid Vices and a Vodka
Lost Talismans and a Tequila
Damned Souls and a Sangria

DEMONIZED

Taming Demons for Beginners
Slaying Monsters for the Feeble
Hunting Fiends for the Ill-Equipped
Delivering Evil for Experts

UNVEILED

The One and Only Crystal Druid

MORE BOOKS BY ANNETTE MARIE

STEEL & STONE UNIVERSE

Steel & Stone Series

Chase the Dark
Bind the Soul
Yield the Night
Reap the Shadows
Unleash the Storm
Steel & Stone

Spell Weaver Trilogy

The Night Realm
The Shadow Weave
The Blood Curse

OTHER WORKS

Red Winter Trilogy

Red Winter
Dark Tempest
Immortal Fire

THE GUILD CODEX

CLASSES OF MAGIC

Spiritalis

Psychica

Arcana

Demonica

Elementaria

MYTHIC

A person with magical ability

MPD / MAGIPOL

The organization that regulates mythics and their activities

ROGUE

A mythic living in violation of MPD laws

HELLBOUND GUILDS
& OTHER MISDIRECTIONS

I

VINCENT PARK was my nemesis.

I don't say that lightly. I'd made the odd enemy in my twenty-two years on this planet, and as a foster kid, I'd encountered more than my fair share of supreme assholes—but I'd never had to cohabit a cubicle with any of them.

"Kit," Vincent said firmly.

His perfectly manicured mohawk of glossy black hair, fondness for sticky notes, and know-it-all attitude had sat three feet from me for eight hours every workday since I'd become an employee of the MPD. Today was no different.

"It stands for *Magicae Politiae Denuntiatores*," he'd corrected me after I'd jokingly called us fledgling Magic Police Department members on our very first day. "It's Latin."

That was the moment I knew I hated him.

"Kit," he repeated with more emphasis.

Well, that and the cargo shorts. Vincent wore cargo shorts every single day. That alone should tell you everything you need to know about him. A blizzard worthy of *The Day After Tomorrow* could hit and in would walk Vinny with his multi-pocketed shorts and frost-tipped leg hairs.

"It's the pockets," he'd told me when I'd asked. "Do you know how much stuff I can carry in these pockets?"

I'd shrugged. "About two half-legs' worth?"

"What do you have in your pockets, huh?" he'd demanded with more intensity than the topic merited.

"Lint, mostly."

"I could save your life with what I carry in my pockets."

That was how things operated with Vincent. He was always trying to one-up me in every little thing. Even pockets.

"*Kit!*" he half shouted, pulling me out of my reverie.

Swiveling on my cheap mesh-backed office chair, I found my cubicle mate standing three feet away. His warm taupe complexion was normally on the fair side, but at the moment, he seemed conspicuously pale.

I offered a polite smile. "Yes?"

He pointed wordlessly at his desk. More specifically, at his black computer mouse sitting neatly on a pad emblazoned with the MPD's severe and unimaginative logo—just like the organization itself.

I glanced at said mouse and repeated, "Yes?"

"There is a *spider*," he said slowly, as though I might not comprehend the words otherwise, "on my *mouse*."

"Oh yeah, I see that." I turned back to my dual monitors.

"Kit!"

"Is that a problem? I didn't take you for an arachnophobe."

"Arachnophobia is an *irrational* fear of spiders."

"Ah. And you don't think you're being irrational?"

"No."

I spun my chair back toward him, eyebrows raised. He wasn't wrong. Any product of natural selection would fear the enormous, eight-legged, yellowish-brown monstrosity with a ten-inch leg span straddling his computer mouse. It was, to be exact, a giant huntsman spider.

Vinny stood a long step back from his desk, glaring at me as though it were my fault his sixteen pockets weren't giving him the courage to move any closer.

Our eyes met, and I could practically read his whirring thoughts. He knew I was responsible. For weeks, he'd come back from lunch to find his desk in an impossible state—covered in strange substances, broken in half, shrunken to a fraction of its size, recolored like an inverted photo. And every time, he'd stubbornly sit in his chair and attempt to work, proving that my insubstantial Psychica "hallucinations" were harmless.

Not that they always were. Just last week, I'd practiced my new Funhouse warp on him, throwing his half of the cubicle into a rough facsimile of the mirror realm from *Dr. Strange*. He'd made it through almost three minutes of clumsy filing before getting so disoriented that the act of reaching for a refracted, upside-down stapler ended with his left leg stuck in a drawer.

Keeping one eye on the spider, he gave me a look dripping in derision, pulled his chair out, and dropped into it. As he reached for his keyboard, the giant huntsman twitched one leg. He flinched.

"Don't like spiders?" I asked conversationally.

He gritted his teeth. Not once in our mythical Jim Halpert/Dwight Schrute battle of wills had he asked me to drop a warp. It was a pride thing, and so far, he was winning.

4 ♦ MARIE & JACOBSEN

Today I would win the war.

"Nobody likes spiders, Kit," he replied, jerkily typing in his password. "Spiders are inherently unlikable creatures."

"Oh, I don't think that's true," I countered. "This one isn't poisonous or dangerous to humans in any way. And her name is Biscuit."

"You name your illusions?"

Technically speaking, my warps aren't illusions. If you took a video of one of my manifestations, nothing would show up because they don't exist in the physical world. They only exist in the minds of the people I target.

For example, when Captain Blythe had caught Vinny manically swatting at a swarm of flies buzzing around his head on our fifth day as cubicle mates, all she'd seen was a flailing recruit—at which point she'd loudly ordered me to stop interrupting my coworker's productivity. That's how Vinny learned I'd been tormenting him all week.

And so our war had begun, though relegated to lunch breaks so I didn't cut into his work. Funny enough, Blythe knew I was still using him for warping practice, but she'd never updated her orders.

Suppressing a gleeful Dr. Evil grin, I watched Vincent deliberately tab through a spreadsheet as though his mouse was an inefficient technological relic he'd never intended to use anyway.

My attention shifted as Lienna's head and shoulders appeared above my cubicle wall—and sweet Flying Spaghetti Monster, was she a sight to behold. Warmth lit her brown eyes, which always had a sarcastic roll chambered and ready to fire. Half a dozen bracelets clinked charmingly as she folded her arms on top of the flimsy wall, rings adorning her delicate fingers and beads hanging from her ponytail of thick raven hair.

"Hey boys," she greeted, then caught a glimpse of Vinny's new eight-legged decoration. "Wow, nice spider, Kit."

"Thanks."

Vinny's jaw flexed. He lifted his hand as though to grab his mouse and prove my warp didn't scare him. I tensed—but he dropped his hand back onto his keyboard.

Lienna stepped into our cubicle, her ponytail swinging as she leaned over Vincent's slim shoulder to get a better look at Biscuit. "That's a *really* good spider. So much detail. Have you been studying arachnids?"

I leaned back in my chair. "I've been visiting the pet store down the street. The owner's pretty cool."

Vincent's gaze darted from Lienna to me. "You know I know you can target more than one person at a time."

"Ready for this afternoon?" she asked as though Vinny hadn't spoken. "Your big exam is in an hour."

"His *retake*." Vincent hammered the tab key on his keyboard. "He failed his first exam."

"Second time's the charm," she told me encouragingly, again ignoring my cubicle mate. "You aced the written exam. Ninety-six percent is what I heard."

I grinned at her. "Did you look up my score?"

"Of course not. But Blythe may have mentioned it."

"I got ninety-eight percent," Vincent announced as though we would care.

I arched my eyebrows at Lienna. "Did she mention it in a 'I knew he was a smart, capable guy and that's why I offered him this job' way, or in a 'I'm surprised that dunce knows how to write his own name' way?"

"Ah. Um ..."

We both knew it was the latter, and I couldn't help but laugh. "I have a better idea what to expect with the exam this time, so—"

"Agent Shen!"

At that whipcrack of a voice, Lienna, Vinny, Biscuit, and I all snapped to attention.

A tall woman filled the opening of the cubicle, her presence assailing us in a rolling tide of stern dissatisfaction at the existence of lesser beings. Gentle waves of soft blond hair framed her lightly tanned face, probably for the sole purpose of luring the gullible public into thinking she might be of a soft, gentle, or blond disposition.

Captain Blythe casually shifted the ten-pound stack of folders on her arm as her laser stare burned a hole through Lienna's forehead.

"I need to speak with you in my office immediately." The blue beam of reckoning shifted to me. "Morris, I'll be waiting for your exam results later. Don't disappoint me again." Her attention switched to Vincent. "Park ... why is there a spider on your desk?"

Vincent went rigid as his gaze flashed to the eight-legged behemoth inches from his hand. He was well aware that Lienna was a frequent spectator and occasional accomplice to my illusory games, but he was also certain beyond the slightest, tiniest, most infinitesimal sliver of a doubt that I would never, *ever* mess with the captain.

Which could mean only one thing.

He and Lienna simultaneously realized that Biscuit was not a figment of anyone's imagination, and they lurched violently away. Lienna tripped over my feet, lost her balance, and sat heavily on my lap. Vinny shoved back so hard his chair tipped over. He fell into the cubicle wall, and with a loud snap, it broke free. He, the chair, the wall—and somehow, his keyboard— crashed to the floor.

Startled by all the movement and noise, Biscuit scuttled across Vinny's desk and hid behind his phone. Silence fell over the bullpen as every agent looked over at the ruckus.

My cheeks ached from the effort of suppressing a jubilant grin.

Blythe's hard stare bored into me. "What did I say about interfering with Park's work?"

I glanced at the big clock on the wall. "Lunch isn't over for another two minutes and twenty-six seconds. So, *technically* ..."

Her eyes sharpened in a way that made me brace for a telekinetic chokehold, but she merely growled, "No pets in the office, Morris."

"Yes, ma'am."

She snapped a glance at Lienna, still seated on my lap. Her lips thinned. "My office, Agent Shen."

Folders cradled in one arm, the captain swept away. Lienna sprang off my lap, shot me a glare, then rushed after Blythe.

I let my triumphant grin bloom. Could that have gone any more perfectly? Not only had I won, but I'd won *with witnesses*. Ultimate glory!

As the regular noise of the bullpen resumed, I pulled a plastic container the size of a small aquarium from under my desk. Cooing reassuringly, I coaxed Biscuit from her hiding spot and into her temporary home. She squashed herself into a corner, imitating Lienna's glare—but with four times the eyes. Could this sassy spidey do an octo-eye-roll *a la* Agent Shen too? Maybe a Kumonga joke would generate one.

"I can't believe that thing is real," Vinny muttered as he righted his chair.

"Wanna pet her? I don't think she bites. No promises, though."

He mouthed two words at me, one of which was four letters and not very polite. My, my.

I set Biscuit's container in the middle of my desk where she'd be in Vinny's line of sight while he repaired his cubicle wall, then sauntered off into the greater bullpen. Time for *my* lunch, which I'd delayed to babysit Biscuit while she'd made friends with Vinny's computer mouse.

The bullpen was the epicenter of everything interesting that happened in the Vancouver precinct. It contained two dozen cubicles and twice as many workstations, though only maybe sixty percent of them were claimed. A pair of glass doors at one end offered a glimpse of the lobby, but I headed in the opposite direction, ducking into the high-traffic hall that connected the rest of the main floor with the bullpen.

The nostril-abusing stench of microwaved fish wafted from the staff room, and I pulled up short. What briny asshole had flouted the cardinal rule of communal microwaving? As I hesitated in the doorway, debating whether to make a run to the coffee shop on the corner or hold my breath long enough to retrieve my lunch from the fridge, a familiar voice poked me in the ear from farther down the hall. I peered toward it.

Blythe and Lienna. They'd stopped to talk to an older male agent. Getting waylaid in the halls was standard around here, but the way Lienna was standing, a few steps behind Blythe with her shoulders drawn in and hands twisted together, was a lot less standard.

Concern blitzed through me. I flicked a glance at my surroundings, found no one looking my way, and with a quick thought, dropped an invisibility warp on every mind in my vicinity.

Vincent and Lienna, and even Blythe herself, were convinced I wouldn't mess with the cap's mind. I actually wasn't sure why they thought that. Did they assume my new job title had transformed me into a more honest and upstanding citizen overnight?

I mean, yeah, it had—fractionally.

As I headed toward the chatting trio, Blythe waved off the older agent and continued down the hall, Lienna following like a beautiful but uncharacteristically anxious shadow. The security cameras could still see me, but I wasn't worried about that; as long as I didn't *act* suspicious, security wouldn't even notice.

I trailed them to Blythe's office, debating the whole way whether I should back off. Whatever this was, it wasn't my business. It probably wasn't even anything important. Maybe Blythe wanted to propose a trade in a fantasy football league they were both secretly part of.

On second thought, Blythe involving herself in anything that used the word "fantasy" was absurd.

The captain strode into her office. Lienna hesitated in the hallway, unintentionally giving me a helpful two seconds to catch up.

I was going to stop there. Really, I was. I didn't want to deceive Lienna or hear something I'd regret. Honestly, I didn't intend to follow her any farther.

Except, as she hesitated with her face turned away from Blythe, her teeth caught her lower lip, biting down so hard the soft pink skin turned white. For that brief moment, she looked small, scared, and too young for the title and responsibilities she carried.

Then she drew in a steadying breath, pushed her shoulders back, and stepped into the office—and I stepped in right after her, unable to leave her to face Blythe alone.

Not that my presence would help since she didn't know I was there.

I scooted straight into the corner of the office. The first time I'd set foot in here, I'd been blown away by the shattering of my expectations. I'd one hundred percent anticipated towering stacks of folders piled to the ceiling, or a futuristic filing system that rotated in and out of the walls like something from an evil genius's lair. Or at the very least, a high-voltage power receptacle where she plugged herself in to charge her android batteries.

Her office had none of those things. It didn't even have a regular filing cabinet. There was a low bank of cupboards beneath the window behind her for storage, some framed achievements and certificates on the wall, and a single photograph on her desk showing three people: a somewhat younger Blythe, a woman who could be her mildly de-aged twin, and a little girl about five years old. Sister and niece, I assumed, though they could easily be three robot clones she kept in storage.

Lienna shut the door, and as she faced Blythe, doubt assaulted me. It would be excruciatingly awkward if either woman discovered my unwelcome invasion. I glanced at Lienna's collection of necklaces, topped by a cat's eye pendant that could block my psychic magic from her mind with a quick incantation. Yeah, I *really* should have thought this through before committing.

But then the captain spoke, and her somber words slapped all regrets out of my head.

"Agent Shen." She braced her elbows on her desk, her ever-present stack of folders beside her. "Your time at this precinct is over."

2

BLYTHE'S WORDS ECHOED strangely through the office. Or maybe that was the sharp disbelief reverberating inside my head.

Lienna? Leaving the precinct?

Unlike me, she didn't seem shocked. Shoulders stiff, she walked to the chair in front of Blythe's desk and sank into it. "What about your offer back in June?"

Blythe drummed her fingers on her folder stack. "The situation has changed. When I made that offer, the Vancouver precinct was critically understaffed. Now, the LA precinct requires additional manpower."

I inched out of my corner so I could see Lienna's expression. The LA precinct's interest in her didn't surprise me. Not only was she a superstar abjuration prodigy, but LA was her home turf. That was where we'd first met—when she'd tackled me to the floor at LAX before escorting me back to Vancouver.

"The LA precinct can recruit from anywhere in North America," Lienna replied quietly. "They don't need me."

"Whether they need you isn't my concern." Blythe thudded her fingernails into her folders as though wishing they were her enemy's eyeballs. "I'll be frank, Agent Shen. As much as I'd like to keep you on my team, I won't fight Deputy Captain Shen for a rookie agent, no matter how talented."

Wait a hot minute. Did she just say Deputy Captain *Shen*?

Lienna pressed her hands between her knees. I stared at the top of her bowed head, scarcely recognizing this meek, hunched-over version of the agent who just yesterday had threatened to turn my femurs into string cheese.

"I want to stay here," she murmured, not looking up to meet Blythe's gaze. "You offered me a permanent position, and—"

"And the deputy captain is offering you the same position in LA or your spot on the Rogue Response team back, whichever you prefer." Blythe turned to her computer and smacked her mouse like a game show buzzer to wake it up. "The LA precinct is larger and you'll have many opportunities to advance your career. You'll do well."

That was the nicest thing I'd ever heard Blythe say, but her dismissive tone still made me wish a thousand paper cuts upon her fingers from her perma-stack of folders.

I shifted closer to Lienna, hovering right beside her chair. If only my psychic powers extended to telepathy. *Fight back*, I'd be brainwaving at her. *Don't take this bullshit lying down.*

Her slumped shoulders slowly straightened. She raised her head, and her brown eyes glinted as she fixed them on the captain. "You offered me a position, and I accepted it. You might not want to fight over a rookie agent, but I won't be a rookie forever, and I'll be worth the fight."

Blythe studied the young woman in ominous silence. "Then prove it to me, Agent Shen. You get one more case, and if you bring it to a satisfactory close, I'll make sure you can stay."

Lienna's spine went ramrod straight. "What's the case?"

"The Grand Grimoire."

"They're under suspicion? For what crimes?"

"That's for you to figure out."

As far as I knew, that guild wasn't on our current shit list, but the Grand Grimoire's whole identity revolved around cavorting with bloodthirsty brutes, so who knew.

"It's the city's only Demonica guild," Blythe added, "and we've seen far too much demon-related chaos over the last few weeks. I expect you to ascertain how they're involved and deliver a solid case for disbandment. Anything less than that and you can book your flight to LA."

Lienna's mouth hung open slightly. She snapped it shut. "I'll begin an investigation, but I don't—"

"I can stall the deputy captain for a week at best. I suggest you get to work."

Fingers digging into her legs, Lienna sat rigidly for a long moment, then pushed to her feet. I backed away, triple-checking that my halluci-bomb was still in full effect. She headed for the door, and I followed on her heels, needing to slip out behind her.

Unfortunately, she opened the door just wide enough for her slender shoulders to fit through.

Silently cursing, I stuck my foot out as she closed the door. It bounced off my invisible shoe, jerking out of her hand. She paused, startled, and I squeezed past her, so close she might've felt the breeze of my passing. Hopefully, she'd assume it was the air conditioning.

In November. That was a thing people did, right? A little winter AC to keep chill?

She tugged the door shut. Her gaze slid along the hallway with a discomforting level of scrutiny, then she pulled her phone from her pocket. The time glowed on the screen.

1:22 p.m.

Panic shot through me. Why was I only remembering *now* that I had an exam in thirty-eight minutes—and it took a solid half-hour to drive to the exam site? In *good* traffic?

Spinning on my heels, I bolted down the hall, leaving an unaware Lienna in the dust.

WHEN I'D ACCEPTED this job from Captain Blythe, it'd seemed like a great deal; instead of going to jail for my underhanded work with KCQ, I got to become a fancy, magical super-cop!

Or so I'd thought.

As it turned out, recruits didn't just get thrown into the field to hunt down bad guys. You had to do a crapton of training, pass a written exam, and then pass a field exam before they let you out of the office for more than a coffee break.

In the meantime, you got to work as an analyst—which, I'd learned very quickly, was code for "paper pusher." I spent every non-training shift reading applications, completing forms, filing documents, and trying not to pass out from sheer, soul-sucking boredom. Spicing up my day at Vinny's expense was the only thing keeping me sane.

During the last five months, I'd discovered I am bizarrely adept at handling spreadsheets. Am I proud of this skill? Hell no. But after repeatedly categorizing guild fines by name, classification, dollar amount, date, and a dozen other variables, I'd become a spreadsheet *god*. Yee-freaking-haw.

And now, almost half a year later, only one thing stood between me and a future in which I never had to look at Overdue Fines Payment Schedule B again: the field exam.

With a slow breath, I bent forward to touch my toes, stretching my hamstrings until they ached. By some miracle, I'd made it to the exam site on time, but now that I wasn't testing a smart car's mettle in a Formula One speed run through mid-afternoon traffic, the nerves were setting in.

The field exam took place at an outdoor paintball arena near Jericho Beach. It was a popular training ground for combat mythics and would've fit right in on the set of *Children of Men* if every surface hadn't been coated in layers of colorful paint splats. Still, the arena was a confusing and slightly intimidating maze of small structures with empty windows and doorways, a two-story watchtower, and an assortment of barricades, barrels, and old cars scattered around as cover.

Off to my left was a raised viewing platform, complete with an awning for rainy days. Seated comfortably on plastic chairs with clipboards in hand were my three examiners. They were accompanied by a handful of other MPD folk who'd be participating in my exam.

Completing my stretches, I faced the first of three challenges, worth the fewest points.

"Mr. Morris," the lead examiner croaked. She was a frighteningly old woman who'd probably been running these exams since the days of Buster Keaton. "Are you ready to begin?"

I gave her a thumbs-up, and a moment later, a foghorn blared sharply. Launching into motion, I raced toward a simple wooden table piled with an assortment of combat paraphernalia. I grabbed the bulky protective vest off the top, pulled it on, and buckled it. The thick belt went around my hips.

Next, I picked up the pistol—not a real one, but a mythic version—dropped the empty magazine out of the bottom, then removed the tiny CO_2 canister. Grabbing a replacement, I screwed it in, then pushed a fresh magazine loaded with seven colorful paintballs into the handle. The gun went into the holster on my right hip and a pair of handcuffs clipped to their proper hook on my left.

I scooped up three wooden artifacts from the table, gave each a quick glance, and inserted them into the remaining available pockets of the vest.

With the table cleared, I took three rushing steps and planted my feet on an X spray-painted in the dirt. Facing a set of four bull's-eye targets thirty feet away, I pulled my paintball gun and fired, unloading the clip. All seven paintballs splattered the target's center, only two hitting the outer ring.

In real combat, those would be sleeping potions instead of paint. The Sandman is handier than Picasso when you're up against actual rogues. Or so I've heard.

Holstering my gun, I pulled the first wooden artifact from my belt, called out the incantation, and whipped it at the next target. It hit dead center and burst into a bright flash of light. Second artifact into the third target—it went off in a swirl of gold dust. The third artifact collided with the final target, triggering a puff of green sparkles.

The first had been a magical flashbang, while the other two had been holding spells to immobilize dangerous suspects. I got points for identifying which artifact was which, successfully activating the spell with its incantation, and actually hitting the target.

I was a psychic, not a sorcerer, but when it came to Arcana artifacts, that didn't matter. Anyone who knew the incantation could activate the spell, though only sorcerers could *make* the spells.

The foghorn bugled again, marking the end of Phase One. I let out a jittery breath. My time felt a bit faster than my first attempt, but the nerves made it hard to know for sure.

"Excellent work, Mr. Morris," the geriatric examiner rasped. "Please move to the second station."

My anxiety ratcheted up again as I strode away from the targets toward an empty patch of dirt near the watchtower. I stopped in the center and waited.

Agent Wolfe, the precinct's only terramage, jogged over. He was an athletic middle-aged guy with thick black hair that hung around his shoulders and bold, blocky features that made me wonder if his ancestors had inspired the Easter Island statues. He wore jeans and a long-sleeved shirt that wasn't nearly warm enough for the damp chill in the afternoon air.

By the way, when I said "athletic," I meant completely ripped and with more stamina than a triathlon champion. Mages had to be in tiptop shape so their energy-draining magic didn't wreck them when they used it.

I set my feet in a combat stance. Wolfe flashed me a toothy grin and matched my pose, his fists held loosely at his sides. In this violent game of make-believe, he was the suspect and I was the agent. All I had to do was get him in cuffs—using nothing but my bare hands.

The foghorn blared.

I rushed Wolfe. He dodged my charge, then kicked my knee. I pivoted with the strike, preventing it from doing serious damage. He grabbed for my gun—which would cost me huge points—and I slammed his arm down and away from my belt.

We exchanged a few quick blows, blocking each other's strikes, then he got under my guard and jabbed his knuckles into my sternum.

Wheezing, I stumbled back, but my protective vest had blunted it. Before he could get another hit in, I tackled him in the gut and we both went down. Rolling across the ground, I wrestled his right arm behind his back and shoved him facedown in the dirt.

He almost threw me off as I clipped the first cuff on his wrist, but I contorted one leg to pin his shoulder and hastily snapped the second cuff on him. The moment he was secured, I threw my hands up.

The foghorn blared. Phase Two complete.

Patting my belt, I found the keys to the handcuffs and unlocked them. Wolfe relaxed his arms as I climbed off him.

"Thought I had you at the end there." Pushing to his feet, he gave me a rueful grin. "Flexible much, Morris?"

"Yoga," I quipped, hooking the cuffs back onto my belt. "I believe that was the detainment pose."

Laughing, he sauntered off. "Good luck with the next round, kid. It's gonna be interesting."

Somehow, that didn't inspire confidence.

Breathing deep to oxygenate my muscles and settle the irritating butterflies in my gut, I faced the tower. In its shadow was another X painted on the ground. My starting point.

Time for the final, most difficult, and most important phase of the field exam. If it went anything like last time, three seasoned agents would kick my unprepared ass up and down the arena with every weapon at their disposal. Including magic.

3

TO BE CLEAR, the goal of this challenge wasn't to kick anyone's ass. It was for the examinee to make it from the starting point to the finish line at the other end of the paintball arena by any means necessary. I could fight, evade, or fly like Superman. All I had to do was traverse from point A to point B.

The ass kicking was just an unfortunate side effect of the agents whose sole job it was to stop me. A job they all took very seriously.

Technically, I could also pass this phase of the exam by incapacitating the agent trio, but I fully intended to go for the less ambitious route. Planting my feet on the X, I went over my plan once more. The first time I'd faced this challenge, I'd been a tad overconfident. I could make myself *invisible*, so really, how could anyone stop me from waltzing straight across the finish line?

As I'd learned, there were lots of ways.

My warp arsenal contains a few different tricks, and I've given each one its own spiffy superpower name. When I rearrange the furniture in a room or, say, slowly make the walls of a cubicle close in on my target, I call that my Redecorator power. Creature Feature is when I summon a three-headed salamander from behind a computer monitor or a noxious alien from the ceiling tiles above the urinal. Smaller herds of vermin, like the aforementioned cloud of flies, are called the Swarm.

My personal favorite, and generally the most useful, is Split Kit—where I make a phony version of myself while rendering my real body invisible and silent. Recently, I'd discovered that I could do this with other people as well, but only if I knew them well enough to replicate and erase their essence.

My powers might not be lethal—as Vincent *loved* to point out, when he wasn't fleeing a venomous space monster that had interrupted his bathroom break—but they could get me through this.

The foghorn blared, and I instantly Split Kit myself, creating two duplicates instead of one. As the fake pair waltzed forward, I hung back, scanning the maze of painted walls and barricades for my enemies, one of whom was clearly a telepath.

Once upon a midnight dreary, a grating male voice intoned inside my head, *while I pondered, weak and weary—*

"Really?" I groaned under my breath.

Over many a quaint and curious volume of forgotten lore—

Stifling a growl, I focused on my Split Kit warps and tried to ignore the familiar voice of Agent Tim. I didn't know his last name—or was that his last name? Everyone just called him Tim.

The poem—emphasis on "Poe"—he was telepathically reciting inside my head was purely to distract me. And damn it, his strategy was working.

While I nodded, nearly napping, suddenly there came a tapping. As of someone gently rapping, rapping at my chamber door.

"'Tis some visitor," I grumbled, hastening toward the shelter of a squat building, "tapping at my chamber door—only this and nothing more."

Tim's amusement tinged his mental voice. *Fancy meeting you here, Kit. Whatchya planning?*

Don't think about it, don't think about it, don't think about it— but if I stopped concentrating, my Split Kits would fall apart.

Oh, two fake Kits, huh? I'll pass that along. Tim gave a telepathic throat clearing. *Ah, distinctly I remember it was in the bleak December …*

Teeth gritted, I struggled to block out his recitation. He would've already alerted his two teammates about my Split Kit hallucinations, but just because they knew the Kits they could see were fake didn't mean they could locate the invisible me.

Had Blythe done this on purpose? Not only could telepaths organize their team's movements, but they could also defeat my greatest magical asset: the element of surprise. I could annoy and misdirect and blind them with all sorts of warps, but the moment they knew it wasn't real, my advantage drastically diminished.

Eagerly I wished the morrow; vainly I had sought to borrow—

Swearing, I raced along the side of the building, my Split Kits keeping pace with me from the center of the dusty "street" between structures.

A figure stepped into the open, fifteen yards ahead of me. Tall, thin, and with short, tightly curled black hair. I recognized Agent Clarice Vingeault, an aeromage who had the looks and general temperament of a kindergarten teacher … unless you were a rogue mythic, in which case you could expect to be engulfed in a literal tornado.

She braced her feet, bent her hands in a Dragon Ball Z-like position, and sent a gale-force blast screaming down the narrow street. It blew me over backward, and my butt thumped hard on the ground.

Crap! She must've guessed I was in the same vicinity as my fake Kits.

Vingeault swept her arms upward, and the wind swirled into a violent maelstrom, whipping dust into my face. I shielded my head with my arms, eyes stinging and watering, and struggled to hold my invisi-bomb.

Let my heart be still a moment and this mystery explore, Agent Tim boomed in my head. *'Tis the wind and nothing more!*

Cute, Tim. Very cute.

Losing my grip on my warp entirely, I shoved to my feet and leaped through the nearest window, out of Vingeault's magical line of fire. I landed in a roll on the paint-splattered floor and came up on my feet.

A flash of motion. I spun around.

My third opponent vaulted the windowsill after me in a flat-out sprint—Agent Daniyah Nader, a tomboyish combat sorcerer, her trademark baseball cap turned backward on her head.

She crashed into me at full tilt. I slammed into the wall, barely managing to shove her off me. Tim was still howling narrative stanzas in my head, but I attempted a warp anyway. Since I couldn't do anything she'd obviously recognize as a hallucination, I threw a vision of the ceiling collapsing at her.

Barely flinching, she pointed a thick silver wand at me and shouted an incantation I couldn't hear over Tim's telepathic caterwauling.

I dove for the floor, invisifying myself as I landed, and the blinding beam of light from her artifact shot over my head and hit the wall with a *pfffff* noise that sounded like it would've hurt a lot if it'd hit my torso instead. I scrambled toward the window, preferring to take my chances with Vingeault's wind.

Grinning, Nader pulled a glass orb from her belt and chucked it to the ground. It exploded in a spray of sparkly purple potion that splattered all over the walls—and me.

I leaped through the window, frantically trying to incorporate the potion into my invisibility so the others wouldn't see disembodied glitter splats running around the arena. My feet landed on the dirt pathway, and I almost skidded straight into Vingeault. As Nader appeared in the window behind me, I whirled in the only direction left to flee.

Agent Tim, that telepathic bastard, stood only a few feet away, pointing a black pistol at me.

I froze, staring down the barrel of a gun held by an irritating agent who, in all likelihood, knew exactly what I was thinking. I couldn't come up with a single warp clever enough to miraculously get me out of this situation.

Smirking broadly, Tim spoke aloud for the first time.

"Quoth the Raven ..." He pulled the trigger, shooting me three times in the upper chest. "'Nevermore.'"

And that's how I failed my second field exam.

I DROPPED ONTO MY BED with a groan and rubbed the sore spot on my collarbone from Agent Tim's paintball gun.

Getting shot was a shitty way to fail the field exam. I hadn't lost to an accomplished agent's badass magic or a superior martial artist's skill. I'd been defeated by boring ol' human weaponry. By supersonic lead slugs. Actually, it was worse than that; they were subsonic paint blobs.

I'd also been surrounded, out-magicked, and out-maneuvered. As soon as my opponents knew about my warping ability, it became practically useless. How could I fool someone into believing a hallucination when they were *expecting* a hallucination? Maybe I'd never pass the exam—not against a telepath/sorcerer combo with a side of mage all working in concert to take me down.

By the time I got home with a paper bag of greasy fast food as my consolation prize, it was after six. Normally, I wouldn't resort to the nutritional equivalent of a deep-fried trash can, but I was hella bummed and ready to drown my sorrows in extra bacon, extra cheese, and extra-large fries.

Get in my belly, you empty, delicious calories.

The inescapable aroma of trans fats permeated every molecule of my minuscule living space—and "minuscule" isn't an exaggeration. This place would give sardines claustrophobia.

An optimistic hipster might call it a cozy micro-apartment, but it was just a junky single room tucked away in the corner of a squat apartment building just off Granville Street, south of downtown. It'd come furnished with a twin mattress on a rickety metal frame, a wooden desk so old you'd need radiocarbon dating to ascertain its manufacturing date, and a mini fridge with an even minier freezer, currently stuffed to the brim with a block of cheese, three frozen dinners, a bottle of ketchup, and a six-pack of Dr. Pepper.

My clothes were jammed in the tiny closet, and there was just enough floor space to unroll my yoga mat—though I had to be careful not to put a limb through the drywall.

But beggars couldn't be choosers, and as both an underpaid MPD analyst who couldn't pass the damn test to become a field agent *and* a former convict who owed a buttload in misdemeanor fines, my budget was so tight I could floss with it.

The only slightly personal décor in my sad abode was a stack of worn books on the safest corner of the desk, far from the untrustworthy microwave and a small pile of nonperishable foodstuffs that took up most of the space. Months ago, Lienna had helped me retrieve the literary keepsakes from my old—and a zillion times swankier—apartment before my landlord pitched them.

As I stuffed a handful of greasy fries in my mouth, a warm feeling that had nothing to do with food overtook my insides. Under the desk where a chair would normally sit were two cardboard boxes that contained my entire movie collection from that same apartment. I'd abandoned the colorful assortment of DVDs and Blu-rays, but unbeknownst to me, Lienna had gone back alone, threatened the doorman into letting her back inside, and boxed up all my movies.

Disclaimer: I have no solid proof she actually threatened anyone, but it seems like a safe assumption. She isn't much of a sweet talker—not that I'm complaining.

She'd returned my rescued collection as a room-warming gift, and I have to admit, this grown man might've gotten a little choked up.

I crumpled my burger wrapper, then grabbed my laptop from the backpack I took to work every day, flipped it open, and navigated to the MPD archives—MagiPol's all-encompassing database and an agent's best friend. If you liked unreliable, outmoded, high-maintenance best friends.

After logging in, I sat for a moment, watching the cursor blink. Someone wanted Lienna to return to the LA precinct, two thousand kilometers away from me. And by someone, I mean a certain Shen of the deputy captain variety.

I typed his name into the search bar. The results popped up with unusual speed: David Shen, forty-eight years old, sorcerer. Current deputy captain of the largest MagiPol precinct on the west coast. His list of career accomplishments was so long I had to click through four pages to skim it all.

Holy crapola. This dude specialized in taking down the biggest, nastiest, murderiest rogue rings and criminal operations he could get his hands on. I guess Lienna's penchant for kicking criminal ass was genetic.

I scrolled back up to the top, where a photo showed a Chinese man with short-cropped black hair and laugh lines around his brown eyes smiling reservedly at the camera. The family resemblance was clear.

Hello, Papa Shen.

A few things made sense now, like Lienna's sorcery skill at a relatively young age and her widespread reputation among the MPD. But one thing didn't make sense. Why was Lienna so dead set on staying in Vancouver when she could work under her dad instead? Was he even more authoritarian than Blythe?

I tried to imagine anyone more authoritarian than Blythe. Stalin? Thanos? It was close.

Chewing my inner cheek, I opened the page for a full database search. *Why* she wanted to stay didn't matter. She did, and I wanted her to stay too. That meant she needed to blow Blythe away with her agency magnificence. And I would help her do it … not that I was an expert on agent-related successes.

Before I could dwell on that depressing reminder of my incompetence, I punched in the Grand Grimoire and clicked the blue and white "Go" button on the right side of the screen. The page went blank as the search ran, then the results poured in.

All 3,120 of them.

If that seems like a lot, you're right. There were sixty-three pages of results, ranging from permits to fines to membership applications to incident reports to tangential references in unrelated cases stretching back over the guild's five-year history.

The MPD *loved* forms. They had a form for everything. I was pretty sure there was a form for printing more forms. But three thousand was still a huge number. So why in the name of all things efficient and comprehensible was one guild filing twelve forms a week, every week, for half a decade?

Actually, that's a relatively easy question to answer.

Demons.

The answer is demons.

The scarier and deadlier something is, the more heavily the MPD regulates it, and demons are as terrifyingly death-tastic as magic gets. The Demonica class is comprised of two main parts: summoners and contractors.

Summoners are sorcerers who specialize in hellbound magic because … money? I guess? They drag devils from their little brimstone houses, bind them into contracts, and sell those contracts to equally bat-shit-crazy folk who think it's cool to wield their own personal Beelzebub. Contractors can be anyone, mythic or human. All you need is a big wad of cash and a soul to sell.

MagiPol has super-duper strict laws on how demon contracts can be constructed. The two most important rules are, one, that the contractor must assume complete control over the demon; like a puppet, it is literally unable to blink an eye without its master's command. And two, the Banishment Clause, which is where the Faustian soul-bartering thing comes in; it states that if the demon outlives its contractor, it must return to hell ASAP, and it can use the contractor's soul as its one-way ticket through hell's back door.

Thanks to those strict regulations, creating a single contract requires a licensed Demonica guild, a licensed summoner, an approved summoning location, an approved summoning circle, a pre-approved contract draft, a pre-approved contract recipient, inspections at every stage, a final contract review, and a final "yes, I can control this demon" contractor license.

Every step involves at least one form plus an administration fee, and when you add it all up, it equals a Himalayan avalanche in paperwork.

I cracked my knuckles and looked at the screen as though I were about to Hugh Jackman my laptop, *Swordfish*-style. Except instead of hacking, which was far outside my range of abilities, I methodically narrowed my search parameters to see what I got. I didn't know what I'd find in this paperwork mountain, but I was going to find *something*.

Then I just had to figure out how to disclose whatever I uncovered to Lienna when I wasn't even supposed to know her case existed.

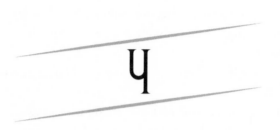

4

"THIS IS NOT A DATE," Lienna declared as she dropped into the seat across from me. A scuffed table filled the space between us, and several other diners occupied identical tables in the cramped deli.

"Of course not," I agreed innocently, unzipping my coat. "Why would you think it's a date?"

She pulled her phone out and held it up to display our latest text message exchange. I'd asked if we could meet for lunch to discuss some research I was doing, she'd agreed, and I'd replied with, "It's a date! :3"

A completely normal coworker interaction.

I grinned unrepentantly. "Don't worry. I'd try way harder than this for a real date."

She fidgeted on her uncomfortable plastic seat, then leveled me with a surprisingly serious stare. "We can't date, Kit. We're coworkers."

Okay, then. We were going there *now*? I'd been joking around.

I'd never hidden that I thought Lienna was talented, accomplished, and hella attractive, and over the past few months, I'd tested the flirting waters with mixed results. Because of those mixed results, I'd kept it to light banter and hints that I'd like to ask her out, hoping for a clear green light before putting her in a position where she might have to turn me down.

But here she was turning me down, and I hadn't even asked yet.

When I didn't laugh off her rejection with an assurance that I was just kidding, her cheeks flushed and she pressed her hands together like she was mashing dough between them.

"It's not that I don't—I mean, you're—" She shook her head violently, then blurted, "It's not allowed, Kit."

I studied her. Honestly, I was less surprised by her refusal than by the blushing and stammering. Had her meeting with Blythe yesterday thrown her that far off her game? I would've expected a brusque promise to replace my eyes with ghost peppers marinated in Tabasco sauce if I mentioned the word "date" again.

Propping my elbow on the table, I rested my chin on my hand. "That's not true."

"What?"

"There's no rule or policy or even a guideline about interoffice dating. Trust me. I had to memorize the precinct handbook from cover to cover before my written exam."

She opened then closed her mouth.

I flashed a smile. "That aside, I was just joking around."

The quintessential dilemma of all men who were about to be shot down: be honest about your intentions and take the rejection on the chin, or pretend you were kidding and spare your pride. I was taking option two.

She blinked, and her blush brightened significantly. "I—Of course. You're never serious."

"Never," I agreed. "Except when I am."

Her uncertainty deepened. "And I was just remarking in general that workplace dating is a bad idea. Our careers are important, and we shouldn't risk them over meaningless drama."

Meaningless? Ouch.

I gazed out the window at the cold pedestrians speed-walking along the sidewalk as though they'd accidentally walked onto the set of *Midnight Cowboy* and wanted out as quickly as possible.

Lienna cleared her throat, then asked brightly, "So? How did the exam go?"

I swiveled back to her happily expectant face, feeling like I'd taken another five-finger death punch to the gut.

"I …" It took me a moment to get the word out. "… failed."

Experiences I'd prefer to never repeat: watching Lienna's expression morph from confident expectancy to disbelief to disappointment, then finally to something that was probably sympathy but looked an awful lot like pity.

"I'm sorry, Kit. You'll get it next time."

"Probably not," I grumbled. "Not unless Blythe is willing to bring in three agents who've never met me and don't know anything about my abilities. I can't beat them if they know what I'm doing, especially against a telepath. Tim had such a strong lock on me that he knew everything I was thinking."

She frowned. "A telepath? That's not very fair."

I sighed. "It's fine."

"No, really, it *isn't* fair. Tim's an instructor—he knows you from training. A rogue telepath wouldn't be able to read your mind so easily. Plus, a telepath puts you at a huge disadvantage because your power relies on deception."

Welcome to the vortex of frustration my brain has been spinning in all day, Lienna.

"The captain is really testing you," she muttered. "Does she *want* you to fail?"

"Maybe she realized psycho warping is a fluff power."

"It's not *fluff*, Kit. Don't you know how terrifying your magic is?"

I scoffed. "Reality warping is terrifying, not my imaginary critters. But I can't reality warp on command, so that's not helpful either."

Back when I was still a convict, I'd accidentally reshaped a silver wand into a metal murder snake with nothing but the godly powers of my brain. Or that's what it had looked like. With every failed attempt to perform a second reality warp, I doubted that interpretation of events even more.

Lienna gave me a hard look, then shook her head. "What did you want to discuss? You mentioned research?"

My attention had drifted to the window again. I scanned the pedestrians, then the traffic, then the far sidewalk.

"Kit? You said you had research to discuss?"

I hastily refocused on her. It was time for the genuinely hard part of this non-date. Burying my worries over how badly this could backfire on me, I channeled maximum Smooth Kit charm.

"I came across something weird while running searches, and I don't know what to make of it." Tugging my phone from my pocket, I pulled up the spreadsheet I'd made last night using my aforementioned spreadsheet wizardry. "Notice anything about those names?"

She gave the short list a quick once-over. "They're all guilds."

"What kind?"

"Sleeper guilds, aren't they?"

I nodded. Sleeper guilds were composed of sleeper mythics, and referred to a complete lack of participation in magic. While magic was super cool, it was also a lot of work and kinda sorta really dangerous, so many mythics opted out—like a solid fifty percent of them.

MagiPol, however, couldn't ignore mythics who claimed to have no interest in practicing magic, and that's where sleeper guilds came in. They were medium to large guilds that didn't do anything mythicy. All they did was keep tabs on their members.

I scrolled the spreadsheet to the next column and passed her the phone. "Take a look at *that* list."

She quickly read it. "I don't recognize any of these names."

"Nope, because they're all sleeper mythics."

She looked up at me, brown eyes glinting as she sensed I was about to drop a bomb on this conversation. "And?"

"And each of those nine sleeper mythics, who aren't supposed to be practicing magic or participating in mythic life, recently got themselves a demon contract."

She sat up straight, and the bright interest on her face was a beautiful sight. "That's unusual. Demon contracts are rare, even among bounty hunters. Why would sleeper mythics have a sudden interest in Demonica?"

"That's what I'm wondering."

"How recent is 'recently'?" she asked, her finger zipping over my phone screen as she investigated the other columns in my spreadsheet. "Could it be a response to the demon activity from two weeks ago?"

Demon activity. What a casual way to refer to the bloodthirsty and enraged demon that had gotten loose in downtown Vancouver, appropriately, on Halloween—a demon without a contract. In other words, the scariest beast next to the *Cloverfield* monster to ever rampage through a city. The resulting chaos had involved a code-black shutdown of the entire Eastside, a police-led evacuation of human civilians, and a three-day hunt encompassing every field agent and every combat mythic in the area.

Fun times.

"I thought that too," I told her, "but the first sleeper to request a contract was three months ago, and it's been steady since then."

"Hmm. Who are the summoners for these contracts? There aren't many licensed summoners in …"

She trailed off as she scrolled to the last column in my spreadsheet, titled "Authorized Summoner." I didn't need to see it to know she was reading the same name over and over.

"Rocco Thorn," she murmured, her hand tightening around my phone. "Guild Master of the Grand Grimoire."

I nodded, playing it cool. When I'd set out to find something suspicious in the Demonica guild's paperwork, I hadn't expected it to be *this* suspicious. There was nothing illegal going on—as far as the paperwork was concerned—but it was strange.

"I did a little comparative searching," I said. "The average summoner requests one to four permits for a demon summoning per year, and on average, only one in three of those results in a successful, approved contract. Rocco Thorn, on the other hand, has been summoning a demon every ten days. Weird, right?"

"Very weird," she muttered, rapidly scanning the spreadsheet from top to bottom and side to side.

I leaned back. "Anyway, that's what I found. Not sure what to do with it, so I guess I'll leave it with you."

She lowered my phone, her eyebrows arching. "You can quit pretending, Kit."

"Huh?"

"Just because you can make yourself invisible doesn't mean you should sneak into private meetings."

I ducked my head guiltily. "I'm sorry. It was a stupid, spur-of-the-moment thing. You looked upset and I wanted to help."

Her lips pressed together. "You shouldn't have been there. I might not even have realized it if you hadn't stopped the door. Though I thought I smelled your cologne before that."

"I don't wear cologne."

Must have been my natural musk. A combination of rich mahogany and 35mm film stock.

She blinked—and inexplicably started blushing again. "Whatever. You still eavesdropped on a private conversation."

"I did, and I'm sorry—really sorry. But I also found something to help your investigation, so that sort of makes up for—"

"No."

"No?"

She pushed my phone toward me. "I can't use this. Blythe gave me this case to prove myself. I can't have you doing my work for me."

I pressed my hands to the tabletop, fingers splayed. "Lienna." I waited for her to look at me. "What Blythe is doing is complete bullshit and you know it. If she won't play fair, you shouldn't either. She'll never know I was the one who ran those searches or made that spreadsheet, so use it."

She hesitated, shifting her weight. "I can't."

"It's a lead. A good one, and you need it. Blythe only gave you a week, remember?"

"Yeah, but she gave it to me, not you. I have to do this by the book, and prove I'm better than—" She cut herself off, jaw clenching as though she hadn't meant to say those words.

Who did she want to prove she was better than? Blythe?

Grabbing my phone, I pushed my chair back. "We're playing hardball then, are we?"

She frowned. "What do you—Kit? Where are you going?"

Alarm sharpened her voice as I strode toward the deli counter. Impatient businesspeople muttered curses as I cut in line, and the drowsy teenager manning the till blinked dazedly at me.

I unzipped my jacket, revealing my MPD badge. "Health and safety. We received a complaint about carnivorous cockroaches in your salami."

The teenager's eyes bugged. Lienna appeared behind me and yanked my sleeve hard.

"We need to speak to the owner," I told the kid.

"*Kit*," Lienna hissed angrily.

"Uh, yeah," the teenager stammered. "He's in the back. Through the door there."

Ignoring Lienna's tugging on my arm, I stepped around the counter and pushed through the swinging door. Behind it, a trio of plastic-gloved chefs hunched over a stainless-steel counter, wrist-deep in a form of meat I hoped would look a whole lot less like cow intestines once they were finished. I made a direct line for a bed-headed guy in his late thirties.

Looking up, he scrutinized us with a heavy brow. "Customers aren't allowed back here."

I pointed at my badge. "We need to talk, Harold."

His eyes widened, then darted to the other two men. "Uh. Let's step outside."

Lienna glared daggers at me as we followed Harold to a fire exit beside a pair of industrial-sized sinks. "What are you doing, Kit?"

"Starting your investigation," I whispered back.

She made a choking noise.

The alley reeked of rotting meat, the hazy stench emanating from a dumpster that didn't look nearly disgusting enough for the odors leaking from it. I rezipped my coat against the damp November chill.

Harold faced us, a sheen of perspiration on his forehead as he squinted over me and Lienna. "Are you two really MPD agents?"

A fair question. The vast majority of our colleagues leaned into the whole "secret government agency" trope pretty hard for their fashion choices, whereas I generally opted for a classic jeans/t-shirt combo. Lienna, of course, favored her eccentric collection of accessories.

"I'm Kit. Agent Morris," I corrected quickly. "This is Agent Shen."

Pending that accursed field exam, I hadn't been officially branded an agent yet, so introducing myself as "Agent Morris" felt super weird, like greeting someone in a foreign language.

"You're the owner of this establishment?" I continued, puffing my chest out and imagining a stick up my ass like most agents had—present company excluded. "Harold Atherton, Arcana mythic and demon contractor, member of Spires?"

Lienna sucked in an almost silent breath as she realized we were standing in front of one of the names from my list—a sleeper mythic who'd recently bought a demon contract from Rocco Thorn.

"Th-that's me," he stammered. "What can I do for you, agents?"

Lienna shot me one more chastising look, then stepped up to my side. "We have a few questions about your demon contract."

His eyes darted wildly down the alley for an escape route. "Uh, yeah. Sure. By that, you mean ...?"

"Your demon contract," she repeated, her agency sternness in full effect—and so much better than mine. She gestured at his torso. "Do you have your infernus with you?"

"Uh ... no, actually."

"You're required by law to carry it on your person at all times, or secure it in a locked class-three safe. Where is your class-three safe located?"

His eye twitched, and he abruptly stuffed a hand in his pocket. "I just remembered, I do have it. Right here, see?"

He lifted his hand, a chain hanging from his fingers. On his palm was a silver disc, the edges carved with twisting runes and the center emblazoned with a large, creepy emblem. An infernus. It looked just like the pictures in my notes, except the emblem in the center was different.

I canted my head, trying to imagine how a whole demon could fit inside it. That's how the magic works, apparently; the contractor stores their demon in their infernus until they need it, like a psychopathic genie in a lamp.

"This is it," Harold added unnecessarily. "Is there a problem? It's all legal. Got all my paperwork approved and everything."

"Your summoner was Rocco Thorn of the Grand Grimoire, correct?" Lienna asked.

"Yeah. He did all the forms, to be honest. I just checked them and signed at the bottom."

"How did you first make contact with Rocco?"

"Uh." Harold squinted. "He … I mean, I looked him up. In the directory."

"When was that?"

"It was … four … months ago. We did a consultation and stuff before starting."

"And what made you decide to seek out Mr. Thorn for a demon contract?"

Harold's eyes bounced between me and Lienna like a theater actor who'd forgotten his lines and was desperately hoping to recall what he was supposed to say before the audience noticed his bungle.

After a too-long-to-not-be-awkward silence, he shrugged. "The world's a dangerous place. I wanted some protection."

"So, get yourself some fancy artifacts," I jumped in. "Selling your soul for a glorified bodyguard is kind of extreme, isn't it?"

"It's my choice." He inched away from us. "Listen, I need to get back to work."

"How is business these days, Harold?" I asked.

"Good, I guess. Lunchtime is always busy."

"So you're making a decent profit?"

He stiffened. "Why does the MPD care about my finances?"

"You're broke," I replied bluntly. "According to your bank records, at least. The cheapest demon contracts *start* at $150,000. So where'd you get the cash?"

"I ... I ..." He pushed his shoulders back, his demeanor turning aggressive. "Am I under arrest?"

Lienna shot me a quick glance. "Not right now."

"Then I'm going back to work."

Not waiting for further permission, he zoomed back through the doors. The moment he was gone, Lienna turned to me and folded her arms.

I arched my eyebrows, projecting innocence. "Suspicious, right?"

She drew in a deep breath, inflating her chest as though preparing to unleash a jilted sports fan's level of shouting—then deflated with a shake of her head. "You really prepared for this, didn't you?"

"Of course I did." My voice went quiet. "Even if I didn't care whether you went back to LA—which I definitely do—*you* don't want to go. I couldn't just twiddle my thumbs and do nothing."

She smiled weakly. "Thanks, Kit."

"Can I ask why you don't want to go back home?"

"I have my reasons."

I wanted to press for a better explanation, but her closed expression warned me I'd get nowhere and only piss her off. "Okay, so what now?"

"You mean you don't have an entire afternoon of interrogations lined up for me?"

"This is your case," I said. "I'm strictly here as your supporting analyst and interrogation assistant. The Igor to your Frankenstein, if you will."

Her eyebrows started to climb.

"Frankenstein the mad scientist," I clarified. "Not Frankenstein the zombie monster. Although Igor isn't actually his assistant in the book or in any of the original movies. In the first film, the assistant is Fritz. So I'm the Fritz to your Frankenstein, which sounds so much better. Alliteration is the key. That's why it's *The Fast and the Furious* and not *The Speedy and the Irritat—*"

Lienna started to laugh. I blinked at her.

"Sorry," she chuckled, pushing her ponytail off her shoulder. "I guess I forgot what it's like to work with you."

"Technically, we haven't worked together. I was a defenseless convict coerced into helping you hunt down my best friend while the MPD threatened me with phony charges."

"Oh really? I thought you were a *guilty* convict manipulating me into giving you a chance to escape custody so you wouldn't have to face the *rightful* charges against you."

"Agree to disagree." I shrugged airily. "What's our next move?"

She tapped her chin in thought. "Anyone we interrogate will brush us off like Harold did unless we have something concrete to hit them with. So ..." She sighed. "More research, I think."

"Research? Sounds like a job for your Fritz."

"This time, let's see what we can find together."

Together? I liked the sound of that.

5

"ROCCO THORN is one sketchy dude."

"Yeah," Lienna agreed, bent over her laptop. "But he isn't doing anything *obviously* illegal as far as I can see."

We'd locked ourselves in a spare boardroom on the precinct's second floor. With a single table, several cheap office chairs, and a projector hanging from the ceiling, it resembled the room where I'd faced the Judiciary Council five months ago.

The remains of our takeout dinner were stacked on the far side of the table, and printouts relating to Rocco Thorn and his guild covered the rest. My laptop was hooked up to the projector, and the white wall across from us was filled with a super-sized version of my spreadsheet—which we'd expanded to include a couple hundred more cells and an ass-load more info, meticulously organized into one overwhelmingly comprehensive data grid.

Unfortunately, we had yet to find anything as suspicious as Rocco's recent bout of summoning.

"All his permits and inspections look good," I said, shuffling through a stack of printouts. "We should check with the inspector, ask him if he's noticed anything suspicious."

"He'll probably tell you he wouldn't have signed off on the contracts if there had been anything suspicious about them," Lienna countered as she paperclipped another stack together. "There are only a couple dozen Demonica inspectors in North America, and from what I've heard, they're all self-important old men who hate it when anyone questions their expertise."

"Helpful." I pulled up the inspector's info. "Looks like his current assignment is in Alaska supervising a contract negotiation. Extra not helpful. Hopefully one of these other documents can shed some light."

We rustled around quietly for a minute as I searched the piles of paper for all the inspector-approved permits. I clipped the bundle together and set it aside.

"Did Rocco go around to the sleeper guilds and post a 'buy one, get one free' demon advert?" I muttered as I pulled a new stack over—Grand Grimoire paperwork instead of Rocco's summoning documents. "Harold said he sought out Rocco, but I'm pretty sure the only truthful things he said were 'uh' and 'um.'"

"He's definitely hiding something." She slapped a paper down with an exasperated huff. "This guild! If nothing else, they need a thorough audit and a few fines so they learn to fill out forms correctly. Most of these were rejected for dumb errors."

"Yeah, like this one." I tapped the page in front of me. "This member application from the end of October is missing the guild history section." I squinted. "It was approved, though."

She peered at the printout. "That shouldn't have gone through. Who approved it?"

I flipped it over to check the signatory on the bottom. "Stephanie Wight."

Tugging her laptop closer, Lienna tapped on the keyboard. "She's an analyst in … Edmonton? Why was this approved by someone in another province?"

We exchanged a look, then dug back into the paperwork stacks. The hands of the boring white clock on the wall ticked around and around as hours slid past. By the time we'd sorted through every form the Grand Grimoire had submitted in the last two years, my eyes were burning.

We had three sets of paperwork. One was all the Grand "Can't Follow Basic Instructions" Grimoire's rejected forms. One was all their approved documentation that seemed legit.

The third and smallest stack was the interesting one. Stephanie Wight, it turned out, had only approved that one form. But agents from Ottawa, Montreal, Winnipeg, Toronto, Seattle, Portland, Sacramento, Salt Lake City, Boston, and Pittsburgh had all, at some point, approved a single form each for Rocco.

He was either a super charmer on par with Jordan Belfort, a blackmailer with dirt on a bunch of different MPD agents, or a forger who never impersonated the same agent twice.

I flopped back into my chair, massaging my temples. "Okay. Rocco probably did something slimy to push these approvals through. Now what? We contact all those agents and find out why they approved the forms?"

Shaking her head, Lienna braced her elbows on the table. "It's possible Rocco bought or blackmailed those agents. If we start asking questions, they could tip him off."

"Good point. So what do we do?"

She looked at the stack of probable forgeries like she'd rather light them on fire than read them again. "We need to catalog who and what each form involves and try to find patterns or clues as to what Rocco is up to."

"Right." I squinted against the eyeball-assaulting fluorescent lights, then pushed to my feet. Crossing to the closed door, I slapped the light switches. All the lights shut off, leaving the projector as the only source of illumination. "*So* much better."

"We can't read paperwork in the dark."

"I know, but we need a break." Stifling a yawn, I returned to my seat beside her. "If I don't stop for a few minutes, my pupils will melt off my eyeballs, and you wouldn't want to be responsible for blinding an up-and-coming master agent, would you?"

"Master agent?" she repeated dryly. "What's that supposed to mean?"

"You tell me." Minimizing my spreadsheet, I started browsing for a movie that wouldn't be ruined by a crappy projector and tinny laptop speakers. "How about this one? The main character's name is Harold, just like our first suspect."

She slouched back in her chair. "Do we have time for a movie?"

"There's always time for a movie." I clicked play. "Start watching. I'll be right back."

I slipped out of the boardroom and prowled the precinct's empty halls for movie-watching supplies. It was after ten, and all but a handful of night-shift agents had gone home for the night. Maybe when I was a full agent, I'd request night shift. It'd be quiet, Vinny-free, and I could watch movies without getting caught.

Five minutes later, I closed the boardroom door and dropped back into my chair. Will Ferrell filled the screen, playing the role of a painstakingly detailed IRS agent. With Lienna bemusedly watching, I unloaded two sodas and five different mini chip bags from the vending machine onto the table. Unfolding my last item, a fuzzy blanket with tassels on the corners, I shook it out.

"Where'd you get a blanket?"

"Borrowed it from Paula's desk. She won't mind." I flipped it over my and Lienna's legs, then leaned back and let Emma Thompson's crisp English accent wash over me. "Have you seen this one before?"

"No," Lienna murmured, also stretching her legs out. "Is it good?"

"Wouldn't have picked it if it wasn't."

We settled in, both pretending the cozy blanket would somehow transform our stiff swivel chairs into a single uber-comfy loveseat. At least, that's what I was pretending.

I selected a bag of pretzels and pulled it open. "Will Ferrell's Harold doesn't remind me much of our deli Harold, but I'm getting serious déjà vu vibes from his IRS coworkers."

"Those cubicles look just like the MPD ones." She nicked a pretzel from my bag. "That room could be the bullpen in the LA precinct."

I stole a glance at her. "Is it nicer than here?"

"A bit. They have a bigger budget."

"But you still prefer it here?"

She hesitated in the middle of selecting another salty pretzel. "Yeah."

I debated whether to ask, then threw it out there. "You don't want to work with your dad?"

Slowly, as though considering each small motion, she brought the pretzel to her mouth and bit off a tiny corner. "It probably doesn't make any sense to you. Seems like I should want to be near my parents, right?"

She was right that it didn't make sense to me, mostly because I'd never known my parents. Maybe I would have wanted to be closer to them if they'd been alive. Maybe not. It'd probably depend on whether they were, you know, decent human beings.

"You don't know what it's like to be under the shadow of everyone's expectations," she continued quietly. "Not just my dad's, but everyone at the precinct. Every single agent in LA knows him and knows me, and they all expect me to be just like him." Staring bleakly at her pretzel, she added almost inaudibly, "I can't breathe in that place."

"Well, I mean, I've never met the guy." I cast her a sideways glance. "But I bet you're as good or even better than he was at your age, and someday, you'll have a résumé just like his."

Her fingers spasmed, snapping the pretzel in half. "No, I won't."

I watched her fish the broken bits from the blanket, unsure what she was opposed to but recognizing the quiet, contained distress on her face. "We'll crack Rocco and the Grand Grimoire wide open, and then Blythe will be begging you to stay."

She managed a flimsy smile. "Rocco, yes, but I'm not sure about the Grand Grimoire as a whole. It'll depend on what we find. Captain Blythe wants a case for disbandment, but taking down a GM doesn't automatically mean the whole guild goes down too."

"We'll find something that'll satisfy the captain."

She fidgeted with the blanket. "The law is supposed to be innocent until proven guilty, Kit. Is *looking* for criminal activity even ethical?"

I hooked my arm over her shoulders and squeezed her gently. "Don't overthink it, Lienna. We know Rocco is rotten, even if we don't know how or why, and any time a GM is implicated in a crime, the entire guild is always investigated. It's standard procedure."

Her shoulders relaxed under my arm. "Right. You're right."

I shifted my arm to the back of her chair, and we settled in to watch the movie. As much as I loved Dustin Hoffman's dry absurdity, my thoughts kept wandering to Lienna. What about her father and the LA precinct got her hackles up? Was it the pressure to live up to her father's illustrious career? Were Lienna and I pushing ethical boundaries by following Blythe's imperious assignment? Were we all just characters in a story controlled by a neurotic author with writer's block?

My eyelids grew heavy; it wasn't easy being a spreadsheet deity, and the hours spent organizing all those cells were finally catching up to me. As my chin dipped forward, a soft weight settled against my shoulder—Lienna's head. She leaned into me, one arm across our conjoined armrests and her eyes closed as the glow from the projector reflected off her smooth cheek.

I let my arm slide off the back of her chair and tucked it over her shoulders. She let out a long, sleepy sigh. Had she pulled a late night yesterday too, working her own angles on the Grand Grimoire in search of a case that would convince Blythe to let her stay? If we didn't find a way to take down the guild, this could be the last movie we watched together.

The door to the boardroom whipped open, blasting us with light from the hall.

I jolted upright, and Lienna jerked straight so fast she almost toppled her chair. We spun around, squinting against the brightness.

As though summoned by my thought of her, Blythe stood in the threshold, framed by fluorescent lighting and her face in shadow. Holy shit, was this woman actually a demon in disguise? I'd been thinking cyborg, but now I was thinking Azazel in Blythean form.

MPD headquarters don't work like standard police stations—we aren't fully staffed twenty-four-seven. We're more about investigating illegal witchcraft and mythic paperwork than traffic stops and B&Es. Thus, aside from an operator on the emergency hotline and a couple of unlucky on-call agents, most of us go home at the end of the workday—including the captain.

But not tonight, apparently.

She hit the light switch, flooding the boardroom with even more light, and I cringed like a hungover college student in an eight-a.m. class.

"Agent Shen. Mr. Morris." Her glare swept between us pointedly. "I don't recall designating any space in the precinct as a recreation room."

"We're working," Lienna blurted, a faint blush rising in her cheeks. "Or, I mean, we're taking a short break, but we've been working this whole time."

"On what?"

"The Grand Grimoire case."

Blythe shifted the stack of folders on her arm. "You've involved Mr. Morris?"

"Agents always have analyst support," I cut in. "They usually have partners too, but all I'm doing is helping with the backend work, which is my job."

The captain's lips thinned.

"Show her what you found, Lienna," I suggested in a low voice.

She jumped as though I'd shoved her. Grabbing my laptop, she exited the still-playing movie and brought up my glorious spreadsheet. Highlighting different columns, she explained our results from start to finish, and I didn't say a word when she presented all our inferences as hers alone.

Because that was exactly what I wanted her to do.

"So," Lienna concluded, "I'm focusing on two leads—Rocco's suspicious paperwork and his sleeper-mythic clients. Harold is my main person of interest. Based on his bank account records, he shouldn't have been able to afford a demon contract. I'd like to dig deeper into his finances, as well as the finances of the other sleeper mythics on our list."

Blythe nodded sharply. "I'll arrange for clearance. Is that everything you have so far?"

"Yes, ma'am."

"Excellent. Now tell me how much of that was Morris's handiwork."

"None," I jumped in. "I was only assisting—printing, organizing, making really pretty spreadsheets, that sort of thing."

"I'm already aware that you're a capable and remorseless liar, Mr. Morris. Agent Shen, however, is doing a poor job concealing her guilt."

Lienna flinched, then quickly reset her expression to neutral. "I wouldn't be at this point without Kit. He's got a sixth sense for uncovering suspicious activity."

"Probably because he's engaged in so much of it himself," Blythe remarked. "If he's proving valuable to your investigation, keep using him. I'd rather see him putting his instincts to good use than tormenting his desk mate."

"My helping out won't affect anything?" I asked quickly. "There aren't any special circumstances with this case?"

She snorted at my attempt to hint at her deal with Lienna. "No, Morris. After all, you're still just an analyst."

It was my turn to flinch.

"Now go home," she barked, "before I have to find exactly which rules you two are breaking and write you up."

I saluted smartly. Blythe answered with a scowl, then swept back into the brightly lit hallway from whence she came.

After waiting to be sure she was really gone, I sagged against the table. Lienna exhaled harshly through her nose as she shut my laptop.

"Well," she muttered, "that could've been worse."

"Yeah, much worse. And hey, on the bright side, I can officially help you on the case now." I waggled my eyebrows. "Feel free to *use me* however you want."

She smacked my arm. "If you want to help, meet me in the parking garage at nine a.m. sharp."

"Oh? Where are we going?"

"Into the field." She gave me her own eyebrow waggle. "So buckle up, Mr. Analyst."

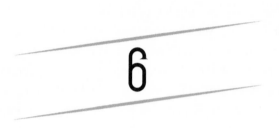

6

THE FIELD. After months of training, studying, exams, and an infinite tsunami of paperwork, I was finally in the field. Not as an agent, per se, but close enough. It was a chance to prove my worth, to take the final step into the unknown, to join the distinguished ranks of all the protectors of justice who'd come before me, to fight crime, apprehend villains, and uncover dastardly deeds of evil hidden behind the closed doors of …

… of a fitness center?

"Are you sure this is the right place?" I asked Lienna.

"Of course."

"Okay, but this," I added in case she was directionally confused, "is a gym."

Standing beside me with her hair in its classic high ponytail, she quirked an eyebrow. "Loads of sleeper guilds are gyms."

"Are they?" I asked curiously as we approached the frosted glass door labeled Spires 24h Fitness. "Why?"

"A few reasons." She tugged the door open. "Gyms blend in, and people can come and go all the time without attracting attention. It's a normal, common membership to have among humans, and no one bats an eye whether you show up every day or only a couple times a year."

Catching the open door with one hand, I glanced over my shoulder at the parking lot, populated by our smart car and a handful of other vehicles, then followed Lienna inside.

The unique aroma of rubber and sweat hit me. It wasn't a pleasant smell, but neither was I opposed to it—my fingers were already itching to grab some free weights. Making sure my Split Kit was a fit Kit and not a flabby one was an important pastime of mine, and while I'd maintained my fitness level since joining the MPD, I hadn't had time for my more intensive exercise routines.

Letting Lienna take the lead, I trailed after her as she approached the front desk. A few people were scattered across the cardio equipment, and two men and a woman were using the weight machines. My gaze turned back to the door, but I couldn't see the parking lot through the frosted glass.

We waited a few minutes, then the guild's GM joined us—a woman in her fifties with the tightest biceps I'd ever seen. Every time her arm flexed, I expected the cuff of her t-shirt to split in half.

Lienna asked all the expected questions, starting with the details about Harold, then expanding into the general membership as she fished for anything relating to the new and extremely expensive fad of Demonica accessories. When the GM only got more and more confused—genuinely confused, unlike Harold—Lienna finally asked outright about a recent surge of interest in Demonica and/or any visits from summoners.

The woman shook her head, her short blond braid bouncing. "We have a few non-member customers who are practicing mythics, but they get thorough rundowns on etiquette."

"What sort of etiquette?" I asked.

"No discussion of magic or mythics on the gym floor." She waved a hand at the rows of cardio machines. "We have human customers as well. Our mythic members support the rules, so even if a summoner got in here to proposition people, someone would report it immediately."

"I see." Lienna jotted that down on her notepad. "And what about Harold?"

"What about him?"

Lienna arched her eyebrows. "His recent demon contract."

"Harold is a *contractor*?" she blurted, eyes wide. "Since when?"

"Five weeks ago. Your guild isn't licensed for Demonica, correct?"

"Of course not." The GM rubbed her palms on her spandex pants. "I'll give him his thirty-day notice right away."

"Please wait on that while this investigation is ongoing. Your guild won't be penalized." Lienna made another note. "Harold's paperwork was all in order. He's not required to alert his guild before getting a contract, but he *is* required to inform you that his class status has changed. That seems to be the only step he missed."

The GM grimaced. "A pretty damn important one."

"Are you familiar with Harold's finances?"

"Not particularly." She paused, wavering over a decision. "I remember him mentioning his business a few times—that sandwich shop. He complained about how expensive it is to run and how hard it is to attract new customers. I don't know if he was just getting his frustrations off his chest or if his business is struggling. He never said either way."

Lienna scribbled that down. "And he never mentioned anything about a demon? Even in passing?"

"I don't know why or how Harold got involved with Demonica, but I'm certain it didn't happen here."

"Do you mind if we look around?"

"Go ahead, but please don't question anyone. As I mentioned, we have human customers as well."

I glanced across the floor. "Do you know which of those bun-busters are mythics?"

"Yes."

I waited a beat. "Will you tell us?"

She pursed her lips. "If you have reason to suspect them of a crime and the appropriate paperwork for an interview, yes."

"That won't be necessary," Lienna said quickly. "Thank you for your cooperation."

The GM smiled. "Anytime."

As the woman headed off, Lienna moved toward the bulletin board on the other side of the counter, and I followed a step behind.

"Is that weird?" I whispered. "That the GM won't let us talk to anyone?"

"Standard," she murmured back, perusing the flyers on the board. "It's a GM's job to advocate for their members. We can talk to any mythic whenever we want, *unless* they're a person of interest or a suspect in a case *and* we're questioning them about that case, at which point we need their GM's permission or a summons for questioning."

"Meaning we should've got that GM's a-okay before talking to Harold yesterday?"

"Depends," she hedged. "We didn't really have a case yet, so technically, Harold wasn't a person of interest when we talked to him. We were just asking about his contract. But now that it's an official case, we have to deal with his GM, and she'll argue that everyone in her guild is a person of interest."

She might be blocking us from everyone else, but it looked like she didn't care too much about Harold now that she knew he'd secretly become a contractor and was on his way out of her guild. I scrubbed a hand through my hair, mentally running through all the procedures I'd memorized during training. "How do we get anything done if GMs won't let us even casually question their members?"

"We work around them. Carefully." She lifted a pink advertisement for a dog-walking service to peer at a page detailing someone's pleading request for a Punjabi tutor. "Any system of law and governing needs checks and balances, and GMs are the biggest power check for the MPD. They can bring an investigation to a standstill."

"Will that be a problem for us, considering Rocco Thorn, the guy we're after, is a guild master?"

"It might be," she replied grimly, leaving the bulletin board and heading toward the change rooms. "And it's the reason we aren't going anywhere near him until we're ready."

"Build case first, piss off GM suspect last. Gotcha."

She ducked into the ladies' room and I gave the empty men's room a quick pass for anything overtly suspicious. We reunited in the hallway.

"Did you learn about GM power dynamics after starting here?" I asked her as we poked our heads into a square room used for yoga and Pilates classes. "Before that, arresting me was your first assignment, right?"

"I've learned a lot, but I already knew about GM roles." She cleared her throat awkwardly. "From my dad."

"Ah." I could see her stiffen at the very thought of Papa Shen, so I nodded at a guy in the corner running through a sun salutation. "Ever tried yoga?"

The tension in her shoulders loosened at the change of subject. "No, but didn't Agent Cutter catch you doing yoga in your holding cell?"

"He didn't *catch* me," I corrected. "He *interrupted* me."

"But that's why you were half naked in the interrogation room that one time."

"Yep."

And neither of us mentioned how she'd stopped dead to ogle me.

We continued our perusal of Spires's facilities, and I kept up a steady chatter about all the different muscle-abusing fitness routines I'd tried, doing my best not to sound like a douchey gym bro. Lienna was rather unimaginatively locked into a mixture of cardio, high-rep weightlifting, and martial arts training.

After letting Spires's GM know we were leaving, we headed for the door. A cold rush of air washed over me, clearing the gym's odor from my nose.

I tucked my hands in my pockets. "What do you think?"

Lienna puffed out a breath. "This guild and its GM probably had nothing to do with Harold becoming a contractor. We need to figure out how, when, and where Harold and Rocco got in contact."

"If Harold refuses to talk, that'll be difficult."

"We might find more clues in his finances once the captain gets us that clearance." She tugged her keys from her satchel. "He paid for his demon *somehow*, and I have a feeling it's important."

Rubbing the back of my neck, I paused beside Lienna as she unlocked the smart car with a press of the fob. My head tilted, gaze skimming her door, then its handle. My eyes narrowed as the twinge of unease in my gut deepened into ominous warning.

She pulled the door open. "Kit? Something wrong?"

I hooked my hand over her elbow and pointed across the parking lot with the other. "Do you see that? That shop has candy!"

"Huh?"

"My blood sugar's low. Let's grab some jellybeans!"

"Now?" she complained as I dragged her away from the car. She swung the door shut and jogged two steps to catch up to me. "Can you stay focused for more than—"

A sound pressed against my eardrums, just out of my range of hearing—then skyrocketed into a shrill, piercing squeal.

I grabbed Lienna around the waist and dove for the pavement.

An explosion boomed through the parking lot, so fast, so violent all I could do was flatten against the ground, one arm across Lienna's shoulders. Shrapnel peppered my back, and the ear-shattering roar deepened into the whoosh of flames.

Limbs trembling and ears ringing painfully, I pushed up on my elbows and looked back.

The smart car's roof was gone, and six-foot-high flames engulfed the interior. Black smoke billowed into the sky, and twisted scraps of metal were scattered across the parking lot. Bits of debris rained down.

I rolled off Lienna, and she pushed herself upright. We gawked at the damage, then shared a terrified look.

Someone had tried to blow us up.

SITTING ON THE CURB beside Lienna, I watched firefighters aim a jet of water at the still-burning smart car. Compact, efficient, *and* highly flammable.

Three police cars were parked beside the firetruck, their lights flashing, but the officers merely loitered around their cruisers. They already knew this wasn't their investigation. A new, unexploded smart car and a black sedan were parked opposite them, having transported four of our fellow MagiPol agents to the scene. One was supervising the firemen, two were inside Spires, and the fourth was walking across the parking lot toward us, a drink tray in his hand.

"How you kids doing?" Agent Brennan Harris crouched in front of us. Middle-aged with an average build, he was one of the most stick-up-his-ass agents I'd met, but my opinion softened as he offered the tray, two steaming beverages lodged in the cardboard. "Have a drink and warm up. I'm almost done here, then I'll take you back to the precinct. A healer is on standby."

"We're fine," Lienna murmured, selecting a drink. "My ears are ringing, that's all."

"You were ten feet from a car bomb." Harris pushed his wire-rimmed glasses up his nose and glanced at the burning vehicle. "Lucky for you two, the explosive force was mostly vertical. Still, if you hadn't hit the deck, you'd both be dead."

I took the second drink. "Lucky no one else got hurt."

"That too. We can't be certain until forensics is done, but our working theory is the air pressure change when you closed the door triggered the detonator. You were supposed to be inside the car at that point, though." He pushed to his feet. "I'll be back once I confirm arrangements for moving the car wreckage to forensics."

"I'll need access to your report and all findings." Lienna sipped her drink. "As soon as you have anything, please."

"This is related to a case?"

"I think so."

He nodded. "Be careful, Agent Shen. Car bombs aren't in the average rogue's arsenal."

As he strode toward Spires, currently evacuated aside from the GM and guild officers, I took a hearty gulp of my drink—scalding my tongue so much I almost couldn't taste it. A molten cappuccino, maybe?

"Car bombs aren't in the average rogue's arsenal," Lienna repeated under her breath, staring down at her drink. "He's right. Who the hell would—or could—do something like this?"

I pried the lid off my cup and blew on the steaming liquid.

"They must have followed us here," she continued. "Or maybe they targeted us after we arrived. We only started this investigation yesterday, and two people knew about it—Blythe and Harold."

My second gulp was a lot more cautious. Definitely a cappuccino, but not molten.

"Harold doesn't seem like the car bomb type. But he also doesn't seem like the demon contractor type." She bit her fingernail, then turned to me. "Kit?"

"Yeah?"

"Say something."

"I don't have any answers, Lienna." I blew on my drink again. "All I know is that someone tried to *Touch of Evil* us and now I can't tell if I'm scared or really pissed off."

Probably both.

"If you hadn't pulled me down, I'd be dead right now." She leaned closer. "How did you know about the bomb?"

A long breath slid from my lungs. My attention was on my cappuccino, but I could feel her gaze raking over me. "I didn't know. But when we were heading inside, I had the feeling we were being watched. When we came back out, I noticed the car door wasn't shut tight, and there were scratches around the lock."

"So you pulled me away from the car to ... what? Scope the parking lot?"

"Yeah." My stomach churned. "It was just a hunch. The scratches might've always been there, and the door being ajar could've been from when you got out. But then ..."

Then I'd heard that sound—one that had catapulted my tightly wound nerves straight up to DEFCON 1. Even as I'd been throwing us down, I hadn't really thought we were in trouble. Part of me had already been trying to think up a way to laugh off my overreaction.

I rubbed my chilled face. "Is this normal? Assassination attempts on day two of an investigation?"

"No. I heard about stuff like this in LA with—with my dad's cases." She again hesitated over the mention of her father. "But he's always going after underground guilds and crime rings and cartels."

"Whereas all we've got is fake paperwork and some unlikely demon contractors. What the hell sort of hornet's nest did we poke?" I chugged my drink and smacked it down on the curb. "Now what?"

"Now we let Agent Harris take us back to the precinct, see a healer, and report to Blythe."

"And then?"

Her gaze swung to the burning car and her expression hardened. "Then we pay Harold another visit. The silver lining of our near deaths is that now we can arrest him. Then we'll find out *exactly* what's going on with his demon contract and Rocco Thorn."

7

POST-LUNCH HOUR RUSH, Harold's deli had an abandoned air to it. Though it was only one thirty in the afternoon, just one customer sat at a table. The same drowsy teenager was behind the till, gazing vacantly at his phone.

Lienna and I marched toward the counter, and the teen looked up. His eyes popped with recognition.

"You haven't eaten the capicola this week, have you?" I asked him.

"N-no. I usually eat corned beef, man."

I stifled a grin at his obvious concern. "Where's Harold?"

"In the back. Hey, veggies are safe, right?"

"Usually," I said, walking around the counter. "But watch out for *E. coli*. That shit's everywhere."

Lienna rolled her eyes, and as we pushed through the swinging doors, she added in a whisper, "You're going to give that kid a complex."

In the kitchen, as before, was our beloved bedheaded contractor, but this time he was working alone. Maybe the other guys had left once the rush was over, which suited us just fine; this was more of a private conversation anyway.

The instant Harold spotted us, his face paled as though he'd seen a ghost—or the two ghosts of MPD agents who were supposed to be ashy smithereens.

"Hey there, Harold." I gave him a teeth-baring grin. "How ya been?"

"You're back," he muttered. "What's the problem?"

"Who said there's a problem?"

"I ... I just assumed ..."

I folded my arms. "Or did you think you'd never see us again? Figured we'd be *taken care of?*"

Bewilderment pulled his eyebrows together. "Huh?"

Lienna poked me in the ribs with her elbow, then canted her head toward the dining area, reminding me that the teenaged cashier was within hearing range. "Let's step outside."

Harold reluctantly allowed himself to be herded through the fire exit. The alley was shadowed and surprisingly dim, the overcast sky gray and dreary. Lienna and I stood with our backs to the exit, and Harold faced us, a few feet away.

"You have two options, Harold," she said coolly. "You can tell us exactly what you did after our first chat, or you can tell us in an interrogation room at the precinct."

He recoiled. "I'm under arrest? What for? I haven't done anything!"

"That's what they all say," I observed.

"We'd love to hear your side of the story," Lienna intoned in a delightfully threatening way.

"What do you m-mean? I didn't do anything. I worked and went home and … and …" He blinked rapidly. "I called Rocco. That's it."

"You called Rocco Thorn?"

"Yeah." He rubbed his hands through his hair, compounding the bedhead quality. "I checked that all my paperwork got filed and everything."

I flicked a glance at Lienna, then looked back at Harold. "Did you tell him we'd come by to speak to you?"

He nodded. "And I asked him if there could be a problem with my paperwork. He said no—it's all filed and signed off and everything." Sweat had beaded on his upper lip, and he wiped it off with the back of his hand. "My contract is legal, okay? Totally legal. Paid for with my soul and everything. I'm not breaking any laws."

"All right." I rocked back on my heels. "I believe you aren't breaking any laws. But that doesn't mean you're squeaky clean, does it? There's something rotten here and it isn't just all this dumpster meat."

Lienna quickly picked up what I was laying down. "It was Rocco's idea, wasn't it? He approached you."

Harold's mouth quivered.

"He bought you," I guessed. "You didn't pay for that contract. *He* paid *you*—money to keep your deli from going under."

"H-how do you know?"

Bingo. I gentled my expression—then dropped a little warp in his mind to brighten the light around me and Lienna, giving us a soft glow. It was a trick I'd used when I'd worked for KCQ to make the shifty, heartless lawyers seem like saviors instead of sharks.

"Rocco is the criminal here," I told him soothingly. "You don't have to go down for his crimes."

Harold shook his head. "N-no. I can't. He'll kill me if I say anything."

Lienna stepped closer, and I subtly amplified her glowing aura. "We can protect you if you let us, Harold."

He was still shaking his head, the motion faster and faster. "No. I c-can't. I haven't done anything wrong. I'm n-not saying anything more."

I exchanged another look with Lienna, and she reached into her satchel to retrieve her handcuffs. This conversation had officially reached a dead end, so it was time to arrest Harold and take him in for a real interrogation.

This would be my first time as the arrester instead of the arrestee. I was a bit too excited to be on the other side of the cuffs.

A grating sound interrupted my anticipation—metal grinding against rock, coming from above us. Harold looked up, and his jaw went slack, eyes bursting wide open.

I stepped away from the wall and craned my neck, sincerely hoping Harold wasn't pulling that old "Look, Tom Cruise doing his own stunts!" trick to make us glance away so he could run like mad in the opposite direction. My gaze shot up to the rooftop two stories above.

"Oh, ball sack," I cursed quietly. "That's not Tom."

Not unless his next role was a hulking shadow with a pair of glowing red eyes. The dark silhouette leaned over the rooftop's edge, staring menacingly at the three of us.

A demon.

I'd never actually seen one in the flesh before, but what else could it be? If it was Tom Cruise, his makeup artist would win all the Oscars.

My brain yanked the Fighting Demons for Beginners page from my mental "combat training" file folder, but unfortunately, it all boiled down to a single word: Run.

The beast swung off the roof, plunging toward us. Lienna and I leaped clear. Slamming down hard enough to crack the asphalt, the demon slashed with a long arm. I reeled back, colliding with Harold's shoulder as the deadly claws whipped toward me—coming so close to my chest I felt the breeze of their passing.

Harold let out a blood-curdling scream.

The demon had missed me because I hadn't been its target. Its claws raked across Harold's chest, and the only reason his ribs were still intact was because I'd knocked him backward.

Looming over us, the demon cocked its arm again. With a half-panicked yelp, I Split Kit myself, sending a fake version leaping in front of the demon's attack while the real me became invisible.

Who knew if psycho warping worked on demons—but the demon's mind wasn't the one I needed to fool, so I stretched the range of my halluci-bomb to its max.

Without hesitating, the demon attempted to gore fake-Kit with its claws. Its arm swung right through the warp, causing the creature to lurch to the side as its uninterrupted momentum threw it off balance.

I took the opportunity to tackle the demon around the waist.

"Lienna!" I shouted. "Get Harold!"

The demon stumbled, and as Lienna grabbed Harold's arm and dragged him behind the dumpster, I leaped away, still invisible, and darted after them. As the demon turned, I threw out another halluci-bomb, again pushing my range as far as I could.

A fake version of me, Lienna, and Harold bolted down the alley, heading deeper into the mid-morning gloom. I'd hastily constructed the warp, so Fake Harold wasn't perfect, but the demon lumbered after them nonetheless, its long tail swinging awkwardly with each step.

"Kit!" Lienna whisper-called.

"Concentrating," I muttered, crouched beside the dumpster as I kept our fake doppelgangers running.

"*Kit!*"

The doppelganger warp had almost reached the end of the alley, so I abandoned it and ducked behind the dumpster, dropping my invisibility as well.

Lienna was pouring a potion over Harold's chest. Blood covered his front, and his lungs heaved with rapid breaths. Swearing, I reached to grab his arm. We had to get out of here before—

The dumpster jolted, then lifted off the ground. It flew sideways, hurled with unbelievable strength, and crashed onto its side—blocking our easiest escape out of the alley.

The demon loomed over us, red eyes burning. It was a seven-foot-tall barbarian with long limbs, a messy mane of black hair, and reddish-brown skin. Two curved horns protruded from each temple and its powerful fingers were tipped with the black claws that had ripped Harold open. Crude leather shorts covered its man—or demon?—bits.

It gazed down at us with an eerily blank expression, then lifted its arm again.

"*Ori te formo cupolam!*" Lienna yelled, pulling her Rubik's Cube from her satchel.

As soon as the spell left her lips, a blue, watery shield erupted from the cube. It flowed out, enclosing her and Harold—and missing me, because I was two feet farther away than I should've been.

The demon's fist slammed into the dome-shaped shield and ricocheted back, throwing it off-kilter. As the demon straightened like an awkward Rocky Balboa, I dropped another invisi-bomb, hiding myself.

The demon struck the spell with its other fist. The blow rippled across the shield and its blue glow dimmed.

"Harold," Lienna shouted, shaking his shoulder with her free hand. "Call out your demon!"

His wide, glassy eyes stared unblinkingly at the attacking creature, blood still leaking from his torso and his face contorted in disbelieving terror as though he'd never seen a demon before. Except *I* was the one who'd never seen a demon before. He was a goddamn *contractor!*

Speaking of contractors—

"Kit!" Lienna's wide eyes swung across the spot where I'd vanished, fear thickening her voice. "Where—"

The demon smashed another blow into her shield, and it dimmed further.

"Hold on!" I called, lunging up.

I sprinted past the demon and into the center of the alley. Fighting that beast wasn't happening. It might be slow and clumsy, but according to my training, it was basically unstoppable. You could rip its limbs off and it would keep coming like Monty Python's Black Knight.

And that was because a contracted demon was basically a lethal marionette—and controlling its every move was a contractor who needed a clear view of the battleground to pilot their demon.

I rapidly surveyed each end of the alley, then looked up at the rooftop the demon had jumped from. Perched on the edge was a stocky man with a Mr. Clean haircut and a punky young woman with half her head shaved. The latter was gripping something small in her hand that was probably an infernus.

Locking my invisi-bomb on their minds, I sprinted toward the fire escape and leaped for the bottom rungs of the retracted ladder. As I hauled myself up onto the platform, the demon rained blows on Lienna's shield. I could hear her shouting at Harold to call his demon out before it was too late, but the wounded contractor seemed incapable of understanding what she wanted.

I sprinted up the first flight of stairs. Halfway there.

Crash.

I looked down. Lienna's shield had failed and the demon's fist was buried in the pavement inches from her legs. She scrambled to her feet, reaching into her satchel for something that could slow the beast down.

Rushing headlong up the rusty stairs, I created a Split Kit and materialized him five feet behind the contractor, a gun in his hand.

"Greetings, assholes," fake-Kit said cheerfully, leveling his equally fake weapon at the contractor's head.

She and her male companion dove sideways as fake-Kit fired his gun, each shot accompanied by an explosive burst—which I was very familiar with, having been shot by a very similar, much more real gun once before. I stole a glance at the alley two stories below, where the demon had frozen halfway through a strike that would've put its claws through Lienna's chest.

That was the thing with puppet demons. If the contractor was distracted or in danger, they couldn't focus on controlling their marionette's movements. And that's why contractors were almost always paired with a champion—as in a musclebound, magic-wielding guardian, not some dude in a hockey jersey, holding a boombox and belting out Queen lyrics.

Mr. Clean's stocky evil twin rolled onto his feet, pulling a long dagger from a sheath on his hip with the same motion. He slashed it through the air as though to disembowel a pesky ghost—and a wall of fire whooshed up, racing for fake-Kit. It engulfed him, the inferno burning white with heat.

If that'd been the real me, I'd have been a blackened matchstick. These lunatics had no qualms about serving up souffléed Kit.

Satisfied that I was dead, the contractor turned back toward the alley, her hand closing around the infernus hanging from her neck.

But that brief distraction had given me enough time to reach the rooftop. Jaw clenched with concentration, I had fake-Kit burst out of the flames and flee across the building. Cursing, the follicle-challenged pyromage champion sprinted after him, hurling fireballs.

Keeping half an eye on that warp, I created another one—a duplicate of the demon down in the alley. It appeared almost on top of the contractor and loosed a bestial roar so loud it would've ruptured her eardrums if the sound had been real.

She flinched, stumbled, and sat heavily on her ass. The fake demon lunged for her—and her infernus lit with a red glow. A streak of crimson light flashed up from the alley and hit the infernus. It absorbed into the disc, then burst back out. The red glow stretched upward, seven feet tall, then solidified into her demon.

The real demon swung at my fake one. Its arm passed through the warp.

The contractor gasped—then grinned. She glanced back to where her champion had chased fake-Kit to the edge of the rooftop and was trying in vain to light him on fire.

"It's an illusion!" she shouted. "Just light up everything!"

Shit.

She shoved to her feet and gestured imperiously with one hand, the other clutching her infernus. Her demon leaped off the roof, and a second later, the crack of its landing reverberated through the alley. Lienna shouted an incantation.

Behind me, fire erupted—a wall of flame stretching the length of the building. The pyromage sent it sweeping across the roof.

Still invisible, I launched forward. As scorching heat built behind me, I sprinted for the only spot that wouldn't be engulfed in an inferno: the spot where the contractor stood. Catching her in a headlock, I squeezed hard. She spluttered and grabbed at my arm, her fingernails raking my jacket sleeve.

My gaze skittered toward the edge of the rooftop, dangerously close, and the alley below.

Horror rammed through my lungs.

In the alley, the demon stood unmoving—but its crushing grip was wrapped around Harold's throat. His legs twitched as Lienna wrenched desperately on the demon's fingers, trying to break its grip.

"Make your demon let him go!" I yelled, locking my arm tighter around the contractor's throat. "Now!"

She yanked on my wrist. Below, the demon didn't move, frozen in place as it choked the deli owner.

"Let him go!" I roared in her ear, frantically debating what to do. Release her? Knock her out? If she was unconscious, would the demon return to the infernus or would it remain in place, still choking Harold? I didn't know!

A hand grabbed my hair—and I realized the fiery wall behind me had died. So had my invisi-bomb. I'd gotten too caught up in trying to save Harold that I'd neglected to keep myself hidden.

The pyromage wrenched my head back and put his dagger against my throat. "Let *her* go."

I dropped a shattered-mirror Funhouse warp over his mind, then rammed my elbow into his gut. Arms flailing, he staggered back toward the building's edge, only a foot away. I half twisted toward him, dropping the warp.

His vision returned to normal, but his heel went off the edge. I lunged for him, a hand outstretched to grab his windmilling arm. The contractor tore out of my grasp, throwing off my balance, and my fingers brushed evil Mr. Clean's sleeve.

He plummeted out of my reach.

Time stalled. The gears in my brain jammed. He was falling—two stories toward unyielding pavement. Falling because of my warp, because I'd shoved him, because I hadn't grabbed him—

The sound of the pyromage's impact below reverberated through my very bones, and at the same moment, a streak of crimson sped up from the alley. The contractor was calling her demon back to her—which meant it was seconds from materializing on the rooftop with us.

I spun around. The punky contractor was two steps behind me, triumph blazing in her face as she clutched her infernus. Crimson light sucked into the silver disc, then surged out again—and my fist slammed into her cheek.

She collapsed, the glow of her infernus dying away. As she sprawled limply, I grabbed her infernus and yanked it over her head. Clutching it, breathing hard, I dropped to my knees at the rooftop's edge.

"Lienna?" I called, my voice cracking.

She was kneeling beside Harold's prone form. At my shout, she looked up. For a second, she just stared at me, then she slowly shook her head.

Unbearable heaviness flooded my body and I braced my hands on the rough concrete, head hanging between my shoulders.

A red glow flashed. I almost whirled toward the contractor, thinking she'd woken up, but the light wasn't coming from her or her infernus. It was streaking across the alley, passing right through the dumpster. Lienna jerked away as the light rushed into Harold's body.

He lit up like a red-tinted Christmas bulb, then the luminescence faded away, and the overcast gloom settled back over the alley.

8

SEATED BACKWARD on an uncomfortable chair with my arms
folded across the back, I stared through the one-way glass at the
small, barren interrogation room on the other side. I was way
more familiar with that room than I wanted to be, having spent
several hours in it when I was a crook instead of an agent.

My gaze shifted across the punk-haired woman sitting in
my former spot, her handcuffs chained to the table. That
should've been Harold, but Harold was dead.

Lienna and Agent Harris were seated across from the
contractor, tag-teaming their interrogation. Since I wasn't an
actual field agent, all I could do was wait and watch. She'd
improved her technique since interviewing me months ago,
not that it was doing her any good against the contractor.

In the interrogation room, Lienna and Harris got to their
feet. The two filed out of the room, leaving the contractor
chained to the table. A moment later, the door to the

observation room opened. As Lienna walked in, I glimpsed Harris stalking down the hall, ire fizzing off him like an overflowing soda can.

Lienna's expression wasn't much calmer as she dropped into the empty chair beside me. "Thirty minutes of interrogation and she didn't say *a single word*. Even you weren't that bad."

"Thanks?"

"At least you talked, even if it was all nonsense. This woman might as well have no voice box."

Nonsense? Was she calling my encyclopedic knowledge of film trivia *nonsense*?

"Maybe I punched her too hard and she can't speak," I suggested. "Give her paper and a pen and see if she writes out her confession. Or maybe a game of charades is in order."

"We don't need a confession. We already have her dead to rights for attacking us and murdering Harold. What we need is information—why she targeted Harold, what guild she belongs to, who she works for. Even her name would be helpful."

"My charades suggestion still stands."

Lienna jabbed an angry finger at the window. "Does she strike you as the kind of rogue who's going to give us anything?"

I took a second to absorb the raw fury etched into the contractor's persistent scowl. I wondered if that's what happened when you spent too much time in close proximity to a demon. You became a living rage emoji.

Dropping my chin onto my folded arms, I stared moodily at the murderous contractor. She wasn't the only one who'd killed today.

A soft touch on my shoulder. Lienna leaned forward to see my face. "Kit? You doing okay?"

"Been better," I admitted.

She was quiet for a moment. "Nothing about that fight went the way we wanted, but if you hadn't been with me, I'd be dead."

"If a real agent had been with you, no one would be dead."

"No, Kit." She squeezed my shoulder. "Demons are difficult to stop and even harder to kill. All I could do was put up a shield and hope for the best, but a demon can't act if the contractor is distracted, and your warps are *extremely* distracting."

I couldn't argue with that. "But Harold died. I should've done more."

"I was right there and I couldn't save him either." She rubbed my upper arm comfortingly. "Don't beat yourself up, Kit. It was a life or death situation."

"Another one," I grumbled. "We've almost died twice today, and we still don't know why."

"We know one thing: Harold's demon contract was real, but his infernus wasn't."

I sat up. "It wasn't? And since when were we doubting his contract was legit?"

"Since he wouldn't call out his demon to protect himself, which would only make sense if he didn't have a demon. But after he died, that red light possessed him."

"Yeah, what was that? It looked like the same streaky red glow as the contractor's demon when she called it in and out of her infernus."

Lienna nodded. "That's exactly what it was. A demon. It was fulfilling the Banishment Clause."

My eyes widened. "That was a demon taking his soul?"

"And returning to the demonic realm, yes. So Harold was in a real contract with a real demon, and it took his soul when he died. *But*"—she tapped a finger on her knee in emphasis—"the demon didn't come out of the infernus in his pocket. It came from somewhere else."

"Did he loan his demon to his best bud or something?"

"Only the contractor can control the demon they're in a contract with. Lending his infernus to anyone would make it as useless as the fake one he was carrying."

We gazed at each other, equally perplexed.

A rap on the door interrupted our silent "I don't get it" commentary. It swung open, revealing a tall, wispy woman in her late twenties with a skater aesthetic. A yellow toque scarcely contained her dark, wavy hair.

"Hey hey," she said pleasantly, strolling into the room. "Heard you've got a mute."

Lienna rose to her feet, her back stiff in a clear "Agent Shen is not pleased" kind of way.

"Agent Suttles," she said quietly. "I haven't completed any forms for a telepath-assisted interview, and we don't have an arbitrator—"

"Calm, calm. I'm just wandering by." The woman winked. "Agent Harris said I should say hello, that's all. You two've had a tough day. I'm Tasha," she added, offering me her hand.

Bemusedly, I took it. "I'm Kit. Analyst."

"An analyst at an interrogation?" Her eyes lost focus, and she abruptly clasped both hands around mine. "Don't hold back, Kit. Let yourself feel, then let it go, or it'll eat you alive."

I blinked. Was this rule-bending mind reader therapizing me?

Lienna shouldered in beside me, forcing Tasha to let go of my hand. "Using your abilities on another MPD employee without permission—"

"Just a quick dip," Tasha cut in, smiling. "Take care of your partner, Lienna. He's not as okay as he looks."

I opened my mouth to protest, then shut it. She wasn't wrong.

"Anyway." Tasha swung toward the one-way glass. "Looky what we have here. Did you tip her off that there are telepaths in the precinct?"

"No."

"Hmm, well, she's already locked down her thoughts. She's meditating."

I glanced again at the contractor, trying to imagine how anyone who looked like they'd sat on a cactus could be in a state of deep, peaceful comptemplation.

Lienna's mouth thinned, but she didn't protest Tasha's attempt to read our rogue contractor's thoughts—which told me how desperate she was for answers.

My favorite poetry-quoting psychic, Agent Tim, was our precinct's full-time telepath. Tasha Suttles, on the other hand, bounced around from precinct to precinct. She'd been kicking around here for about three weeks.

Telepathy wasn't a common psychic power, and neither was it popular among the mythic community. It's kind of funny when you think about it. No one cares that giant corporations are harvesting information about every facet of our lives, but the moment a telepath walks into the room, we're up in arms over our precious privacy.

My dislike of Agent Tim had nothing to do with his telepathy, though. I disliked him because he was a smug jerkwad and largely responsible for my second flunk on the field exam.

Anyway, during my studies of procedure and protocol, I'd learned that almost a century ago, the North American and European coalitions of guild masters had basically decided that, hey, using telepaths against suspects is all sorts of sketchy. They'd thrown up a big stink, and as a result, there were a whole bunch of rules about when, where, and how the MPD could utilize telepathy against suspects and convicted criminals.

And Tasha's presence in this room was flouting basically all of them.

I rubbed my chin. Having once been a suspect at the MPD's mercy, a big part of me was all about protecting suspects' rights and reigning in MagiPol's unchecked power. But another part of me didn't care about the rights of this particular rogue, who'd murdered Harold, almost murdered me and Lienna, and caused me to kill her champion.

I suspected Lienna was keeping her mouth shut because she felt the same way.

Arms crossed, Tasha faced the window, squinting at the contractor. Gradually, her squint deepened.

After a few minutes more, she sighed. "This woman is a closed book. She's meditating so hard I'm surprised she isn't levitating off her chair. I think she's been trained for this kind of thing."

"Who trains people to handle telepaths?" I asked.

Tasha turned away from the window. "I've heard some guilds do it—Psychica guilds and security guilds. But mostly rogues."

"So she's a dead end," Lienna grumbled.

"For now. But I can check in again on her. Maybe catch her off guard. You can't close down your mind forever."

"My observance of the political arena would beg to differ," I quipped.

Tasha smiled. Lienna didn't.

The telepath waved. "I'll continue on my way to the lunchroom, then. Nice checking in on you rookies. Take it easy, yeah?"

She shot me a pointed look, then bustled out the door.

As it clacked shut, Lienna dropped back into her chair. "Agent Harris is having an analyst comb through all contractor records for a match on this woman. If her contract is legal, we'll find her. And Captain Blythe got us clearance for a deep finances search, so Agent Harris will pull in another analyst to review records for Harold, Rocco, and his other clients."

I peered sideways at her. "Being the analyst on this case, shouldn't I do some of that?"

"You're staying with me. If we come face to face with another demon, I want you there to distract the contractor."

Because that had gone *so* well today. "But—"

"You're my partner for this case, Kit," she growled. "Quit trying to weasel out of it."

I perked up. "Partner?"

Her instant regret at her word choice was written all over her face. "Harold had a real contract but a fake infernus. Rocco Thorn prepared his contract and infernus, meaning he's at least partially responsible for whatever was going on with Harold's contract."

"And after we talked to Harold yesterday, he told Rocco," I added. "This morning, someone tried to splatter us all over the parking lot outside his guild."

"Then this contractor"—Lienna gestured at the one-way glass and the stone-faced woman on the other side—"killed Harold before we could take him in for questioning. I'm not sure if she was waiting for us to show up, or if we just have bad timing."

"*Really* bad timing, I think."

She rose to her feet again. "Either way, our next move is clear."

"Yep." I stood as well. "Rocco Thorn is suspect *Numero Uno*. Are we talking to him next?"

Her expression was as bleak as mine. "Yes. And let's try not to almost die this time."

"Will do, partner."

She responded with an eye roll, because of course she did.

I grinned. "Shall we get going then, partner?"

"That's going to get really old really fast," she warned, heading for the door. "Really, really fast."

I slipped ahead of her and opened the door, holding it ajar with a sweep of my other arm. "After you, partner."

She gave me an even more magnificent eye roll that could have been crowned the Supreme Queen of All Eye Rolls. "Don't make me hurt you."

Classic Lienna.

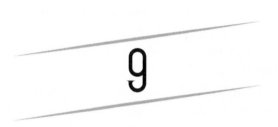

9

"SO, UH." Lienna cleared her throat. "How are you doing, Kit?"

I looked over at her, trying to ignore the way my knees kept bumping the glove compartment of our quantum-realm smart car, identical in every way to the one that had unwillingly blown its top this morning.

Don't think I didn't notice how bespectacled Agent Harris drove a black sedan that no doubt boasted enough luxurious leg space to satisfy a giraffe. Were the smart cars for rookie agents only?

"I'm fine," I replied.

She tapped her fingers on the steering wheel in a nervous, fidgety, un-Lienna-like way. "Do you want to talk about anything?"

"Like what? I mean, I'm having fun imagining what it'd feel like to punch Rocco's teeth into the back of his throat, but I should probably refrain."

"Yeah, don't do that." She flicked on her turn signal and switched lanes after a cursory shoulder check. The gloomy overcast from this morning had broken up, dotting the sky with blobs of gray cloud that kept drifting across the setting sun. "I'm here to listen if you need to ... share."

My forehead scrunched, and I had the sudden feeling this conversation would make more sense if I were stretched out on a lounge chair while Lienna sat beside me with a pad of paper, taking delicate notes as I dabbed my eyes with a tissue. "Are you asking because of what Tasha said?"

She glanced at me, half alarmed, half sheepish, then focused on the increasingly dense rush hour traffic. Awkward discomfort radiated off her, and I couldn't help a smile. She had many strengths—kicking bad-guy butt, scaring lesser mythics, out-geniusing other sorcerers, delivering frighteningly creative threats—but heart-to-heart conversations involving human emotions wasn't among them.

Still, she was trying, and I appreciated it. "I'm doing okay. Ready for whatever happens at the Grand Grimoire. I think."

She chewed her lower lip.

"Are *you* okay?" I asked. "You have a lot riding on this case." And so far, it wasn't going smoothly.

"I've never gone after a guild master before," she admitted quietly, directing the car off the main road and onto a significantly dicier side street. "And even if we get him, I don't know if Captain Blythe will be satisfied."

"Because she wants the whole damn guild disbanded." I ran my fingers through my hair. "Do you know what she has against it?"

"Purely Demonica guilds like the Grand Grimoire tend to be trouble. The type of people who become demon contractors aren't usually docile personalities. Aside from that, I'm not sure, but we're about to walk into a viper's nest."

"Well, if shit hits the fan, I'll just warp some minds to get us out."

She arched an eyebrow. "What about warping some reality?"

I grimaced. "Sure, no problem. I'll whip up a trebuchet out of thin air."

"Why a trebuchet?"

"Why not? If you ask me, modern society could only be improved by a larger quantity of trebuchets in day-to-day life."

She rolled her eyes, then craned her neck to scan the buildings lining the street. "Let's hope this interview doesn't degenerate to the point of requiring medieval war engines."

I looked down at the thick folder on my lap. It contained everything of interest about Rocco Thorn that we'd dug up so far. Unfortunately, the only obvious indicator of lawbreaking was a handful of dubitable paperwork, and that worried me.

Lienna parallel parked between a van, which definitely looked like it was used to kidnap children, and an orange-ish sedan spotted with rust like a decrepit leopard. We climbed out of our mini-mobile onto a street barely wide enough for a vehicle to drive down it without smashing mirrors off the parked cars. The gutters were littered with trash.

The road itself was on a hill, with the buildings roughly embedded in the slope, giving everything a lopsided look, as though it'd been drawn by a toddler. Across the downward-slanting street, a white three-story building boasted ugly bars on the windows. A green awning with faded gold letters in a font straight out of an eighties arcade game read, "The Grand Grimoire."

It didn't look very grand.

"Feels like a place you'd go to buy a human kidney," I observed as we approached the door. "Is that what their front is? Black market organs?"

The MPD requires every guild to have a front—a non-mythic business behind which the guild can operate. Some rely heavily on their fronts for income. Others, not so much.

Judging by the Grand Grimoire's pathetic excuse for a storefront, it fell into the latter category. The interior was a dimly lit dust-mite paradise. A handful of outdated board games populated the shelves, a couple decks of cards with faded price tags were stacked on top, and the cash register, which could have passed for an antique, was unmanned. A windowless door, most likely leading to the guild's inner workings, lurked behind the counter.

Lienna found a "ring for service" bell beside the aged cash register and smacked it.

Nobody came.

While she rang it again, I inspected a second-hand box containing Operation—that game where you have to exercise fine motor skills to perform medically dubious procedures on a plastic man sporting a clown nose and a Charlie Chaplin haircut. Vintage board games are a strange lot, man.

Lienna continued to abuse the bell, growing grumpier by the ding. I opened a faded Mouse Trap box and inspected its dismal contents.

"Where the hell are these guys?" she growled, still going to town on the bell like the most enthusiastic member of a really lame all-percussion band.

"I don't think they're coming. But there's probably a dog close by that's drooling like a maniac."

She didn't reply. Sure, everyone gets a chuckle from a lazy Sean Connery joke, but class it up with a Pavlov reference and all you get are crickets.

Abandoning the bell, she marched around the counter, rummaging through her satchel as she went. "Well, if they won't open this door, I will."

Before she could kick it down or blow it up with her Rubik's Cube, the lock clunked and the door swung open, nearly bowling her over. In the threshold loomed a burly dude with a brush cut, a bushy beard, and a silver infernus dangling around his neck in plain sight.

"What do ya want?" he grunted. "We're closed."

"Ah, shucks," I said with a snap of my fingers. "I was really hoping to add this incomplete Mouse Trap game to my extensive collection of completely useless shit."

Lienna, always more professional, held up her badge. "Agent Shen, MPD. The comedian is Agent Morris."

"What do ya want, *agents*?" our greeter asked again, dripping false civility all over his crumb-peppered beard. Based on his appearance and demeanor, I decided his name was Butch. He seemed like a Butch.

"We're here to speak with your guild master," Lienna informed him.

"Mr. Thorn isn't in right—"

"Don't bother," she interrupted sharply. "We're coming in whether you like it or not. If you want to tell me Rocco Thorn isn't here, go right ahead. But when I find him in there, not only will your idiocy be glaringly transparent, but I'll arrest you for obstruction. Got it?"

Good lord, her tongue was almost as dangerous as her magic. I loved it.

Butch didn't look impressed, but he shoved the door open a little wider. "Then come on in. The MPD is always welcome at the Grand Grimoire."

Sarcasm didn't suit Butch.

We followed him past a few abandoned offices, through another door, and up a dark staircase to the building's second floor, where we found a room best described as the hybrid offspring of a biker bar and a frat house.

Ten tough-looking men, replete with tattoos, facial hair, and leather outfits, lounged on a trio of couches that might have just been pulled from the local garbage dump. Some recliners and the odd coffee table made up the rest of the furniture. Stuffed against the back wall was a collection of laptops and computers spread out over a couple of tables. A golden sunset shone through the big windows, undermining the dark and brooding vibe they'd been going for when they'd painted the walls a deep maroon color.

"Do all demon contractors dress like *Sons of Anarchy* extras?" I whispered to Lienna. My question garnered nothing but an elbow to the ribs.

"Wait here," Butch instructed before stumping back through the door we had come in. His loud footfalls moved upward to the next level.

A recliner creaked as a man-shaped mountain rose to his feet, doing his best to stare Lienna and me down. He was easily six and a half feet tall and had the musculature of a silverback gorilla who liked beer a bit too much. Leather gauntlets covered his thick hands, the wrists banded in runes—a combat sorcerer?

"You two lost?" His voice rumbled across the room like thunder.

Lienna flashed him her badge. "Not at all."

I stepped in beside her, showing support without getting aggressive about it, my hands tucked casually in my pockets.

"MPD," the gorilla sneered. "Did I miss filling out a form? You gonna arrest me?"

My partner bristled. "If you give me a reason, I'd be happy to introduce you to the precinct's holding cells—assuming you haven't visited them before, which I doubt."

"But luckily," I jumped in, "we're here for a quick word with your GM. It's about paperwork, yeah, but *everything* with the MPD is about paperwork, so what can you do?"

I smiled and shrugged, inviting him in on the joke. He hesitated, then grunted. Tugging his leather jacket straight, he lumbered back to his recliner.

"Thought I was gonna have to tackle him," a hoarse smoker's voice drawled from behind me. "Glad you two have your heads on straight."

Turning, I found an older, wiry guy who clearly spent a lot of time outside. Between the suntanned hide on his face and the salt-and-pepper scruff dotting his jaw, I couldn't guess his age. Somewhere between forty and eighty was my best estimate.

I had no idea who he was except that he *wasn't* Rocco Thorn.

"Name's Leroy," the mystery mythic added, offering us each a handshake.

"Agent Shen," Lienna replied.

"And I'm Kit."

"Agent Morris," my partner corrected.

"Kit's fine."

"Good to make your acquaintance. Is there anything I can help you with while you wait?"

"Are you guys always this welcoming?" I asked. "Or just Koko over there?"

I nodded at the ape man, who was giving us the dagger-eyes treatment from his recliner.

"Now, that's an insult to the memory of Koko. She could use sign language, after all."

I couldn't help but grin. A man who could trade Koko the gorilla jokes was my kind of dude. Even if he was a grisly Grand Grimoire member.

"The guys have been a bit sensitive lately," Leroy mused, glancing at his guildmates and lowering his voice slightly. "Last time a pretty little lady came in, they were left smarting afterward—in body and in pride."

"Oh?" I prompted. "What happened?"

"I wasn't here—it was in the middle of the hunt for that unbound demon a couple weeks ago—but from what I heard, this petite thing came in with her champion, asking to join the guild. The guys were skeptical, as you might imagine."

"What happened?" Lienna asked curiously.

"The little lady thoroughly enlightened them—with her demon."

I was instantly sad that I hadn't gotten to see that beatdown for myself.

"Hell of a contractor, she was—but you should know that." He gave a shrug that was somehow amused and perplexed at the same time. "She and that same demon of hers killed the unbound one a few days later."

His words pinged off a memory—everyone in the precinct gossiping about the "unusual" contractor who'd "appeared out of nowhere" to kill the escaped demon on Halloween.

"Do you mean that Page girl?" Lienna asked. "Didn't—"

The whining of door hinges interrupted her. Butch stepped out of the stairwell and beckoned us in with a silent bob of his beard. Looked like it was time to say hello to Rocco Thorn, the overactive summoner with an inexplicable surge of customers from sleeper guilds.

And the scheming scumbag who was probably trying to kill us.

BIDDING LEROY ADIEU, we followed Butch back into the stairwell. He grouchily ushered us up one more flight, down a hallway, and into an office near the back of the building. A steel desk hunkered in front of the room's only window, which presented a delightfully drab view of the narrow, junky street below.

Behind the desk was the Grand Grimoire's guild master. A large man in his early fifties, he wore a sleek black suit that looked like it had been deliberately tailored to fit a hair too small so it'd stretch across his broad shoulders. His thick blond beard complemented an unmistakably Scandinavian complexion, giving him the look of a Dolph Lundgren clone who'd forgotten to shave for three months.

As we entered, another man walked out—a slender, t-shirt clad millennial with messy black hair spiked out in every direction. He shot us a distinctly hostile glare on his way by.

The door swung shut behind him. Butch hadn't come in with us, not that I'd expected him to.

"Have a seat, agents," Rocco said in a deep, gravelly voice. "Make yourselves comfortable."

Judging by the state of the chairs he was offering us, I didn't expect sitting to be a more comfortable experience than standing, but I didn't argue. Lienna and I sat—and my worst fears about the butt-cheek torture I was about to endure came true. These weren't chairs. They were spiteful slabs of unfinished wood masquerading as chairs.

Rocco scooped together the papers scattered across his desk. "I apologize for the mess. I was just in a meeting with my first officer."

Mr. Millennial was the first officer here? I would've expected someone with more facial hair.

"We won't take up too much of your time," Lienna said, opting for a charade of courtesy to kick things off. "We have a few questions regarding a case we're investigating."

He folded his hands on top of his papers. "I hope I can be of assistance."

His words sounded sincere, but I didn't trust them any farther than I could throw the overly muscled, demon-summoning Viking.

"You're listed as the summoner for Harold Atherton."

"Yes," Rocco agreed before she could pose a question. "I summoned his demon on October seventh and sealed his contract on October fourteenth."

Information that was freely available in the documents and permits.

"When did you first meet Harold?" Lienna asked.

Rocco studied her with deep-set eyes. "I'm afraid that information is confidential. I must protect my clients' privacy. I'm sure you understand."

Her fingers tightened on our folder of research. "This is a murder investigation, Mr. Thorn. I require your cooperation."

"Do you have an official summons for me?" His pleasant expression didn't change, nor had he so much as blinked at the mention of murder. "Unless I'm being subpoenaed, I can't violate my clients' privacy."

My jaw clenched. We couldn't bring Rocco in because we couldn't link him to Harold's murder. Yet.

Lienna flipped her folder open. "Then let's discuss the other summonings you've performed over the past three months. It's been a busy season for you."

"It has. A very successful one, if I do say so. I'm pleased to have provided contracts to so many mythics in need of one."

"Where did you find all these new clients?" she asked tersely.

He smiled. "How my clients find me is confidential, Miss Shen."

"*Agent* Shen," she snapped.

"What kind of recruiting are you doing?" I interjected. "How do you advertise your services? Craigslist?"

"Advertising isn't required." He leaned back in his chair. "I'm the only licensed summoner in the greater Vancouver area. My only competition retired fifteen years ago, and he didn't need to advertise either. Would-be contractors find us. It isn't difficult."

I held eye contact with him, watching for a tell. "Why do you think you've seen a sudden spike in business?"

"The world is a dangerous place."

That was word for word what Harold had said about why he needed a demon contract.

"Generally speaking," he continued, "new clients hear about me through word of mouth. My past clients all speak very highly of me."

"Really?" Lienna murmured. "And which past clients should we contact to confirm that?"

"All my contracts and their recipients are filed in the archives. Feel free to reach out to any of them." His cool smile returned. "I have nothing to hide."

My fingers started to curl into fists, but I forced them to relax. I hadn't spent a year around KCQ's slimy lawyers not to recognize Rocco's brand of bull.

"You seem to be hiding a lot," Lienna growled softly.

"Client-summoner privilege, my dear. Serve me with a subpoena and I'll answer your questions."

The bastard knew arresting a guild master without a solid case against him would cripple the investigation. GMs had more protections under the law than any other mythics to prevent unscrupulous MPD agents from targeting them.

Lienna jerked a photo from her file and held it out. "Do you recognize this woman?"

Rocco glanced at the snapshot of the punk contractor taken from our interrogation room. "I've never seen her before."

"She's not a client?"

"No."

"A guild member?"

"Obviously not."

"An employee?"

"Still no." He arched an eyebrow. "There are no women associated with the Grand Grimoire—not to suggest we discriminate. Demonica rarely appeals to the fairer sex," he added in the most sexist way possible.

Lienna's jaw flexed.

"What about Page?" I jumped in, buying my partner time to cool her temper. "One of your guys downstairs mentioned her—the contractor who killed the unbound demon."

"Robin Page? She joined our ranks around Halloween but moved on very quickly. Unfortunately, the Grand Grimoire wasn't a good match for her despite her abundant talent."

"Where is she now?" I asked. Thanks to my endless research over the last couple of days, I knew which of our local guilds were licensed for the Demonica class, and I could count them on one hand. If Robin Page wasn't with the Grand Grimoire, she had to be with one of the others.

Rocco's deep-set eyes glittered in a way that sent a chill down my spine. "I believe she's now a member of the Crow and Hammer."

Another chill followed the first. The Crow and Hammer—the selfsame group of delinquents that had brought down my old guild, sent me fleeing for my life, and triggered the rollercoaster of events that resulted in my forced employment with the MPD.

"What can you tell me about the murder victim?" Lienna asked.

"What murder victim is that?" Rocco asked, not taking her bait.

"Harold. He's dead."

Surprise that might've been genuine shifted his bold features. "I'm very sorry to hear that. I didn't know him well, but he seemed like a good man."

"He refused to call out his demon when he was attacked," my partner revealed. "Why didn't he use it to defend himself?"

"Controlling a demon takes months to learn and years to master. If he was scared or panicking, he might not have remembered the incantation for calling his demon from the infernus."

It was a plausible explanation, especially since Harold had been slashed open by the attacking demon and probably more concerned about blood loss than incantations. Lienna flicked a glance at me, subtle frustration tightening her eyes.

"Rocco," I said, slouching back into the torture chair. "You're a demon expert, right?"

He raised his thick eyebrows. "As much as any summoner can be."

"Then tell me, what does it look like when the Banishment Clause activates?"

"You mean when a contractor dies?" He braced his elbows on the desk. "If the demon is outside the infernus, it will immediately shift into its incorporeal form, possess the contractor's body, and disappear. If it's inside the infernus, it will jump straight from the infernus to the contractor's body."

"Is there a distance limit on that?"

"What do you mean?"

"How far away can the demon be from the dead contractor for the Banishment Clause to work?"

"There's nothing in the contract language that limits distance, so the only possible limit would be on the demon's magic—whether it could sense that its contractor was dead. Distance between demon, infernus, and contractor weakens the connection."

"And how fast can a demon travel in its incorporeal form?"

"Very quickly, but I'm not sure of the actual speed."

That wasn't enough information to help me calculate how far away Harold's demon had been when he'd died.

"Why was Harold carrying a fake infernus?" Lienna asked out of nowhere.

Again, Rocco didn't give anything away. "A fake? I assure you, the one I gave him was very real."

"Well, he wasn't carrying that one."

"I can't imagine why." He offered another hollow smile, this one edged with challenge. "Do you have any questions I might be able to answer without groundless speculation?"

Mocking us and dismissing us at the same time. That fantasy of knocking his pearly whites into his tonsils infiltrated my brain again.

Lienna pushed to her feet, clutching the folder with one arm. "Expect your summons for questioning soon, Mr. Thorn."

"Am I a suspect in poor Harold's death?" he asked with patently false innocence.

"That's confidential," she quipped scornfully, and I almost applauded.

Rocco gave a small, derisive bow from his seat. "I'll look forward to it, then, Miss Shen."

Spinning on her heel, she swept to the door. I rose more slowly, keeping my gaze on Rocco.

He smiled coolly. "Mr. Morris, I wish I could say your new employment suits you, but your talents are wasted at the MPD."

Had he looked into my guild history—and criminal record—before attempting to kill me, or had he heard about me from my former guildmates? It wouldn't surprise me if he'd had dealings with the ol' KCQ crowd. He was a snake in a businessman's clothes, just like them.

"Are you familiar with my specific 'talents'?" I asked neutrally.

"I'm afraid not."

I gave him a cool smile of my own. "Then I look forward to giving you a demonstration, Mr. Thorn."

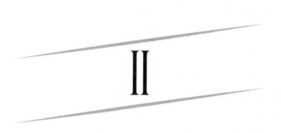

II

I EYED LIENNA'S white-knuckled grip on the steering wheel and hoped she wasn't too tense to direct our replacement smart car through the streets.

"Well," I ventured, "that didn't go great."

She growled wordlessly.

"He didn't give away anything." I drummed my fingers on my knee. "Other than coming off as a scheming, backstabbing creep, but we can't arrest him for that."

Glaring out the windshield at the rows of taillights in our path, she pried one hand off the wheel to shove her ponytail over her shoulder. "Do you think a more experienced agent could've gotten something out of him?"

"He dodged our questions like a pro. The guy knows what he's doing. My old GM was the same way."

She flicked on her signal and waited for another driver to make room for our dinky-toy car.

"Why does it seem like all we're doing is adding more questions to this case?" she grumbled.

"Chin up, partner," I said in the cheesiest possible tone, flashing her a grin. "We've been at this since nine a.m. Let's take a break. Plus, I'm starving." I pointed through the windshield at a boxy, bright blue truck parked on the curb a block ahead. "That souvlaki food truck serves a mean chicken skewer, if you want a quick dinner."

"Sure."

She squeezed into the right lane, then parallel parked between two sedans a few cars up from our mobile food destination. We climbed out, and a chilly wind pushed us toward the truck. The mouth-watering aroma of grilled chicken hung over the lineup of hungry customers, and my taste buds were already preparing themselves for tangy tzatziki sauce.

We moved to the back of the line, which extended into the opening of an alley. That was the downside to working during the evening rush hour. Everything was busy.

I zipped my jacket up under my chin. "Did you finish watching the movie last night after you got home?"

"No." She kicked at a rock on the sidewalk, avoiding my eyes. "I figured we could watch the rest of it together sometime."

I opened my mouth to invite her over to my place, then checked myself. Firstly, she'd made it clear she had reservations about dating me—though whether those reservations were work-related, relocation-related, or something else, I didn't know—and asking her over might give the wrong impression. And secondly, my "place" consisted of a single room with only a bed for seating, which would *definitely* give the wrong impression. Thirdly, and most ironically, I didn't own a TV.

"That'd be fun," I said, the words sounding lame even to my ears. "Just let me know when."

How did people *do* this? Navigate these strange waters of "co-worker," "friend," "possible romantic interest," and "person I find extremely attractive and want to get closer to"? How did you progress from one to the other without risking the entire relationship? It was like that incomplete game of Mouse Trap I'd found at the Grand Grimoire: the rules were complicated, half the pieces were missing, and the whole situation was a delicate balance that led to an inevitable trap.

Having lived most of my life as either a down-trodden foster-kid outcast, an unemployed runaway outcast, or a mythic con-artist outcast, my romantic relationships had all been brief and with a lot more romance than relationship. It usually went: meet, flirt, Netflix and chill, then drift away once words like "exclusive" and "boyfriend" cropped up.

I'd never tried to date a co-worker *or* a friend before. These were uncharted waters, and it didn't help that Lienna was so hot and cold with me that she could star in a Katy Perry music video.

On the hot side, she blushed when I flirted with her, joked and bantered with me, seemed to like spending time together, and ogled me whenever I took my clothes off in front of her. Oh, and there was that time I'd been under an empath's influence and she'd let me kiss her for a lot longer than would've made sense if she hadn't liked me kissing her.

On the cold side, she rarely shared anything personal, didn't initiate interactions as much as I did, and had made it explicitly clear that she didn't want to date me for reasons unknown.

Aside from a few unilluminating mentions of her father, I knew absolutely nothing about her family.

"What are you counting?"

I blinked at Lienna, then realized I'd been ticking off my list of her hot/cold behaviors on my fingers. "Uh, the number of Death Stars in the *Star Wars* franchise," I lied.

Before she could criticize my counting skills, the weather came to my rescue. A gust of wind blasted down the sidewalk, carrying a wave of fallen leaves and paper garbage. I flung my arm up to cover my face, stepping backward into the alley.

A flare of blue light shone around my arm, and as the wind died, I lowered my hand. "Did you see that light?"

Lienna didn't reply, and I leaned out of the alley's mouth to peer down the street, wondering if a cop car was trying to squeeze through the traffic jam. All I could see were red taillights.

Dropping back onto my heels, I grimaced. "This line is barely moving. Maybe we should—"

"*Kit.*"

I looked over at her, confused by her harsh tone. "What?"

"I can't move."

My confusion deepened. "Huh?"

"*Can't move!*" Her limbs vibrated strangely. "A spell!"

For a second, I just stared—then understanding kicked in. "The wind—the light—that was a spell?"

My head whipped around, and I scanned the well-lit sidewalk and much darker alley, but there were people everywhere, with no way to identify a mythic attacker.

"Let's get out of here," I said quickly, looping an arm around her shoulders. If she couldn't move, I'd carry her—except when I pulled on her, she was as immobile as a stone statue.

I wrenched with all my strength, but she didn't budge an inch. My wild movements startled the people around us, and they shifted nervously away.

A tiny, pained sound escaped her as I pulled again. "Won't work," she forced out, barely able to move her mouth. "Need—"

A barrage of exclamations from the nearby crowd interrupted her:

"What's happening?"

"Is it going to fall?"

"You two, get out of the way!"

The shouted words startled me out of my "how to move Lienna" urgency. Turning, I found Lienna and myself alone at the mouth of the alley. Everyone else had drawn back, but they weren't weirded out by my and Lienna's mime act. They were all staring fearfully at something above my head.

I looked up.

Six feet overhead, a power line ran between the two old buildings—and it was sparking wildly at both ends. White sizzles danced across the line, and as I gawked in horror, a fiery flare raced from one end to the other and exploded in a shower of sparks.

"Move! Get away!"

Everyone from the food truck line was shouting at us—but Lienna was locked in place by a spell.

"My bag!" she hissed. "Red pyramid."

Her satchel was trapped under her elbow. I yanked it open and dug inside. Wooden Rubik's Cube, stun marbles, sunglasses, a scarf, a notebook, pens, a packet of tissues. I dug deeper, sparks raining down on us as the power line crackled loudly. Every flare was accompanied by a deep *vrrooo* noise that vibrated through me.

How come she never had this much difficulty locating an artifact in this bottomless pit of chaos? Was there some sort of unfathomable organization system to the clutter?

A deluge of sparks rained over me as a loud crack ran through the power line overhead. My fingers wrested free something small and triangular: a marble-sized red pyramid with a different rune on each side.

"Put—on—me!" Lienna gritted out.

Realizing the spell must need skin contact, I extended the pyramid toward her face.

"It's gonna fall!" a bystander shouted.

Hands grabbed my arms, dragging me away. The human spectators were trying to save us. Another Good Samaritan attempted to pull Lienna to safety and almost fell when she didn't move.

Snarling, I tore away from the gropey do-gooders and lunged toward Lienna, hand outstretched. The oscillating buzz of the power line deepened to a new pitch.

I pushed the artifact against her cheek, my other arm clamping around her waist.

"*Ori infringo potentiam!*"

At the same time as her gasping words, electricity exploded from the power line and one end broke free. It swung down, blue light bursting off it.

I leaped backward, and Lienna's feet came off the ground.

The burning, blazing power line swung right through the spot where she'd been standing. I slammed down on the pavement, my arms clamped tight around her, as the line hit the wall of the opposite building with a boom, a crack, and a wave of white-hot sparks.

Only because I'd fallen backward, and only because my gaze was aimed at the sky, did I see him.

Crouched on the rooftop, a few feet above the power line, was a bald man with a dark goatee, curved sunglasses, and a long black jacket. The instant I saw him, he slipped out of view.

As worried bystanders milled behind me, I slowly sat up. My arms were still banded around Lienna, holding her tight to my chest. She angled her head to see my face, her eyes wide and glassy with receding fear.

I rubbed my thumb gently across the red mark on her cheek where I'd pressed the small pyramid artifact. Somehow that turned into my hand cupping her warm cheek.

Her fingers were digging into my shoulders. Her lips parted. A soft press of my palm tilted her face up a shade more. I leaned in toward her.

Flashing red light erupted, glaring across every surface, and a firetruck blared its horn. I jolted straight, twisting to see two firetrucks forcing their way through the bumper-to-bumper traffic.

Sucking in a breath, I scooped Lienna up and stood. She didn't protest as I strode away from the alley and the violently sparking power line.

When I reached the smart car, I put her in the passenger seat, then circled around and got behind the wheel. Though I slid the seat back as far as it went, my knees still hit the steering column. I performed a quick shoulder check and pulled sharply into traffic.

Lienna cleared her throat shakily. "It looks like the car bomber isn't done with us yet."

Us? I wasn't so sure. I'd been close by, but it felt like my death would've been collateral damage rather than a targeted assassination.

I kept that thought to myself. Lienna had enough to worry about already.

12

"'**ROBIN PAGE**,'" I read aloud. "'Female. Twenty years old. Arcana, sorcery. Demonica, contractor. Recently awarded a bounty of one-hundred-and-forty-thousand dollars for slaying an unbound demon.'"

We were back at the precinct—miraculously alive and unzapped—and Robin Page's photo filled a corner of my monitor.

The young contractor definitely didn't look like a candidate for the Grand Grimoire. No tattoos, no leather, no piercings. Not even a scowl. Instead, she sported large glasses, short brown hair, and a comfy sweater. She looked like a teenager cosplaying as her favorite librarian.

Sitting beside me in Vinny's vacant chair, Lienna leaned closer to my desk. She'd recovered her composure following the assassination attempt an hour ago, though she was still pale.

"Robin Page killed the unbound demon *by herself?*" she asked.

"Looks like it." I scrolled down the page. "She's been a contractor for ... six months. That's it? She joined the Grand Grimoire on October thirty-first, killed the unbound demon on November second, then left the Grand Grimoire on November seventh."

"And joined the Crow and Hammer, according to Rocco."

"Actually ..." I opened an attached file. "There's a transfer request here, but the Crow and Hammer hasn't filed any of the pursuant paperwork for inducting her."

Lienna made a thoughtful noise. "What about her previous guild?"

I clicked around until I found it. "A guild called Indivision, located in Burnaby." Opening the guild's info page, I scanned its description. "A combo academic/sleeper guild."

We exchanged a meaningful look.

"Another contractor from a sleeper guild," she murmured. "Was Rocco the summoner?"

"Nope. It was some dude from Seattle. Maybe she didn't like the look of Rocco and decided a Starbucks-adjacent summoner would be safer."

Lienna sat back in Vinny's chair. "A coincidence, then? Robin Page is an unlikely contractor, but she doesn't match all the criteria of Rocco's other clients. And, unlike Harold, she has no issues wielding her demon effectively."

By "criteria," Lienna meant "financially wrecked." Agent Harris had sent us the preliminary findings on a deep dive into the bank accounts of Rocco's clients, and all nine sleeper-mythics-turned-contractors shared an affinity for empty-wallet syndrome. Before his death, Harold had confirmed that Rocco had paid him off, and I was betting the summoner had waved wads of cold hard cash at his other "clients" too.

Robin Page, on the other hand, was doing okay for herself, monetarily speaking. Prior to that six-figure demon bounty depositing in her account, she hadn't had much in savings, but she also had no debt, unlike the mythics Rocco targeted.

"You weren't kidding that she can manage her demon," I muttered, skimming the report on the unbound demon's demise. "Death by decapitation. Ouch. She went all Robespierre on it. And it looks like Blythe was on the scene to collect the dead demon. Do you think she met—"

"What's that?"

Lienna pointed over my shoulder at a section titled "Linked Files." The top link was a recent case number. I clicked it and an investigation page popped up. I took one look at the first photo under "Evidence" and almost upchucked the drive-thru chicken wrap I'd picked up on our way back to the precinct.

The picture showed a blood-sprayed concrete lot edging the harbor, bodies scattered across it. At a pier in the background, a speedboat was spewing flames and black smoke into the sky.

"What the hell is this?" I mumbled.

Lienna scooted her chair closer, our armrests bumping as we read the case details.

"A group of unidentified rogues believed to be members of Red Rum," she summarized, "were found dead on November third. Investigators think they died in a conflict between criminal parties, and one or both was responsible for the unbound demon. The scene showed signs of demon combat."

Red Rum. That was the rather conspicuous name for one of the most feared rogue guilds on the West Coast. They were not, as I had originally hoped when I'd first heard their name, a guild full of *The Shining* fanatics.

Nope, they were a murder guild. A globe-trotting gang of smugglers, assassins, and thieves, they preferred to stick to their fleet of expensive boats out in international waters. Whenever one of their ships dropped anchor near a city, there was always a mess to clean up afterward. Not like glitter and leftover pizza boxes. More like dead bodies and ruined lives.

Red Rum was called a guild because that was the easiest way to describe it, but it didn't follow any guild rules or regulations. It was a criminal organization that openly defied the MPD and did whatever it wanted—and killed anyone who tried to stop it, regardless of whether they were a mythic, a regular old human, or an MPD agent.

"Kit," Lienna said quietly, "look who reported the Red Rum bodies."

I dragged my stare off the gory photos and down to the line she was indicating.

"'Darius King,'" I read. "Guild master of the Crow and Hammer."

"The same guild Robin Page joined a week after killing the unbound demon." Lienna rubbed her face. "Darius King discovered the mass murder of the group suspected of unleashing an unbound demon, and the girl who killed that same demon joined his guild a week later. What are the chances that's just a big coincidence?"

"Pretty close to zilch."

"That's what I was thinking. But"—she squeezed her temples—"what are the chances *that* pile of suspicious coincidences has anything to do with the pile of suspicious coincidences surrounding Rocco Thorn?"

I twisted my mouth. "Not sure on that one. The only link between them is Robin Page, and she was only a member of the Grand Grimoire for a week. It doesn't seem like—"

"Hey hey!" A head appeared over the top of the cubicle wall, Tasha's yellow toque accompanied by a pair of big blue headphones hooked around her neck. "I was afraid I'd missed you two."

"We're working late," I informed her unnecessarily.

"Good, because I swung by your mute contractor's cell a few times. She finally got tired of meditating and I got something. She's still crazy well-guarded so it's not particularly coherent, but better than nothing, right?"

With a flourish, she passed Lienna a sheet of paper torn from a notebook. At first glance, Tasha's notes looked like the hectic scrawls of a hyper-stressed PhD student in a lecture: a lot of unrelated phrases, words, and numbers, plus Tasha's descriptions of the contractor's emotional state. I skimmed down the list, growing more confused and frustrated with each line.

"This is it?" I asked. "There's nothing here that says, 'Rocco Thorn hired me to kill Harold Atherton and obliterate two MPD agents.'"

"'Fraid that's all I could get. I'll try again tomorrow, or you can file all the paperwork to allow me into the interrogation room with her. I can do a lot more with access to the suspect." She waved as she sauntered away. "There's a martini at Scully's with my name on it. See ya later, kiddos."

I slumped back in my chair. "This is useless. Nothing here suggests she's heard of the Grand Grimoire, let alone met Rocco. And our interview with him gave us a ginormous goose egg. All we did was confirm he's got nothing to worry about."

Lienna studied Tasha's page of notes. "Is there anything special about Burrard Street?"

"Burrard? I don't know. It's a main drag that runs all the way from downtown into Kitsilano. A few guilds have addresses nearby, I think." I peered at her. "Why?"

"It's the only word that appears on this list more than twice."

Sitting forward, I bent over the page, bringing my head so close to Lienna's that I could smell the flowery scent of shampoo drifting from her hair. "That doesn't say Burrard *Street*. It just says Burrard. There are lots of other 'Burrard' things around town. A train station and a park, I think. Lots of businesses, like Burrard Sushi or Burrard Copy Centre."

"We'll have to investigate all of them." She sighed, sounding less than enthused. "It'll take more time than we have with Blythe's deadline, but we're out of leads unless we want to make contact with Rocco's other clients. Considering what happened to Harold ..."

Going near his clients could easily result in more dead suspects, especially now that Rocco knew we were investigating him.

I studied the repeating "Burrard" on Tasha's notes, then turned to look at my screen, still displaying photos of the butchered Red Rum rogues.

"Lienna," I said slowly, "is Red Rum one of those rogue guilds that might train their assassins in anti-telepathy measures?"

"I think so, yes."

"In that case, before we start scoping copy centers, maybe I should make a call."

"A call? Who to?"

"I happen to know someone with a boat and a lot of reasons to keep track of any dangerous, rogue-run vessels that might be hanging around the harbor." I looked up at her. "Or more specifically, any Red Rum ships that might be anchored in the Burrard Inlet."

THE BURRARD INLET cut into the mainland, acting almost like a river that separated Vancouver's downtown from the municipalities of North and West Vancouver. But what interested me far more than its geography were the various commercial anchorage points in the area, where ships could idle for days or weeks while waiting for berths in the Port of Vancouver.

One of those ships, I'd just learned, was a vessel known to belong to Red Rum—at least as far as the rogue underground was concerned. The MPD had missed that memo.

It's all about who you know. And I knew a smuggler who clandestinely transported rogues out of Vancouver before the MPD could put them in cuffs. Thanks to this profitable hobby, my smuggling friend was familiar with the various ships loitering about the inlet.

Vera was waiting as Lienna and I walked down the wooden dock where she moored her boat. Even from a distance you could tell she was tall—at least six feet, plus the poofed-up blonde hair she kept shaved on the sides. A jean jacket hid her numerous colorful tattoos.

The dock was a private rental just south of Deep Cove. During the summer, the small community brimmed with tourists looking for a quaint coastal experience, but in mid-November, it was practically a ghost town.

Standing on the deck of the refurbished fishing boat that doubled as her floating residence, Vera glowered in a distinctly unwelcoming way.

"Saw us coming, huh?" I said, stopping at the edge of the dock.

"A big advantage of being a seer," she snapped, "is avoiding people I don't want to talk to."

"Yet here you are, talking to me."

Her scowl deepened. "I told you to stay away from me, Kit."

Vera hadn't always been this hostile. In fact, we'd once worked marvelously well together while stealing back her artifact collection as my payment for her shipping me off to Thailand. But at some point after that, her attitude had taken a hard one-eighty. And that point had been the exact moment she'd found out about my new employment.

Freshly out of custody, I'd swung by to inform her of the good news—that I wasn't going to spend the rest of my sad, cinema-free existence in a MagiPol-issued jumpsuit. The fact that I was now Johnny Law, however, meant I was fundamentally incompatible with the anti-MPD smuggler, and she was not shy about making her feelings on the matter known.

That had been our last conversation, until I'd called her an hour ago for information about Red Rum vessels.

"You owe me a boat ride," I reminded her.

"I gave you that ride. You're the one who made me turn around."

"Let's call it a mulligan."

"No."

I flashed her my charmingest grin. "It's for a good cause."

"Still no." She crossed her arms. "Unless this boat ride has nothing to do with the rogue ship you were pestering me about, then maybe."

I sucked air noisily between my teeth. "About that …"

"*Hell* no," the seer growled. "I'm not taking *Clifford* anywhere near those psychopaths."

I glanced over to ensure *Clifford* the boat was still tied to the dock. Preventing Vera from sailing off to avoid me was the main reason I'd dragged Lienna out here, despite it now being past nine o'clock.

"Come on, Vera," I coaxed. "You know what I can do. No one on that Red Rum ship will even see you."

"Except they might, and I don't have 'help idiot agent with suicide mission' on my to-do list tonight."

Lienna stepped up to my side. "Maybe you'd prefer to reconsider your answer in a jail cell."

I shot my partner an angry look. Vera might not be the most cooperative smuggler in the world, but that didn't mean I wanted to threaten her.

The seer looked down at Lienna. "You must be Kit's little agent crush. Shen, right?"

Woah, hey. No need to be throwing around the c-word, Vera.

"*Agent* Shen."

This was going so well.

"Nice to meet you, *Agent Shen*," Vera sneered. "Now get lost, because I'm not—"

Heaving a sigh, I dropped an invisi-bomb on them, turning all three of us invisible.

Lienna and Vera shrieked in fright. Vera reeled backward, narrowly avoiding a plunge into the Pacific, while Lienna scrabbled at her chest for her anti-magic necklace.

For me, making myself invisible was about as exciting as riding a tricycle down a mild decline. For them, it was a terrifying delve into a disembodied existence where they couldn't hear their own voice or see their own flesh.

I watched them flail, then released the warp. As the two women panted for air, I said, "Vera, I need your help with this. Even if I had access to an MPD boat, I'd have to file so much goddamn paperwork that I'd be a middle-aged soccer dad before I got a mission approved."

Lienna righted herself and punched me squarely in the shoulder, mumbling some very unkind epithets about my methodology under her breath.

Vera's glower returned. "I—"

"And," I added, speaking over her, "that seer gift of yours will raise any red flags on the way. At the first sign of danger, we can turn back."

Vera could only see a couple of minutes into the future, but one hundred and twenty seconds could make the difference between escaping alive and making new fishy friends at the bottom of Burrard Inlet.

Her lips pressed together, gaze snapping between me and Lienna.

My partner folded her arms. "If you help us with this, I'll forget you exist."

The seer ground her teeth so violently I could almost hear it over the water sloshing against the steel hull of her boat.

"Fine, I'll do it." She directed a humorless, shark-like grin at me. "But I sure hope you know what the hell you're getting into."

13

DARKNESS BLANKETED the inlet's salty waves, the water as black as pitch. Downtown Vancouver to the south and North and West Vancouver opposite it were the only points of reference, aside from the glaring lights of anchored cargo ships.

According to Vera, the ships in the inlet ran their engines twenty-four-seven, even when moored for weeks, dumping pollutants into the water while their anchors ravaged the seafloor. Big business over the environment. Sounded pretty standard.

Our target was a smallish cargo vessel glowing with lights like a rusty, depressing cruise ship covered in barnacles and evil. A few dozen shipping containers were stacked in front of the towering bridge, and using Vera's binoculars, I could make out at least ten people moving about the deck.

Surprisingly busy for a ship idly waiting for a berth at port.

When we'd set out, I'd thought I'd have to exhaust my brain making me, Lienna, Vera, and her boat invisible to Red Rum for our entire approach, but I hadn't factored in the darkness or the experience this ship's captain had with sneaky nighttime sailing.

Lienna and I flanked Vera, who manned the wheel. Every light on the boat was off, rendering us no more than a rumbling shadow on the black water as we navigated by the lights of other ships. The salty wind carried all the cold of the November ocean and then some, whipping at my clothes and burning my cheeks.

"You know," I said to Vera, "your boat is neither big nor red."

"What?"

"Clifford," I clarified. "You know, the big red d—"

"I know who Clifford the Big Red Dog is," she interrupted. "I didn't name the boat. The guy I bought it from did. I think it was his dad's name or something."

Well, that was far less interesting than I'd hoped.

As we drew nearer, I steeled myself. Once we got in range of the ship's lights, I'd have to drop a wide-range invisi-bomb— and I'd have to time it perfectly. Start it too late, and someone might spot us before we vanished. But start it too soon, and I'd waste my stamina, increasing the risk that I'd run out of mental juice and my warps would begin looking like Kandinsky paintings.

"Now, Kit," Vera whispered.

Lienna gripped her cat's eye necklace and chanted, "*Ori menti defendo.*"

At her nod, I cast my warp out, mentally stretching to catch all the minds on the ship. Vera sucked in a terse breath as we and the boat disappeared. Lienna could shield her mind from my powers with her artifact, but Vera had no protection. Luckily, she'd practiced functioning while invisible for our artifact-stealing excursion. As long as I didn't spring it on her without warning, she could handle it for a while.

She shifted the engine down to trolling speed and we drifted closer. The cargo ship, which hadn't seemed that big next to all that dark, open water, loomed above us, bright lights shining off the tall bridge. And it became abundantly clear that it was painted red. *This* behemoth was Clifford, not the glorified dinghy we were sneaking in on.

Once we were in the ship's shadow, I dropped the warp so Vera could see what she was doing. Delicately maneuvering her boat right up beside the vessel's hull, she handed the wheel over to Lienna and pulled out a strange black object. It looked like a cross between a gun and a power tool.

"What's that?" I asked, goggling.

Aiming it at the ship's railing thirty feet above, she replied matter-of-factly, "Grappling gun."

"You have a *grappling gun?*"

"I have a lot of fun smuggler's toys. Now shut up."

She fired the weapon. The grappling hook flew into the air, a thin rope trailing behind it, and disappeared over the top rail. She yanked on the rope to draw the hook against the railing, tugged it again to ensure it was firmly locked in place, then passed the gun to me. I hefted it in my hands.

So. Cool.

As the boat rocked with the waves, Vera directed Lienna and me to grip the gun, then pointed out the switch for the winch.

"Don't let go unless you wanna get wet," she added helpfully as she activated the winch.

Motor whirring, it heaved us off the deck of Vera's boat. Thank Neptune for upper body strength, because holding on wasn't particularly easy. My shoes gripped the steel side of the cargo ship well despite the cold ocean spray, and Lienna and I hopped along the hull while the winch did all the lifting work.

Thirty feet up, we swung over the railing—if the thigh-high barrier could be called a railing—and I tugged the grappling hook free. I tossed the gun back down to Vera.

Safely invisible and tucked behind a shipping container for extra security, Lienna and I waited as Vera directed her boat away from the Red Rum ship. When I could no longer make out its shape, I dropped its invisibility. A weight lifted off my mind.

Unfortunately, that meant we were now stranded on the ship. But Vera had promised not to go far, and she was trustworthy.

Right?

"How are you doing?" Lienna asked, adjusting her necklace. "Are we still invisible?"

I put a hand to my chest in mock indignation. "What do you take me for? Some mythic hack?"

That got me nothing but an expected roll of the eyes. Time to focus on our mission: find something that could link Red Rum the international rogue guild, Rocco Thorn of the Grand Grimoire, Harold Atherton the dead deli contractor, the nameless punk contractor-assassin, Robin Page the mysterious demon-slaying contractor, and/or the Crow and Hammer.

Putting it that way, did it seem like we were grasping at some really dangerous straws here?

We crept between the shipping containers toward the bridge. After so long on the dark water, the glaring lights all over the ship stung my eyes; the thing was lit up like a stadium for Monday Night Football. It was around the same length as a football field too, its massive size absorbing the choppy waves. The deck rumbled beneath my feet with the vibrations of its engine.

Despite the ship's size, I counted seven Red Rum assholes in our first three minutes of creeping around. Each rogue had a prescribed route, either along the perimeter or between the storage containers, but none were moving with much gusto. Clearly, they were just following routine and didn't expect to be boarded, James Bond-style.

The first guy, whom I almost walked into as I rounded the corner of a container, was a couple inches shorter than me but twice as wide. And not in a spherical way either. He was wide in an exceptionally "Arnold Schwarzenegger of the eighties" kind of way, with a handlebar mustache and a scowl to match.

With roughly the same grace as an intoxicated flamingo, I sidestepped the mustachioed, musclebound goon, while Lienna dodged him on his other side.

We continued along the deck, Lienna checking each container as we went, probably hoping to find a "SECRET ILLEGAL DEMONICA" label or something like that. But no such luck. And there was no way we were breaking into any of them; they were all thoroughly locked down to the deck and to each other with steel lashing bars.

"So," she muttered, "below deck or up to the bridge?"

"The bridge is a lot less real estate to search."

In unison, we turned toward the rusted steel staircase that led up to the bridge. I really hoped we'd find an old guy in a navy blue suit with a perfectly trimmed white beard and a monocle standing at the helm. Creating a warp to hide the opening of the door, I slipped through with my partner and closed it behind us.

The wide room, lined with windows that provided a broad view of the ship's deck and its patrolling guards, was significantly dimmer and warmer than the deck. The command center stretched from end to end, and a mind-baffling number of buttons, dials, screens, blinking lights, and other very technical-looking odds and ends filled it.

Oh, and three people, none of whom had the Captain Crunch sensibility I was hoping for. In keeping with the tough-guy aesthetic that pervaded Red Rum, all three rogues looked like they ate nails for breakfast and shit out unflattering metal sculptures of their worst enemies.

One of them—an ugly dude in his forties wearing a skintight black t-shirt tucked into his blue jeans—was sitting backward on the swiveling captain's chair as he spoke to the other two.

"... *told* Fivel not to stick his finger in anything an alchemist has touched, but did the idiot listen? Nope. And that's why he's Fourvel now."

The other man laughed, but the old woman, a cigarette in her mouth and a pair of sunglasses that looked like they'd come from the glove compartment of a mid-nineties minivan perched on her head, merely blew smoke into the air and leaned back in her chair beside the command center.

"Anyway," the talkative guy went on, "what was I saying? Right. Fourvel said he'll be done tonight, and Mandeep finished this afternoon, so we're almost clear to head out."

The old woman put out her cigarette on a panel of buttons and pulled another one from the pack in her pocket. "Anyone else we're waiting for?"

"Just Ortega."

This sounded a lot like a conversation that was wrapping up, which wouldn't help Lienna and me figure out their evil plans.

"We need to keep them talking," I muttered.

Lienna shook her head. "How? If Tasha were here ..."

We didn't have a telepath, but we *did* have a psycho warper who'd been tormenting his cubicle mate with psychic experiments for the past five months.

"I'm gonna try something," I whispered.

Her alarm was instant. "Now isn't the time for a fake monster or a cute Keanu Reeves reference."

"Wait, are you saying that Keanu is cute or that a reference to Keanu would be cute?"

"Kit," she growled.

I waved away her concern. Or was that annoyance? "Shh, let me try."

Homing in on the three rogues, I created an image of the punky, scowling contractor who'd almost killed us. But rather than a full-color, real-life duplicate, I made the warp as close to invisible as I could. It was like an almost transparent projection of the contractor.

While experimenting on Vinny, I'd discovered that if I did one of these super-faint warps around him, he'd end up thinking about whatever I showed him without noticing the warp. It was my own special brand of subliminal marketing. One time, I'd parked a cute little phantom puppy beside him for a solid ten minutes. He never looked at it, but half an hour later, I caught him watching a "Puppies Being the Absolute Kewtest!" video on his computer.

Oh, the things I could accomplish with this trick if I had looser morals.

The ugly guy and the chain-smoking mob boss were now discussing the upcoming maintenance of the ballast tanks and bilge pumps. I made the subliminal warp a bit more solid, my head aching from the complexity of creating a semi-transparent fake woman while simultaneously keeping the real Lienna and myself fully transparent.

"What about Janie?"

The sudden question came from the previously mute third rogue, who was leaning on another bank of instrumentation with his arms crossed. He was tall, middle-aged, athletically built, and had movie-star stubble and a cold, steely gaze. The sleeves of his black dress shirt were rolled up, revealing a myriad of frightening tattoos. I was pretty sure one of them was a vampire baby murdering a unicorn.

His partners in crime looked over at him.

"What about her?" the old woman asked.

"You said we're almost ready to go. We just gonna leave her?"

"Yeah," the ugly dude barked. "That's what happens when you get your ass caught by the MPD."

"What if they crack her?"

"They won't." The old woman squinted and looked behind her as though she'd heard something unexpected, then flicked the ash from her latest cigarette onto the floor. "She's a write-off now. Forget about her."

Mr. Nightmare Ink grimaced. "She and Miguel were the most powerful team we had."

"Miguel is dead, so he wasn't the pyromage he claimed to be," she retorted, waving a bony hand impatiently. "And Janie isn't our only contractor. Gilmore has been training with the new infernus. One demon will be enough firepower for now."

"Yeah, he's ready to rock," the ugly dude said. "He let me take it for a spin. Not as easy as I'd thought it would be."

The tattooed one smirked. "I tried it out too. Wasn't that hard."

Take what for a spin? It almost sounded like they were talking about Gilmore's demon, but no one else could use a contractor's infernus. Right?

The old woman scrutinized the bridge again, then pushed off her chair and took a step to peer behind a navigation console. "You shouldn't be fooling around like that. We're already down an infernus."

Ugly Guy grunted. "Who'd've thought the MPD would get nosy over a deli owner, for Christ's sake. But we won't have to worry about the new batch. At least, that's what—"

The old woman raised her hand imperiously, silencing him. She gave the bridge another slow perusal, then dropped a casual observation that made my heart plunge into my stomach.

"We're not alone. There's someone else in here."

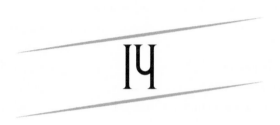

14

"I CAN FEEL THEIR MIND," the old woman croaked. "They're close by."

Seriously? She was a *psychic*?

Lienna tugged my wrist, and as we backed toward the door, the two men joined their female counterpart in looking around the room for the intruder she sensed.

"They're trying to escape," she told them. "Alert the crew."

The ugly dude pulled a radio off his waistband and spoke into it as he marched toward us, sweeping the room with his eyes. "We got an intruder on our hands. Everyone on your toes."

A string of "copy that" responses crackled back at him. How much did I want to bet the lazy, inattentive mood of the men on the deck had switched into ultra-militant mode?

Lienna put her hand up to the door handle and waited for my signal. I created a warp of the closed door, then nodded.

We slipped out, zoomed down the steps, and bolted between shipping containers.

As I'd feared, the Red Rum goon squad was swarming the deck, and not in the incompetent, haphazard fashion I would've hoped for if I'd had time to hope for anything. They were crisscrossing the deck in a methodical grid. Less than ideal.

Time to summon Vera and her boat back.

As Lienna swerved between containers and into the ridiculously narrow gap between a double-high stack and the portside railing, I pulled out my phone. Black water sloshed below us in a sinister way as I squeezed in after her, fumbling to open the messaging app where I'd already prepped an SOS text.

It took some balance to navigate the precarious perimeter without bumping a container or falling over the rail. And unfortunately for me, holding an invisibility warp for almost twenty minutes, plus trying to send off a text message with numb hands chilled by the frigid ocean wind, didn't leave much free brainpower for footwork.

Right as I hit send on my message to Vera, I tripped over my own toes and bumped the container, my shoulder thudding against it with a hollow bang that echoed over the water.

"Here!" someone bellowed. The Schwarzenegger-esque goon appeared at the railing just ahead of me and Lienna, cutting off our escape. "Gilmore! I heard something over here!"

Gilmore? Wasn't he the "firepower" with the infernus that the fossilized nicotine addict had mentioned?

Lienna moved forward, closing the distance between her and the Arnie rogue. Her hand dipped into her satchel for a weapon.

A figure stepped from between the stacks of containers and into the bright lights shining down from the bridge. The guy was about my age, with shoulder-length blond hair and a clean-shaven face that reminded me of Spicoli from *Fast Times at Ridgemont High*. A silver pendant dangled around his neck.

Well, if it wasn't Gilmore. Fan-freakin'-tastic.

Lienna pulled up short as the contractor joined his comrade, squinting into the shadowy gap between the containers and the railing where we lurked. Lienna and I awkwardly backed up.

"Nothing here," he told Arnie.

"Stella says they're invisible."

"How are we supposed to find them if they're invisible?"

Arnie extended his right arm, a shiny gray cuff glinting around his thick wrist. "*Ori obsideo!*"

Dark pink light flickered over his cuff, then a beam of sparkling fuchsia blasted straight at us. Lienna ducked, but my overworked brain wasn't as fast at coming up with a viable dodge maneuver in the cramped space—meaning I tried to duck and dodge at the same time.

The good news: the sorcery attack missed me.

The bad news: I pitched sideways, hit the container, bounced off, then careened over the pitiable excuse for a safety rail.

My stomach leaped into my throat as I plummeted through thirty feet of darkness and into the icy salt water below.

Several months ago, I'd gone for a late-night summer swim in this same inlet, and I'd wondered if that experience was the coldest I'd ever been in my life. But now I realized I'd never known what the word "cold" really meant.

The instant I plunged into the frigid black liquid, every muscle in my body seized. If they hadn't, I would've gulped down an entire lungful of water from the compulsive gasp that shook my core. "Cold" was an entirely inadequate descriptor. It felt like my soul had been dipped in liquid nitrogen and my entire body had turned into an ice statue like a cartoon character in a slapstick Christmas special.

Survival instinct kicked in, and I struggled upward with deadened limbs. My head broke the surface and I wheezed, unable to control the fast, deep hyperventilation. Panic competed with blank-brained shock, and all I could do was tread water and try not to inhale any of it.

Shouts. A flash of pink light. Then a huge splash a few feet away, heard more than seen.

"They're in the water!" someone yelled.

Waves rippled wildly, faintly lit by the ship's lights, then Lienna surfaced beside me, gasping in the exact same way. I wanted to help her, but I was shivering so violently I could barely keep my head above the waves.

Two silhouettes leaned over the rail a dozen feet above us. More men joined them, jeering at the MPD ducks in the water, helpless and hypothermic.

"Get 'em, Gilmore," one of them called.

In answer, red light flared. The eerie glow expanded and solidified into a demon with glowing red eyes, perched on the railing. I couldn't make out its details, but I could definitely see that it was lean, mean, and horned.

I tried to think of a distraction—I was supposed to be the perfect mythic for fighting contractors, wasn't I? I just had to distract Gilmore. One little distraction. Just one!

But my shocked, frozen, exhausted, moments-from-drowning brain had nothing. The demon sank into a crouch, ready to leap into the drink after us.

A deep pop echoed across the water, and fiery orange light blazed somewhere behind me. A Nerf-ball-sized object flashed out of the darkness like a rocket and exploded against the hull in a fireball that made our mysterious car bombing look like a firecracker.

Flames rained down, sending me ducking under the water, and I resurfaced to the sound of shouts from aboard the ship.

"Kit! This way!"

A hand pulled on my arm, and I awkwardly swam with Lienna, panting, teeth chattering, limbs quaking with shivers.

I didn't spot Vera's boat until the seer shouted at us to hurry. Abruptly realizing I was moments from escaping this liquid arctic hell, I kicked harder. Vera reached down and grabbed Lienna's hand. She hauled her up, then they both dragged me aboard together.

I collapsed half on top of Lienna, flattening her to the deck. She didn't complain, breathing hard and shaking even harder.

Vera's feet thudded past us, then the boat's engine roared. The bow lifted as she did the nautical equivalent of flooring it, and we bounced across the waves, leaving the Red Rum ship behind.

A few minutes later, the boat slowed again. When Vera crouched beside us, Lienna and I hadn't moved, my arm across her middle and my head pillowed on her elbow.

"Come on, Kit. Get up. You'll warm up better below deck."

"Warm?" I slurred woozily. "I need the warm."

Lienna sat up, still breathing heavily. "What the hell kind of artifact was that? You almost blew up their ship."

"That was no artifact." She smirked. "That, Agent Shen, was a rocket-propelled grenade—with some alchemic enhancements. I told you I have a lot of toys."

Lienna and I gawked at her.

Vera waved impatiently. "Now get down there and dry off before I have to roast you idiots over a spit to thaw you out."

I had so many questions, but warming up was far more pressing than the no doubt badass story behind Vera's RPG launcher. Lienna and I levered to our feet, and leaning on each other for support, we stumbled toward the narrow stairs leading below deck.

IN THE SMART CAR yet again.

The streets were nearly empty of traffic as Lienna drove us back to the precinct. We were returning to do … something. Paperwork, maybe? File a report? We should probably report a ship from a notorious criminal guild in the local harbor, not to mention the most recent attempt by said criminals to wipe Lienna and me from the face of the planet. That seemed reasonable.

Damn, I was tired. Like, bone-deep, brain-fried exhausted. My chin nodded forward, fatigue blanketing my limbs. If it hadn't been for the sporadic shivers still racking my body, I'd have already been asleep. As I held my hands out to the stream of hot air blasting from the car's vents, my sleeves pulled up, baring my wrists.

I was wearing a black hoodie with a glittery purple skull splashed across the chest and a pair of plaid pajama pants, both too small. Lienna was wearing a knitted wool Christmas sweater and fire-engine red leggings, both too large. Claiming she couldn't trust us to return her stuff, Vera had offered clothes she "wouldn't be seen dead in." So generous.

Glumly, I stuffed my cold feet into my wet shoes and leaned down to tie the soggy laces. The whole interior of the car smelled like seawater and damp cotton.

Lienna, ever law-abiding, signaled her turn as our Lilliputian vehicle sloshed through a puddle in front of the ramp that led down into the MPD's parking garage. We rolled to the bottom and stopped at the security station, a barricade arm blocking our path. The booth was manned by Trevor Eggert, the only non-mythic on the Vancouver precinct's staff.

He popped his head out of the window, his genial smile punctuated by a caterpillar mustache. "Good evening, agents. Are you two young'ns returning that car for the night?"

He acted like he was a middle-aged uncle—an impression cemented by his mustache—but in reality, he was barely thirty. I knew because I'd asked.

"We are," Lienna confirmed, pulling her badge from her water-spotted satchel. She held it up, and Eggert dutifully jotted down her badge number before hitting whatever secret button opened the gate. As the red barrier swung upward, bright light flashed through the smart car's interior—the blinding high beams of another vehicle.

Eggert's startled shout registered an instant before the vehicle slammed into the rear of our car.

I whipped forward, my seatbelt locking. Lienna stomped the brake pedal so hard I felt the thud through the floor, but we were still moving—the vehicle behind us was shoving our lightweight car deeper into the garage. The squealing tires protested as we slid.

An engine revved, our vehicular assailant pumping the gas. Bracing my limbs, I told myself not to panic as the smart car's nose headed straight for a massive concrete pillar. It slammed into the obstacle, the impact jarring through me.

Just as I realized our car was pinned, something slammed into its roof with the approximate force of a falling grand piano.

The aluminum caved inward. A hideous metallic shriek pierced my ears, then black claws punctured the metal and tore across it, the tinfoil roof dipping even lower.

Okay, *now* it was time to panic.

"Get out!" I shouted.

Lienna flung her door open and leaped clear. I followed suit, landing on my hands and knees, then shoved upright and spun around.

A demon was crouched on the smart car, its weight slowly caving in the roof.

15

A DEMON.

In the MPD's parking garage.

Murdering our defenseless smart car.

And presumably, we were next on its hit list.

It was shorter and slimmer than either of the two demons I'd faced today, but that didn't make it any less terrifying. Reddish skin stretched over rippling muscles, long horns sprouted from its head, and its thin barbed tail snapped side to side like a whip.

Oh, and a pair of huge, hellish bat wings arched off its back, thick membranous skin stretching between flexible ribs.

The demon pulled its long claws out of the metal and swung its bestial face toward me, revealing those telltale eyes that glowed like hot embers. Then it looked the opposite way, locating Lienna on the vehicle's other side—out of my easy reach.

The beast's wings curled inward, limbs coiling as it prepared to pounce.

Panic shot through me. Invisifying her was a risk when she wasn't using her cat's eye necklace to shield her mind from my magic, so I did the next best thing—I created half a dozen Lienna duplicates. Her doppelgangers all leaped out of the same spot where the real woman stood, forming a confusing crowd around her.

The demon froze, and my focus shot to the SUV that'd rammed us. The windows were tinted but I could just make out the silhouette of a man in the driver's seat. I took a fast step toward the vehicle and—

A low, hoarse growl rolled through the demon's throat. That didn't seem right. Weren't demons supposed to be silent? Something about their contracts locking up their voice boxes like an Elizabethan chastity belt?

As six fake Liennas and a single real one bolted away from the two vehicles, the demon sprang across twelve feet like it'd launched off a diving board instead of a crumpled car roof. It landed, wings flaring and clawed toes tearing into the concrete floor, then lunged again.

Straight at the real Lienna.

It was like my warps weren't even there. Like Lienna had a homing beacon on her back, drawing the demon straight to her.

A wordless shout burst from me as the demon swung its talons at her fleeing back. She twisted in mid-step, terror on her face, her satchel slipping off her shoulder.

The demon's talons caught the falling bag instead of her flesh, ripping through the hemp. Clangs rang out as her artifacts bounced across the floor.

She pitched forward, landing hard on her hands and knees— and the demon's next strike flashed over the top of her head in a blur. How was this thing so fast? It was in a whole different league from the demon that'd killed Harold.

"*Ori menti defendo!*" she yelled—the incantation for her cat's eye necklace. She was all but begging me to protect her—to hide her.

Stretching my range as far as it could go in case the contractor wasn't the person in the SUV, I made us invisible. The demon slid to a stop a few feet away from Lienna, who crouched on the ground, unmoving.

The demon's head tilted one way, then the other. A pause. A low rumble in its chest.

It sprang straight at Lienna. Her scream rang out as she wrenched away. Blood splattered across the floor as she slammed down on her side.

Flinging my hand out, I threw up the meanest Funhouse warp I could visualize. The air fractured like shards of glass. The floor turned to shiny ripples. All the colors inverted. The parked cars bulged weirdly, like reflections in a warped mirror.

The demon barely even blinked.

Lienna rolled desperately as it gouged tracks in the concrete, missing her by inches. She threw her torn bag in its face, more of her possessions flying in every direction. Slipping on the floor, she lunged for her Rubik's Cube on the ground a couple yards away.

No—there wasn't enough time! The demon was too fast!

And my warps weren't doing a damn thing to stop it.

Holding on to the SUV's hood, I called on every ounce of brainpower I had left and created a warp of the parking garage floor turning into goopy quicksand—except I wasn't trying to fool anyone's mind.

I was trying to change reality.

Once and only once, I'd altered the fabric of the universe on command, and I needed to do it again *right now*.

I had a second. Less than a second.

I bent every molecule of my mind to it—and nauseating dizziness rolled over me, a tremor running through my limbs. Sudden weakness swamped me, and as I fell onto the SUV's hood, the demon launched right through my insubstantial warp.

Lienna grabbed her cube, but the demon was right behind her. She had no time to speak the incantation, no time to evade, no time to do anything as the beast's claws streaked down, its talons gleaming with her blood.

BANG-BANG-BANG!

Rapid-fire gunshots exploded through the garage and the demon lurched as bullets peppered its back.

Eggert stood halfway between the guard station and the demon as he emptied his pistol's clip into the beast. The demon did a one-eighty to face the security guard, its upper lip curling in a snarl. Thick, dark blood oozed from the scattered holes in its body and the tears in its wings.

Eggert kept pulling the trigger, the gun clicking, the magazine empty.

The creature's tail snapped, then it strode toward the guard—and even though the demon was supposed to be a mindless puppet whose every movement was controlled by its contractor, a distinctly vicious gloat contorted its features at Eggert's white-faced terror.

It bore down on him, and all I did was stand there, hands braced on the SUV's hood as my vision swam, my overextended powers fizzling and my brain in a fatigue spiral.

A flash of movement. At the same moment that the demon sprang, a saucer-sized metal disc slid across the floor like an air hockey puck and hit Eggert's toes.

Green light spiraled out from it. A circle three feet across, swirling like an emerald vortex, opened under his shoes and sucked him down into the floor like an otherworldly vacuum. The demon's reaching claws swiped the air inches from the vanishing guard, then it thrust its hand down into the vortex after its prey.

"*Ori spatium claudo!*" Lienna shouted.

In a blink, the vortex retracted into the disc—and the demon threw itself backward with a roar, dark blood gushing from the stump of its arm, severed by the spell. Still bellowing with fury, it launched at Lienna with a sweep of its wings, propelling itself at an even more impossible speed.

"*Ori te formo cupolam!*"

A watery blue dome formed over her, and the demon rammed it with the full force of its charge. The barrier shimmered in warning. The demon smashed the dome again. It didn't seem to care that it was missing its hand and wrist, or that thick blood was dribbling from the stump.

Lienna clutched her Rubik's Cube as the glow of her barrier dimmed. Three more hits. Maybe less.

The contractor. The only way to stop a demon was to stop the contractor.

I vaulted over the SUV's hood and whirled toward the driver's door, prepared to punch in the window to get at this demon-wielding bastard. Before I could reach for the handle, the door swung open.

I jumped into the gap, fist drawing back to smash this guy's face in.

With a burst of blinding light, something hit me in the gut like the hottest punch ever. Searing pain shot down my legs, and the next thing I knew, I was on the ground. My blurred vision snapped up to the man standing over me, his blue-tinted sunglasses reflecting my pallid face. An infernus hung from his neck, glinting against his dark coat.

His foot came down on my stomach and electricity blasted through me. My limbs convulsed, lungs locked, burning pain scorching my innards.

Twenty-five feet away, Lienna shouted something, her voice high and desperate.

The man stomped on me again, and another surge of excruciating voltage seized my muscles. Electramage, I realized hazily. The same bald, goateed electramage who'd tried to drop a power line on Lienna's head earlier today. And he was also a contractor.

"That's an interesting ability you have," he said in a growly voice edged with arrogance. Pushing his boot into my gut, he pulsed short waves of electricity through me. "I bet a regular contractor wouldn't stand a chance against you."

My arms twitched and spasmed. I couldn't even reach up to push his foot off me.

A smirk twisted his face. "Demons can see even in complete darkness. Looks like they can see through your illusions too."

Heavy thuds punctuated by the click of claws drew closer. The demon appeared, its good arm raised and its thick fingers curled around Lienna's neck. She hung in its grip, gasping for air as she wrenched on its hand in a scene horrifically reminiscent of Harold's final moments.

The electramage smiled, his attention on my partner. "We finally meet, little miss Shen. I can see the family resemblance."

Her eyes rolled toward him, her mouth gaping as she tried to get air past the demon's crushing grip.

"How old are you? Twenty-three now?" His own question seemed to infuriate him, his hands balling into fists and mouth twisting. "Thirteen years too long."

He raised his arm. Crackling white light raced over his hand and up his wrist. The air sizzled with a building charge. All the hair on my body stood on end. The electricity gathering in his clenched fist intensified.

He was going to kill Lienna. I knew it without a doubt, knew it in my gut.

Distract him. I had to distract him.

My eyes squinched as I created a warp. A man appeared beside the electramage. Medium height, medium build, and with the face of Lienna's father, identical to the photo I'd studied from the MPD records.

The electramage faltered, his weight lifting off my stomach—only to slam back down, crushing my diaphragm.

"Nice try," he snarled, swinging his fist toward me instead to unleash that lethal charge at *my* chest.

The temperature in the parking garage dropped—and out of nowhere, a barrage of ice shards shot at the electramage like spearheads fired from a cannon. He staggered off me, arms shielding his face as ice shattered against him and rained down on the floor.

An ice-flinging mythic charged out from between two parked cars. It wasn't a warp this time, though I desperately wished I'd been responsible.

No, it was my cubicle mate Vincent, complete with his cargo shorts, mohawk, and hands full of sparkling ice. As he raced for us, he flung a frozen sphere at the demon. It expanded as it flew, and when it hit the demon square in the face, the ice block surged over the beast's head.

The demon dropped Lienna to claw at the Jack Frost visage that had replaced its ugly demon mug.

Vinny jumped between Lienna and me and dropped into a protective crouch as he hurled ice shards at the demon and electramage both, driving them back. The ice block on the demon's head shattered and it roared furiously.

A door slammed. An engine revved. Then the SUV reversed, dragging our smart car several feet before the mangled bumpers disconnected. Tires squealing, the SUV shot away, tearing up the ramp toward the exit ass-end first.

Red light flared as the demon dissolved into a crimson glow. The light streaked after the escaping SUV and disappeared along with the roar of the engine.

"Hold on, Lienna!" Vinny pulled a small roll of twine from a pocket of his cargo shorts and wound some around her blood-covered arm. "Help is coming. You'll be okay."

I watched him cinch the makeshift tourniquet tight around her upper arm, scarcely able to believe it. Under different circumstances, I would've laughed, because who the hell carried *twine* on them? But Vinny had told me he could save my life with what he carried in his pockets, and here he was, saving Lienna's life instead.

Because I hadn't.

16

EVERYTHING WAS GARBAGE.

I mean, I was still alive, which was less garbagey than the alternative of being un-alive, but everything else was garbage.

My magic was a joke, for starters. Lienna had said I was the perfect mythic to take on a contractor, but I might as well have been performing a mediocre "Single Ladies" routine for all the good my warps had done against this one. Add a few bolts of electricity to the gut, and I hadn't even been able to save myself.

And reality warping? Forget that shit. The only time I'd ever successfully warped reality was before I knew it was a possibility. Maybe my abilities had come with one reality warp only, like a "get out of jail free" card for manipulating molecules at my whim.

"You were lucky." Scooter, the precinct's healer, prodded my bare stomach, and I flinched with each gentle press. "Internal bruises and burns, but no serious damage."

Oh, sure. My intestines had been tenderized, then cooked to a nice medium rare. No big deal.

The tall, spindly mythic with bright red hair down to his shoulders had joined me at my bed in the infirmary room a few minutes ago. I winced as he pressed again on my blue and purple abs, grateful for the privacy curtains that encircled the hard-as-concrete bed.

Scooter turned toward his big ol' bag of Arcana supplies. "I'm going to dose you with a round of potions for pain relief and accelerated healing. I recommend forty-eight hours of bed rest. Contact me immediately if your pain worsens or you start feeling dizzy, nauseated, chilled, disoriented, that sort of thing."

The word "nauseated" did terrible things to my writhing stomach. I already felt plenty sick and dizzy, but that had nothing to do with the boot-to-gut beating my stomach had taken and everything to do with pushing my mental stamina to the max.

"Got anything for the ringing in my ears?" I asked, rubbing one in vain. Gunfire in an echoey parking garage hadn't done my eardrums any favors.

"Sure, but it'll make you deaf for about six hours."

"Never mind."

Scooter force-fed me four potions that tasted like dill pickles, fish oil, concentrated balsamic vinegar, and a radioactive tire fire, respectively. Reinforcing his instruction that I rest, he pushed through the curtains, leaving me alone. He bustled around out of sight for a few minutes, then the infirmary door clicked shut.

I was deeply tempted to lie back on the bed and give in to the intense exhaustion permeating my aching bones. Instead, I sat forward and braced my elbows on my knees. Gooseflesh rose on my arms, but I couldn't bring myself to put Vera's purple skull sweater back on. Even that was too cheerful for my Eeyoreish state of mind.

My head dropped forward into my hands. How much more could I screw up? From allowing Harold to be murdered in front of us, to accidentally killing the pyromage champion, to failing to get anything out of Rocco, to falling overboard while escaping the Red Rum ship, to being completely helpless against the electramage contractor and his demon.

Why had I thought I could do any of this? "Master agent," my ass.

Just look at Vincent and the way his ice projectiles had sent the rogue running. I'd spent five months trying to prove my psychic magic was just as valuable as his elemental magery, but I'd never actually believed it. My pride just hadn't let me admit that I was inferior to a smug, over-pocketed, know-it-all kryomage.

Heaving an exhausted sigh, I pushed off the bed, then looked dismally at my still-damp shoes and decided against putting those on either. Wearing only a pair of plaid cotton pants that revealed a daring amount of ankle, I padded barefoot to the curtain and pushed it aside.

The precinct's infirmary was a small room crammed with enough stuff to make it feel as claustrophobic as Vera's boat. Three medical bays partitioned by curtains used up most of the space, and a long counter with a sink and cupboards above it filled the rest of it. Moving to the curtain beside mine, I parted the blue fabric enough to peek inside.

Lienna lay on the bed, her ugly holiday sweater splattered with blood and one sleeve cut away. Blue Arcana runes marked her bare arm, but the wounds that had cut deep into her forearm were now faint pink lines. Magic was amazing stuff, mine excluded.

Reassured she was alive and in one piece, I was about to retreat, when her eyelids fluttered tiredly, then popped open. She sat up so fast I felt dizzy on her behalf.

"Kit! Are you okay?"

Why was she worried about *me*?

I pushed the curtain open enough to step closer to her bed. "How are you doing?"

"I'll be fine. Scooter already fixed my arm." Her brows pinched with concern as her gaze dropped to my bruised stomach. It must have looked bad; she didn't even blush. "Oh man, that looks nasty. Did Scooter give you anything for the pain?"

"Yeah, I'm fine. You're the one who—what are you doing?"

She'd flipped the blankets off and was swinging her race-car red legs over the edge of her bed. "I have to take care of something."

"You need to rest. You lost a lot of blood and—"

"Not that much. It looked worse than it was. Besides, I fully intend to sleep in my own bed tonight."

"Ah." I didn't move from her path. "Well, I fully intend not to allow that."

Surprise flickered over her features, followed by stubborn displeasure. She halted in front of me, glaring. "Really."

"Really," I confirmed.

I wasn't actually stopping her from leaving—all she had to do was step around me and push the curtains aside—but she was facing off with me on principle.

"You might not have heard," I continued, "but that electramage contractor with the wonky demon was after *you*."

She frowned.

"He knew your name. He knew how old you are. I was just in his way, but he was after you."

"That doesn't mean—"

"He knew your dad."

Her eyes widened.

"He mentioned your family resemblance, so I created a warp of your dad to distract him and he reacted pretty strongly. Whatever his beef is, it's personal." I arched an eyebrow. "And that means going home is a no-go, partner. That psychopathic asshole might know where you live."

Her frown returned. "Okay, but I still need you to get out of my way."

I planted my hands on my hips. "I just said—"

"I know, I know. I'm not leaving the precinct."

"Oh." I backed up, allowing her to stride past. She headed straight for the door and I followed, my bare feet slapping the cold linoleum.

As we headed into the hallway, she shot me a look over her shoulder. "You don't need to come."

"That remains to be seen." Sticking my hands in my plaid pockets for warmth, I shadowed her to the elevator. "Where are we going?"

She shot me an irritated look that derailed partway—at least judging by the way her gaze dipped down to my pecs then zoomed away. Her cheeks flushed.

"I'm going to get Eggert," she said stiffly as she punched the down button.

"Oh, that—*Eggert?* Shit, I forgot about him!"

How the hell had I forgotten about the way she'd made an entire human being disappear into a vortex? I was blaming my memory lapse on the brain fog from overdoing the psycho warping tonight.

"What happened to him?" I asked as the elevator chimed and the doors slid open. "Did you suck him into a parallel universe or something? Is he being tormented in a seven-dimensional spacetime existence?"

"No, nothing like that." She stepped into the elevator and hit the B3 button. "Well, not *exactly* like that."

"Exactly like what, then? An *eight*-dimensional spacetime existence?"

"I'm not supposed to talk about it."

"It looked like a portal straight out of *Portal*." I eyed her as the elevator descended. "It was, wasn't it?"

She scrunched her nose up in a way that was adorable but also very suspicious. "I can't answer that. It's classified."

"Sure, yeah, you'd tell me but then you'd have to kill me or whatever," I said dismissively. "But I literally witnessed Eggsy vanish into the freaking floor. And now we're taking a quick trip below ground to 'get him' after his impossibly portaltastic excursion? Come on, Lienna, fill me in."

Exhaling sharply, she glanced up at the security camera in the elevator's corner, but everyone at the precinct knew the cameras were video only, no audio. "If I tell you about this, you need to promise you'll never mention a single word of it to anyone. Ever."

I raised my right hand. "Scout's honor."

"This isn't a joke, Kit. If anyone finds out …"

Did she mean "if anyone finds out about the maybe-a-portal" or "if anyone finds out we talked about the maybe-a-portal"?

The elevator slowed to a halt and chimed cheerfully as the doors opened to reveal the second lowest basement level. I racked my brain to recall what I knew about B3. "Is this the containment floor?"

"No, that's one more level down. This floor is used for research, experiments, and some types of training. And storage as well."

Yet again, I was denied a glimpse of the containment floor. I'd only ever heard it mentioned in passing, and no one would explain what it was. The handbook didn't even acknowledge its existence.

Still, this was closer than I'd ever gotten before.

My first impression of B3 gave me a very *2001: A Space Odyssey* vibe. Plain, unmarked doors stood at even intervals along a stark, white, painfully bright hallway that extended for about forty yards before terminating at a black door that almost definitely housed a malevolent and sentient abyss that would eviscerate your essence and scatter it across the quantum realm for all eternity.

"So was it actually a portal like the video game?" I asked, my voice echoing, along with the embarrassing *pat-pat* of my naked feet as I walked.

She watched the doors pass, each one marked with a Roman numeral. "What video game?"

Right. I didn't think Lienna had ever played a video game in her life. Maybe a Mavis Beacon typing game, at best. "It's a game where you use portals to teleport around and solve puzzles before a homicidal robot reduces you to atoms in the name of science. Every portal has an entrance and an exit."

She considered this for a moment. "That sounds pretty similar. Maybe I should try it out sometime."

"You—" I cut myself off before I invited her to my place. I'd already decided that was a bad idea.

"The part I threw at Eggert was the entrance artifact," she told me as we passed the endless line of doors. "The exit point is linked to it, and that's down here. The two ends have to be fairly close together. That's what I'm working on, actually—extending the range. Getting it to work all the way up in the parking garage was a bit of a stretch."

"Have you ever sent a person through a portal before? Eggert won't be turned inside out or anything, will he?"

"He'll be fine. It works instantaneously; if you enter one end of the portal, you've already arrived on the other side." Finally selecting a door, she entered a long code into the panel on the wall beside it. A low buzz indicated that the door was now unlocked, and she pushed her way in.

The room inside matched the hallway outside: a sterile, crisp, white space with squint-worthy lighting. A sturdy wooden table with metal legs sat in the corner near the door, one side stacked with a variety of artifacts and Arcana tools. On the other side was an expensive-looking machine that could've been the lovechild of the killer laser beam in *Goldfinger* and one of those claw games you find at arcades that entice you into spending twenty bucks to win a stuffed animal worth fifty cents.

Lienna grabbed something off the cluttered end of the table and tossed it to me. "This is an entrance artifact."

I caught the object and turned it over in my hands. It was a pitch-black disc about twice the size of a coaster with a deeply etched five-pointed star in its center. Runes dotted every square centimeter of both sides, each one cut with astonishing detail and precision.

Crossing the room to another door, this one engraved with an intricate seven-pointed design filled with runes, Lienna placed her hand in the center and murmured something very Latin under her breath. The rune glowed faintly, then she grasped the handle, turned it, and pulled the door open.

Light washed through what looked like a storage room. The shelves on each side were stacked with more Arcana paraphernalia, but that wasn't what caught my attention.

Eggert, his mustache bristling as he squinted, was sitting in the middle of the floor.

Busy rubbernecking, I almost didn't notice the large piece of smooth wood fixed to the ceiling. On it was carved a three-foot-wide circle spell filled with an even more complex arrangement of runes than the small portal entrance artifact.

Ah, that must be the portal's exit.

"Well, hey there." Eggert pushed to his feet and dusted off his pants as though being teleported out of a demonic battle and into a dark closet was par for the course. "Happy to see you two still kicking."

"You okay?" Lienna asked, stepping back and waving him out of the closet. "You didn't hurt yourself when you landed?"

"I took a bit of a tumble here, but nothing's broken." He entered the room, peering around. "Where are we?"

"Precinct basement. Lienna teleported you down here," I answered distractedly.

"Teleported?" he repeated in a hushed tone. "Wow."

My neck craned back to observe the portal exit. "Why's it on the ceiling?"

She prodded my arm to get me to move out of the way of the door. "Because otherwise, you'd be upside down when you came out of it, obviously."

I blinked. "Right. Obviously."

"That demon there still roaming around?" Eggert asked. "Oh, hold on."

He zipped back into the closet and reappeared holding the bloody, dismembered demon hand that had gone through the portal with him. Holding it gingerly by a claw, he offered it to Lienna. "You probably don't want to leave it in there, hey?"

"Maybe just, uh ..." She glanced around the room for any place other than her hands to put the severed appendage. "Over there. Under the table."

Eggsy tossed the macabre hand where directed, then the three of us traipsed out.

"By the way, Kit," the guard murmured. "Your shoes are missing. And your shirt."

"I'm aware."

Lienna locked the door to her experimentation lab before facing us. "Gentlemen, you should know that practicing portal magic requires top-level clearance from the MPD, and revealing anything about modern portals is strictly forbidden. No one can find out about my experiments."

"Including the captain?" I asked, my eyebrows shooting up.

"She assigned me this room for abjuration testing, but we didn't discuss what kind." She frowned sternly. "So if you mention my work down here, or portals in general, to *anyone*, you'll be risking all our lives."

I made a zipping motion across my lips while Eggert nodded fervently and swore on his mustache to never utter a word.

We took the elevator back up to the office level, at which point Eggert headed straight for a bathroom; poor guy had been locked in the closet for a couple of hours while Lienna and I had gotten treatment. Seemingly out of habit, we walked to my cubicle, where I sank into my chair and Lienna took Vinny's.

Speaking of Vinny, he was probably still assisting the cleanup crew in the garage. I hadn't realized he was working late tonight, but as he'd pompously explained while helping me limp to the infirmary, Agent Harris had selected him as the most capable and trustworthy analyst to search the archives for the identity of the punk contractor we'd apprehended—which he'd been dutifully working on all evening, minus a short, professional break for dinner.

"Kit?"

My head jerked up. I'd almost nodded off while silently hating Vinny.

"What's up?" Lienna asked gently. "You okay?"

Okay? Definitely not, but if I could sit here quietly for a few minutes without any crashes, bangs, explosions, electricity, portals, or demons, I might relax enough to—

The door to the bullpen crashed open.

A folderless Captain Blythe strode inside, her blond hair fanning away from her face as she barked a string of curse words that roughly amounted to the question, and I'm paraphrasing here, "What shit-for-brains psychopath thought it was a good idea to attack my precinct with a demon? And how in god's ass did we stop it?"

I slumped back in my chair and groaned. It'd already been a long night, and I had the foreboding feeling it would only get longer.

17

WE EXPLAINED to Captain Blythe that we didn't know who the shit-for-brains psychopath was and begrudgingly admitted that Vinny, the annoyingly heroic kryomage, was the only reason we were alive. Our superior's blue streak of deeply unprofessional language continued throughout the conversation, but between her profanities, she informed us that she expected a complete report the next morning, then ordered us to hit the hay.

Per Blythe's instructions, Lienna and I slept in the infirmary. It didn't take much tossing and turning for me to determine that the infirmary beds were fitted with the same mattresses as the holding cells. Memory foam constructed with rough cement and thumbtacks, by my estimate.

I managed a restless six hours of shut-eye before waking up aching, wincing, and with a throbbing headache. There'd be no more sleeping in that state. I got out of bed, worked up enough mental juice to make myself invisible—mainly to spare myself any awkward questions about why I'd come to work wearing a pair of too-short PJ bottoms and nothing else—then trudged through the now bustling precinct to the men's locker room.

There I showered before dressing in a t-shirt and black sweats stolen from Agent Cutter's locker. I was disappointed that the garments didn't smell of cedar chips and woodsmoke, but at least the resident lumberjack was only slightly more massive than me, so the clothes fit-ish. Retracing my invisible steps to the infirmary, I fell back onto the bed and passed out again.

Getting nearly murdered too many times to count really tuckered a guy out.

I woke sometime later, groggy but slightly more refreshed. What time was it? My phone had died after my dip into the Arctic—sorry, *Pacific* Ocean. Finding out the time without my handy pocket device would require leaving the infirmary again, but the sickbay was the best place for me. Out of the way, demon-free, and where I couldn't screw anything up or get anyone killed.

Fine. I was also hiding out in here to indulge in a private pity party, but cut me some slack. My first almost-official case as an agent, and the *only* part I'd done right was the spreadsheeting.

I stared up at the blank white ceiling. When Blythe had offered me the deal of becoming an MPD agent to escape jail, I hadn't thought about the logistics. For example, the attempted-murder rate skewed a wee bit higher than I'd anticipated.

Ditto for the general viciousness of the mythics I'd be up against. I'd known about the existence of mythics for all of eighteen months, and over a year of that had been spent with scheming psychic lawyers and their cronies; the level of mythic firepower in my sphere had been mild to moderate at best. My psycho-warping powers and I were not equipped, magically or mentally, to handle real-world rogues.

Like the mages. And the demons. And the portal-experimenting abjuration prodigies.

Maybe I wasn't cut out for this line of work.

Stewing in my inadequacies, I didn't register the clack of the door until the curtains around my bed were being swept aside. Framed by a halo of fluorescent light, Lienna strode toward my bed. Her angelic aura intensified by a magnitude of ten when I noticed the bag of takeout food in her hand.

"Lunch," she declared, holding out the bag with a flourish.

I sat up, the flimsy blanket falling into my lap. My oversized, borrowed shirt was wrinkled, but I didn't care as I zeroed in on her offering. My fingers made desperate grabby motions as I claimed the bag for myself and pulled the top open.

"Donairs?" I gasped reverently. "*Two* of them? Lienna, I think I love you."

"One of them is for me."

"Oh." I tried not to look too disappointed as I extended one of the paper-wrapped bundles of deliciousness toward her. "Here you …"

Trailing off, I completely forgot what I'd been about to say because her cheeks had flushed a rosy pink.

She snatched the donair from my hand and turned away to sit on the edge of the bed. I watched her unwrap it, then pulled the second one from the bag. We ate in silence. Or rather, I shoveled the hot, spicy donair into my mouth so fast I couldn't make any intelligible noise.

Crumpling her wrapper, Lienna stuffed it in the bag. "Feeling better? Blythe is expecting us in ten minutes."

I choked on my last bite. Thumping my chest, I managed to swallow it down. "Ten minutes? Thanks for the warning."

Her blushing, defensive shyness was nowhere in sight as she brushed the crumbs from her hands in a businesslike way. "She wanted our report first thing in the morning, and it's almost noon. She won't wait much longer."

My stomach grumbled unhappily, threatening to make itself the epicenter of *Donair's Revenge: Gastrointestinal Apocalypse*, starring Acid Reflux, Tummy Cramps, and Digestive Regret.

I cleared my throat, wishing I'd eaten slower. "You don't need me for that, do you?"

She frowned. "Of course I do. This is our case."

"No, this is *your* case. The case that'll win you a permanent spot at this precinct so you don't have to go back to LA. I'm just your glorified assistant. Your Igor, remember?"

"My Fritz, actually."

I waved a hand. "You need a real agent as your partner to finish this. I'm better suited to desk work."

She gazed at me intently, then grabbed the front of my shirt and shook me. "I trust you to watch my back. That hasn't changed. Stop beating yourself up because one of the most powerful mythics I've ever seen got the better of you."

My head bobbed back and forth from her literally trying to shake some sense into me. The Lienna-induced Kit-quake wasn't helping the unstable situation in my gut. "The most powerful?"

"Yes. Mages have so much magical firepower that they don't typically want or need to become contractors. And electramages are especially lethal. Add in an illegal contract, and ninety percent of the precinct wouldn't have stood a chance against him."

My eyebrows rose. "Did you say an illegal contract?"

Nodding, she gave me another brief shake. "Get it now? Your warps *were* distracting the contractor, but the demon didn't need the contractor to direct its movements. It was acting semi-autonomously."

Was that why the demon had been growling, roaring, gloating, and enraged during the fight? Not to mention it'd been way faster than a demon being controlled by its contractor.

Part of the reason the MPD monitored summoners and their contracts so carefully was to ensure they adhered to all the super-strict Demonica regulations. Demons were supposed to surrender *all* autonomy to their contractor. Anything less was a ticking time bomb of carnage waiting to happen.

"By my best guess," she continued, "it's an illegal contract where the demon follows simple commands instead of being puppeted. The contractor tells it what to do, it goes and does it, and he's free to focus on other things. It's extremely dangerous for everyone, including him. Demons almost always find a loophole in loose contracts and kill their contractors."

I rubbed both hands over my face. "So who the hell is this lunatic? And why does he want to kill you?"

She finally released my shirt. "I don't know. I don't think I've ever seen him before."

"He knew you, that's for sure. And like I said, he knows your dad—or knows *of* your dad. Can you ask him?"

"Ask who?"

"Your dad. Ask him if he knows why an electramage contractor is trying to kill you. That's the fastest way to find out who—"

She pushed to her feet, turning away so I couldn't see her face. "That won't be necessary."

"Really? It seems pretty necess—"

"If this contractor's issue with me is personal, then it's not related to our case, and that's what I need to focus on."

"But he's trying *to kill you.* He almost succeeded twice, possibly three times if he was behind that car bomb, and he has a de—"

"Our meeting starts in two minutes. We need to go."

I threw the blankets aside, anger buzzing through me. "Lienna—"

"Not—not right now, Kit." She looked back at me. "Please. Just not now."

Our eyes met, and my anger drained away. Her mouth was tense, her brows drawn, her brown eyes dim with anxiety. She knew she was making no sense. She knew she was being willfully blind to the danger she was in, but she needed to focus on something else.

I swung off the bed and tugged my lumberjack-sized shirt straight.

For now. I'd leave it be for now. But as soon as I had the chance, I was getting to the bottom of this, even if that meant erecting a conversational trebuchet to break down the castle-quality barriers she'd built up between her professional life and all the mysteries of her personal life she was hiding from me.

ARMS FOLDED over her chest, Blythe listened silently as Lienna spoke. Standing beside my partner, I kept my mouth shut and let her do the talking. Blythe and I didn't see eye to eye at the best of times, so it was better that I didn't interject, even though some lighthearted commentary would've gone a long way in breaking up this heavy discussion of violence, death, attempted murder, and dangerous criminal organizations.

While Lienna brought the captain up to speed, Blythe kept her laser stare on the young agent, the width of her desk between them.

"So," Lienna concluded, "it looks like Red Rum is directly responsible for Harold Atherton's murder, but Rocco Thorn is the one who tipped them off that we were investigating Harold."

Blythe nodded slowly. "Do you have evidence that Rocco Thorn contacted Red Rum?"

"Not yet."

"Did the Red Rum rogues mention Thorn?"

"No."

"Can you connect the electramage contractor to Thorn?"

"No."

"Do you have *any* concrete evidence?"

"No," Lienna admitted unhappily.

Blythe folded her arms. "So far, you have a dead suspect, an unidentified contractor in custody who won't talk, a car bombing by an unknown party, a Red Rum ship in the inlet for unknown reasons, and another unidentified contractor who attacked you at a food truck and then in our parking garage. What's the connection between them?"

"Harold," Lienna answered.

"Us," I said.

The captain's eyebrows rose.

"Lienna and I," I clarified, "are the only clear link between all those things, but that's because we don't know what the actual connection is yet. Harold isn't the lynchpin between Rocco and Red Rum. He was collateral."

Lienna chewed her lower lip thoughtfully. "The Red Rum rogues talked about 'trying' what sounded like an infernus, and they mentioned 'losing' an infernus. That could've been a reference to Harold's murder, since his death activated the Banishment Clause for his contract."

"He was carrying a fake infernus," I added, "which suggests he never intended to wield his demon. He couldn't afford an actual demon anyway. He was broke and having money troubles with his business."

Lienna nodded. "Could Rocco be doing illegal contracts for Red Rum and hiding them behind his legitimate contract work? That would explain why he's had a sudden surge of clients who are all sleeper mythics."

The captain slowly raised her eyebrows. "Why would Red Rum need a public façade of summoning when they've been performing illegal summoning in secrecy for years? You two are grasping at straws, but whether you're right or wrong, conjecture can't cinch a case."

"Okay," I agreed reluctantly. "But if we bring in Rocco for a real interrogation, we could—"

"No." Blythe looked between us. "Agent Shen, I believe you're already aware of this, but I'll spell it out for Mr. Morris's sake. We don't kick wild lions in the teeth unless we're absolutely certain those lions will be locked in cages immediately afterward."

I frowned.

"In other words," she said in exasperation, interpreting my frustration as confusion, "prematurely arresting Thorn could cripple your case. The same goes for Red Rum. We're not touching them unless you have rock-solid evidence of capital crimes. Anything less isn't worth antagonizing a rogue guild of that size."

"We're just going to let known criminals do whatever they want unless we can *prove* they're up to bad shit?" I asked incredulously.

"Exactly, Mr. Morris. If you can't grasp the difference between suspecting a crime has occurred and proving it, go back to your spreadsheets." Rising, she circled her desk. "Get me evidence, or this case is dead in the water."

Stepping past us, she opened her door, a clear signal that we were supposed to exit.

Lienna walked out, and I followed behind her as she headed for the bullpen. It was brimming with busy agents and analysts. Lienna stopped beside my cubicle, and I looked from her to it and back. Was she returning me to my proper place, just like Blythe had cuttingly suggested?

"Are we done?" I asked disbelievingly. "You're just giving up?"

She stared at the floor, her shoulders drooping. "Captain Blythe is right," she whispered, avoiding my eyes. "We have no hard evidence of anything except Harold's murder, and the contractor who killed him is in custody. The rest is just suspicious behavior and hearsay."

"Then we go back to the drawing board." I lowered my head to catch her eye. "We start again with Rocco's sleeper-guild clients. We look at his paperwork. We pull up everything on Red Rum from the last year and look for clues."

She lifted her anxious brown eyes to me, biting her lower lip.

I gently gripped her shoulders. "We know he and Red Rum are doing something with demons, and we *will* find the evidence we need. We aren't giving up. I won't let you, Lienna."

Half an hour ago, I'd tried convincing her that I didn't belong in the field, but I'd been too deep in my own pity party to realize Lienna needed me.

Her warm hands closed around my wrists. The way she was looking at me made me suddenly aware of the fact that I'd pulled her close. My gaze roved across her face. Yes, we were in a bustling room full of our coworkers, but when the beautiful woman you have a huge crush on looks at you like *that*, those details stop mattering.

A loud throat clearing jarred through me. I looked over at none other than Vincent leaning out of the cubicle, his eyebrows arched and mouth pushed into a disapproving frown.

"I see you're up again," he observed. "Recovering okay?"

Why did he have to sound sort of concerned? It was harder to loathe every particle of his being when he wasn't acting like a complete tool. Speaking of his particles, I bet every one of them had a microscopic mohawk and teeny weeny molecule-sized cargo pants.

"Peachy keen," I answered, stepping a more professional distance away from Lienna. "I even got out for a walk and visited the pet store."

"Glad to hear you're—" Vincent's eyes narrowed. "The pet store?"

I nodded. "They've got a new reticulated python named Peanut."

"Reticulated pythons are the longest snakes in the world," he muttered, as though being armed with reptilian trivia would defend him against a surprise visit from Peanut during his next lunch break. "Even longer than the green anaconda."

"Fascinating," I said with a spreading grin. "Are you a snake guy, Vinny?"

"No ... why?"

I gave an airy shrug. "No reason."

"Anyway," he half growled, waving away his inevitable slithery encounter, "do you know the identity of that electramage contractor? Is he a suspect in your case?"

"We're not sure yet," Lienna answered, more subdued than usual. "He could be connected to Rocco Thorn. He's probably the guy who planted the bomb in our car after we questioned one of Rocco's clients."

"Rocco Thorn, the guild master of the Grand Grimoire?" Vinny grimaced. "GMs have no respect for the MPD. And they all seem to be in league with each other, blocking due process at every turn."

In league with each other?

"GMs are supposed to balance the MPD's power," Lienna said in the same flat, slightly bitter tone as someone who said winning wasn't important after losing a race. "They play an important role in—"

I grabbed her arm. "Yeah, balance, roles, whatever. Let's go, Lienna."

"Go where? Kit?"

Leaving Vinny staring after us and probably wondering if he should do an internet search on how to snake-proof his desk, I dragged her across the bullpen and into the hallway before she yanked her arm free.

"Kit! What are you doing?"

I seized her hand and pulled her back into motion. "We *do* have a lead. I completely forgot about it with the whole Red Rum ship excursion, but what got us thinking about Red Rum in the first place?"

It took her a second. "The report on the unbound demon and all those Red Rum bodies!"

"And the guy who reported it was Darius King, GM of the Crow and Hammer." I pulled her into the elevator's open doors as it disgorged a trio of analysts carrying their lunches. I punched the button for the parking garage. "It's like Vinny said. GMs are all in league with each other."

"I don't think that's accurate," she muttered.

"But the idea that GMs are more connected than other mythics is accurate, right? If anyone might have an inkling about what Rocco is up to, why not another GM in the same neighborhood?"

"Especially a GM who's also connected to Red Rum. He found the bodies." Her eyes lit with that resolute, mischievous glint I loved. "Do you think Darius will talk?"

"Oh, almost definitely not, but it's worth a try."

The elevator doors chimed open, but Lienna didn't exit. "You really should've told me where we were going."

"Why?"

"Because all my stuff is upstairs, and I need to sign out a new vehicle."

"Oh. Right." I sheepishly waited for the doors to slide closed again. "Will they give you another car after what happened to the last two?"

"I think so, but let's try not to destroy this one, because I doubt I'll get a fourth."

As the elevator carried us back up, I grinned. "You got it, partner."

She didn't roll her eyes, instead giving me a tight, determined grin.

That didn't fix anything, but I felt a hell of a lot better about going out into the field again. And I vowed that, this time, I wouldn't screw it up.

18

THE CROW AND HAMMER guild was tucked away at the western edge of the Downtown Eastside—an area well known as the city's nastiest neighborhood. Gloomy gray clouds blanketed the sky as our car wound through the dingy streets, and the afternoon light was beginning to weaken.

We'd lost an hour stopping at my place, then Lienna's to get proper clothes. She'd also needed a new satchel for all her Arcana knickknacks—though what she'd grabbed was not new, but actually very old and worn. I suspected it was the predecessor of her last bag, brought out of retirement after its replacement's tragic demise.

Going to her home had been a risk in case the goateed lightning bolt and his demon were lying in wait, but I'd invisified us and we'd been quick.

Lienna pulled Smart Car III—a newer model that, believe it or not, actually had a back seat!—up in front of a three-story brick building. Barred windows on the upper levels diminished its curb appeal, and the wooden door sat back in an alcove as far away from the sidewalk as the architecture would allow.

My gut jumped nervously as I gazed at that door. This guild and I had a past, though somewhat indirectly. They'd tagged my former pal Quentin, a super-empath who'd turned out to be crazy-evil. My old GM had retaliated, and in response, the Crow and Hammer had mobilized its far more impressive combat force and obliterated KCQ.

Not that the Crow and Hammer had a reputation as "impressive." The water-cooler talk at the precinct suggested the guild was a haven for misfits, troublemakers, former rogues, and ex-cons. They were like that semi-delinquent kid at school who'd failed a few grades and missed classes half the time, but always showed up to kick the smaller kids' butts in gym class.

Anyway, in the domino chain of events leading to my employment at the MPD, the Crow and Hammer was the callous finger flick that'd sent the whole sequence into motion.

Lienna and I approached the shadowed alcove. Painted on the solid wood door was a crow and—wait for it—a hammer.

"Do we have a plan of attack?" I asked my partner.

"Nope."

"Then we're winging it. My favorite."

And in we went.

The Crow and Hammer's business front was that of a bar. It had that knockoff Irish pub vibe where everything was wooden and all the lights emitted a dim, orange glow. A long bar stretched across the back, stacked with an unusual assortment of bottles.

As we wound between the empty tables, a pair of saloon doors behind the bar swung open. A young woman around my age with wild red curls tied into a top bun backed through the doorway, carrying a bulky step stool.

Clearing the threshold, she turned around, spotted the two people standing on the other side of the bar, and let out a loud, startled squawk. The stool fell out of her arms. Judging by the loud and highly colorful curse she shouted next, it'd landed on her foot. I winced sympathetically.

"We're closed," she barked, her eyes watering as she stepped over the dropped stool. "So take a hike."

Would Lienna and I always have this problem? Maybe we needed to get on the suit-and-tie bandwagon with the rest of our colleagues.

"Is Darius King in?" my partner asked.

Faint surprise registered on the redhead's freckled face, then her expression closed. "Who's asking?"

"The MPD."

"Oh really." She folded her arms, a hip cocked. "Got identification?"

Lienna pulled her badge from her replacement satchel and offered it for the bartender's inspection. I tugged my jacket zipper down to flash mine but didn't hand it over.

Tucking her badge away again, Lienna asked, "So? Is he around?"

"No idea."

"You work here, don't you?"

"Yeah, but I'm not usually in at this time." The woman waved at the bottles everywhere, then at the shelves behind her, which were conspicuously empty. "I'm doing extra cleaning."

"What about Robin Page?" I asked. "Is *she* around?"

"No."

"Where is she?"

"How should I know?" The woman cocked her hip in the other direction. "I'm a bartender, not a babysitter. I don't take attendance."

Well, her unhelpful response at least confirmed that she considered Robin—the suspicious young contractor who'd joined the Grand Grimoire, killed an unbound demon, then jumped ship to the Crow and Hammer a week later—to be a guildmate.

"Can I help you two with anything else?" the redhead added as aggressively as possible.

My goodness, this bartender had a bad attitude. She rivaled the Grand Grimoire's grizzled apes for anti-authority hostility.

"How about a piña colada?" I asked lightly. "With a cute little umbrella like—"

"No umbrellas," she half snarled, slapping her hands down on the counter. "I said we're closed, so if you want to day-drink, go find a bingo hall."

I choked back a snort.

"We need to talk to your guild master," Lienna said curtly. "Can you please check whether he's in the building? If you won't, we'll have to search it."

We didn't have a search warrant, but the bartender didn't know that—and hopefully didn't realize we needed one.

The redhead blew air through her nose. "I'll check. Wait here."

Striding the length of the bar, she cut toward the staircase in the corner, then paused and called over her shoulder, "And don't touch anything!"

"You got it, barkeep," I called back.

She flipped me the bird, then sped up the stairs and out of sight, leaving Lienna and me alone with half a liquor store's worth of unguarded alcohol. I sighed wistfully. What did a guy have to do to get some coconut and pineapple in his life? Move to a tropical resort?

Still tired after our hellishly long and life-threatening day yesterday, I pulled out a stool and slid onto it while we waited. Lienna hesitated, then perched on the stool next to me.

Blatantly ignoring the redhead's orders, I turned a bottle of white wine around to read the label. "Do you actually think Rocco sicced the electramage contractor on us?"

"The timing fits." She lined up a row of matching vodka bottles. "The electramage is probably the one who bombed our car yesterday morning, and Harold admitted he told Rocco we were investigating him. That's just enough time for Rocco to call someone in to eliminate us."

"But it doesn't explain why the electramage has a beef with you." I peeked at her profile from the corner of my eye. "He said something about 'thirteen years too long.' Did ten-year-old you kill this guy's goldfish or something?"

She shook her head. "I've been racking my brain all morning, and I can't remember ever meeting him before. But I think …"

I waited a moment, then asked, "You think what?"

Picking at the corner of a bottle's label, she exhaled slowly. "If you're right that he reacted strongly to the sight of my father, there's a chance he's after me because of my dad."

Duh. There was more than just a *chance*. But I didn't say that, opting to nudge her into opening up a bit more. "What do you mean?"

"My dad has put away a lot of criminals in his career. Powerful ones who thought they were untouchable." She cleared her throat. "It's almost cliché how many of them threatened revenge on him and our family. It happened on a yearly basis."

"*Yearly?*"

She nodded. "But it was never really a concern. Almost all those mythics were executed. On top of that, I went to a private mythic school with excellent security, so there was no way rogues could get to me."

"But you're not at a private school anymore."

"I haven't been for years," she countered, picking almost frantically at the label, "and no one has ever bothered me. Why now? And why here, so far from LA?"

"Why not ask your dad? He'll know all his cases, and a murderous electramage with an illegal demon contract is bound to stand out."

Her face tightened. "I can't, Kit."

"Why? Are you not on speaking terms?" I frowned. "Doesn't he want you to go back to the LA precinct to work with him?"

"Yes."

"Then why—"

She tore a chunk of label off the bottle. "Kit, *please*. I can't ask my dad, end of story."

So much for opening up. I braced my elbows on the counter. "Fine."

We sat quietly, and I watched Lienna rip strips off the label, piling them in a little paper mountain on the bar top. How big was this building? That bartender was taking her sweet time.

"Don't give me that look, Kit."

"What look?"

"*That* one." She started shredding the tiny label pieces. "That's your 'thinking' face."

"You don't want me to think?"

Normally, such a response would have garnered an eye roll, but she seemed too focused on breaking that poor label down to an atomic level.

"You make that face when you're trying to figure something out," she said. "Or some*one*."

I propped my chin on my palm, saying nothing. The disconnect in her typically logical mind baffled me. She knew the electramage contractor and her father were tied together somehow but refused to contact Papa Shen about the investigation or give me the tiniest bit of information about her family life. She was hiding something.

So, yes, I was absolutely trying to figure her out.

"I ..." she whispered. "I just can't talk about it, okay?"

"It's fine." I couldn't stand her anguished expression, and I didn't want to make her uncomfortable. If she was going to talk, she'd do it on her own terms.

The silence between us stretched, growing painful, but I didn't know how to reassure her.

"It's ..." Her voice went even quieter. "It's just that he's so respected and successful."

I hesitated, unsure how to interpret her statement. "Is being respected and successful a bad thing?"

"No, but he's the perfect agent—a great leader, skilled sorcerer, and top investigator. Everyone in LA looks up to him, and I was so proud to be his daughter."

I didn't miss the past tense on that last statement. "He's not a perfect agent, then?"

Her face was alarmingly pale. "He's taken down rogue guilds and put away loads of dangerous criminals. He's even outed corrupt agents."

Why were her words at complete odds with her tone and body language? Was she defending her dad or condemning him?

I covered her hand with mine, toppling her leaning tower of microscopic label bits.

Her shoulders folded inward, her head bowing. For a long moment, she didn't say anything. "I worked on one of his cases. My last case as an analyst. Dad's investigation involved this rich asshole who was going to get off due to a lack of evidence. Dad had given up, but I didn't want to let him down, so I kept digging for anything we could use to nail the charges."

Her hand curled into a fist beneath mine. "I wanted to be an agent just like him. I'd dedicated my whole life to becoming the best sorceress possible, better than anyone, so when I joined the MPD, I could get promoted to full agent and join his team right away."

I waited as she struggled to speak. Her throat worked, trying to get out the words—words that hurt like knives, judging by the way her face was crumpling.

"Dad took a bribe in return for destroying key evidence in the case." Her clenched fist opened, her fingers curling tightly around mine. "I found other cases of his, one every couple years, where the charges fell through for similar reasons—a lack of evidence. In most of them, the suspect was rich but not notorious or well-known."

"Shit," I whispered.

"I confronted him." She breathed deeply, unsteadily. "He said it wasn't a big deal because they weren't violent criminals, and he was just looking out for our family's future. And he said if I told anyone about it, I'd ruin both our careers. I'd never escape the stain of his bad name, and neither would our family. The truth would destroy my mom."

She looked up at me as though meeting my eyes was the hardest thing she'd ever done. "So I closed the case, the guy got off with a misdemeanor fine, and Dad recommended me for immediate promotion to the Rogue Response team."

And her first job on the Rogue Response team had been to capture a runaway psychic passing through LAX. She'd arrested me, flown me back to Vancouver, and accepted the position Blythe had offered.

All to stay away from her father.

I remembered how much of a hard-ass she'd been when I'd first met her. How judgmental of my criminal behavior and con-artist activity. How intense and almost paranoid about doing everything right.

That all made a hell of a lot more sense now.

"I did *nothing*, Kit." Tears filmed her eyes, but she furiously blinked them away before any could fall. "You're the only person I've ever told. Everyone thinks he's amazing, but he's let criminals off for personal gain. And I let him get away with it because—because I'm just as selfish as he is."

Her voice broke, and I slid off my stool to wrap her in my arms.

"You're not responsible for what your dad did," I murmured, holding her tight to my chest. "And you're not selfish. You were protecting yourself and your mother. I know you believe in law and order with every fiber of your being, Lienna, but you can't use that as your measuring stick for every single decision."

She peeked up at me, guilt and grief shadowing her eyes.

"Sometimes, law and order and right and wrong come in second to surviving." I squeezed her gently. "You're surviving. Just because you aren't in physical danger doesn't mean it isn't survival. You did what you needed to do, and that's okay."

Sucking in an unsteady breath, she wiggled an arm out of my hold to rub her eyes as though to ensure no stealthy tears would escape her control. "Is that what you were doing with KCQ? Surviving? You seemed to care about justice, but you worked for a criminal guild anyway."

"I was surviving," I agreed. "Worrying about right and wrong is a luxury some people don't have."

"A poignant and hard truth, certainly."

At the unfamiliar male voice, I leaped backward, accidentally pulling Lienna off her stool. It wobbled violently, almost toppling over.

The speaker was an impeccably dressed man in his late forties or early fifties. With well-groomed salt-and-pepper hair and a short beard to match, he was the epitome of a silver fox. He stood behind the counter across from us, nonchalant as though he hadn't somehow, impossibly, entered the room, walked along the bar, and positioned himself three feet away without either Lienna or me noticing.

His cool smile was affable, but the casual, confident way he held himself put me on edge. This was a man equally comfortable shaking your hand or slitting your throat.

And I had no idea which to expect.

19

DARIUS KING. With his cool poise and dangerous allure, I had no doubt this guy was the leader of a guild full of troublemakers, rogues, and ex-cons.

"Welcome to the Crow and Hammer, agents," the silver fox murmured in a deep, pleasant voice. His gray eyes appraised us. "I must say, Captain Blythe doesn't usually send fledglings into my den. Is Agent Harris ill?"

"I'm Agent Shen," Lienna said, ignoring his question. "This is Agent Morris. You must be Darius King."

"At your service." He made a sweeping gesture across the bottle-laden bar. "Please forgive the disarray. Can I get either of you a drink?"

I perked up. "Could I have a piña col—"

"No, thank you," Lienna said over me. "No drinks, just answers."

Darius picked up a bottle of cognac and gave it the same assessing examination he'd given us. "Answers about what?"

"Robin Page. We heard she's a member of your guild, but her transfer paperwork is incomplete."

"Ah. My AGM is critically overworked. The forms are in progress, and as I'm sure you're aware, the MPD offers a grace period of thirty days for Class C filings."

He knew his stuff. I had the sudden feeling this GM would be harder to crack than Rocco Thorn.

"Why did Robin Page join your guild?" Lienna asked, changing tracks.

Darius's smile returned, this time accompanied by an amused sparkle in his eyes. "I poached her."

"Sorry?"

"I encountered her during the search for the unbound demon on Halloween. Recognizing her remarkable talent, I offered her a place at my guild."

That was a more honest answer than I'd expected. "Did you know she was a member of the Grand Grimoire when you invited her?"

"I did." His eyebrows rose slightly. "I won't pretend I didn't see the advantage in adding a contractor like her to my roster, but it wasn't my only motivation. The Grand Grimoire is no place for an inexperienced young woman, no matter how gifted."

"And you think your guild is a better place for her?" I surmised.

"A safer one." He pulled a tall Collins glass from beneath the bar and set it on the counter. "While around half our membership is licensed for bounty hunting, we also have many members, including young ladies like Miss Page, who are pursuing other aspirations with their magic."

Lienna hitched her satchel strap over her shoulder. "Did you confirm the legality of Robin's contract before inducting her into your guild?"

Darius selected a bottle from the mess on the bar. "I confirmed her contract was MPD-approved. Should I have investigated more thoroughly? Overseeing contracts is the responsibility of the MPD's Demonica inspectors."

"I was just wondering if you found it strange that a contractor with six months of experience was able to kill an unbound demon that the best combat teams in the city couldn't handle."

"Not to lessen Miss Page's accomplishment," Darius replied as he poured an ounce or two of what looked like white rum into the glass, "but she got very, very lucky. The unbound demon had already suffered injuries from its previous encounters with combat teams, mine included."

He swapped the rum for a bottle of simple syrup and added a splash to the glass. "What I'd like to know, Agent Shen, is whether you're skirting the questions you want to ask me, or whether you've yet to realize what questions you should be asking."

She tensed warily. "And what should I be asking?"

Instead of replying, he turned and walked through the saloon doors, vanishing into the back. I stared at the swinging doors, then glanced at Lienna, but before either of us could say anything, he returned, carrying a carton of what looked like milk. He gave it a shake, then added half an ounce to his drink.

"What questions should I be asking?" Lienna repeated.

A faint smile played over Darius's lips. He added a drizzle of brown liqueur to his cocktail. "It's your job to ask the questions, Agent Shen. This is your investigation."

Damn. He was a wily silver fox, wasn't he?

Cracking open a can of vanilla soda, he poured half of it into the glass, then scooped in some crushed ice. I watched him with narrowed eyes. He didn't trigger my "skeevy manipulator" spidey sense the way the Grand Grimoire's GM had, but I knew he was manipulating us, nonetheless.

"You discovered the bodies of the Red Rum rogues responsible for the unbound demon," Lienna ventured. "Robin joined your guild right after. Was she involved in the massacre of the Red Rum rogues?"

Pausing, the GM met her probing stare. "No."

"Was she involved with the unbound demon in any way besides killing it?"

"No."

"Was she involved in Rocco Thorn's summoning business?"

He shrugged. "Not as far as I know. If you want to learn more about the Red Rum case, I suggest asking Agent Harris. He was the lead investigator."

Lienna pressed her lips together, and I knew what she was thinking. Robin Page was the only link between the Grand Grimoire, Rocco Thorn, Red Rum, Darius King, and the unbound demon. Her involvement might be coincidental, but we needed to know for sure.

"Where is Robin?" I asked.

"If you wish to interview her, you'll need to present me with an official summons first."

I swore under my breath.

Lienna widened her stance slightly, as though bracing for a fight. "How well do you know Rocco Thorn?"

Darius pulled out a tool that resembled a stick with four prongs on the end and inserted it into his drink. "I'm familiar with him, but our interactions have always been strictly related to guild business."

Pressing the stick between his palms, he spun it rapidly back and forth as though trying to start a fire in the glass. The icy mixture foamed up.

I was frustrated, anxious, tired, and wary, but damn if my mouth wasn't watering. Had I been this thirsty when I'd come in? Because I was dying for a drink.

"Even so," I said bluntly, "you have to be aware that Thorn is sketchy as hell, right?"

Breath hitching at my sudden change in tactics, Lienna shot me a questioning look.

Darius's eyes met mine, and though he didn't speak, his silent amusement seemed a lot like confirmation. He scooped more ice into the glass, filling it nearly to the top, then resumed swizzling it.

"Do you know anything about him participating in illegal Demonica?" I pried further.

"Frankly, there are *always* rumors of illegal Demonica circulating about the Grand Grimoire. Accuracy and specificity are chronically lacking among gossipers, however."

"What about involvement with Red Rum?"

His eyebrows arched. "That's a dangerous accusation, Agent Morris."

I watched him intently. This guy could and would waltz conversational circles around us without giving away a single thing he didn't want to reveal. But I also suspected he appreciated honesty and directness.

"I can't say what Mr. Thorn might be up to," Darius finally said. He stuck a bushy sprig of mint leaves into his glass. "But I can say he's a smart man."

Where the hell had he gotten that mint? I hadn't seen any on the counter.

"A smart man," he continued, "would only deal with Red Rum in one of two ways: buying or selling. Anything else is a noose waiting to drop over your head."

Lienna pressed her hands to the counter. "That's all you'll tell us? You're a GM. Don't pretend you're clueless about the illegal activity in your own backyard. Don't you want a criminal like Thorn brought to justice?"

No, that wasn't the right angle. I stepped closer to the bar. "Don't you want a liability like Thorn out of your territory?"

Darius smiled like a cat in the milk, and a slight shiver ran down my spine.

"A GM's choices become his guild's choices, to the benefit or detriment of his guildeds." Reaching under the counter, he pulled out a festive red-and-white-striped straw and stuck it in the drink. "Have you met Rocco Thorn's first officer? A man driven by idealism and clear-sighted goals, who has his guild's best interests at heart."

Darius slid the drink across the counter until it was directly in front of me. "It isn't a piña colada, but I hope you enjoy this cocojito. It's my own recipe."

I blinked at the frothy white drink with its mint bouquet garnish, the soda fizzling and the outside of the glass lightly frosted.

"Have a lovely afternoon, Agent Morris, Agent Shen."

And just like that, the wily silver fox of the Crow and Hammer disappeared through the saloon doors, the carton of coconut milk in his hand. This time he wasn't coming back; our interview was over.

Lienna let out an explosive breath. "Well."

"Well," I agreed, wrapping my hand around the icy cocojito.

"That was interesting."

"Very," I murmured, lifting the drink so I could inhale the minty-fresh coconut aroma.

"Kit, are you even listening?"

"Sure," I whispered dreamily, directing the straw toward my mouth.

She crossed her arms. "Agents can't drink on the job."

"Good thing I'm not a real agent yet." I took a long sip, and oh my tropical goddess, the smooth coconut, biting mint, sweet vanilla, and teasing hint of bitter cocoa. It was like a boozy Christmas beach party dancing in a delicious grass skirt on my tongue. "This is *amazing*. Can I join this guild?"

"Kit," she growled.

I took another long sip, then offered it to her. Her scowl deepened. Fine, more for me. Maybe these Crow and Hammer ruffians weren't so terrible after all.

"The bad news," I said, focusing now that my tastebuds were satisfied, "is that he gave us nothing but hints. The good news is that they were good hints."

"If Rocco is working with Red Rum, then he's either buying or selling," she inferred. "Wanna bet he's selling?"

I tried to answer affirmatively but only succeeded in blowing a bubble into my new favorite drink of all time. Oh well, she was piecing this together just fine on her own. She didn't need my confirmation.

"And wanna bet it's the 'new batch' we heard about on the ship?"

Resentfully prying my lips from the straw, I answered, "Yup. He's selling something to do with infernuses ... inferni? Which is it?"

"Infernuses. Inferni sounds ridiculous."

"Touché. Infernuses. And his sleeper-guild clients are involved somehow."

"Yeah." She leaned against the bar. "But we still only have suspicions and hearsay. No hard evidence. We can't go after Rocco without it."

"Darius told us where to look next." I smirked. "Ol' Viking Beard is risking his guild with his scheme, and his first officer wants to protect the guild. As second-in-command, he's got to have *some* idea what's going on. All we have to do is get him to talk."

Lienna pushed away from the bar. "Let's go."

"Slow down, skipper. There's no need to rush." I slid back onto my stool. "Take a breather. Let's think this through. Concoct our mighty plan."

She rolled her eyes. "You just want to enjoy your drink."

I took a luxurious sip of coconut-vanilla bliss. "Damn right I do."

20

PARKED HALF A BLOCK down the road from the Grand Grimoire, Lienna and I were staking out the guild from our car like a pair of hard-boiled film noir private eyes from the forties. Our proximity to a building full of combat-hardened, demon-wielding mythics had me on edge, but a glimmer of excitement penetrated my general state of apprehension.

My first stakeout.

Sure, we were MagiPol rookies, not scruffy, misanthropic detectives. And, yes, we were in a car the size of a Costco beach ball with sunset-stained, early evening cloud cover overhead, rather than in a classic, beat-up sedan during a midnight downpour. But still—give me a trench coat, a pack of cigarettes, and a shadowy black-and-white filter, and it would be perfect. Maybe toss in a flask of whiskey for good measure.

Hey, I'd already broken the "no drinking on the job" rule today, right?

"We can't sit here forever," Lienna muttered, almost to herself. "We don't even know if Tae-min is in there."

Though I'd forgotten about it until Darius's hint, Lienna and I had already met the Grand Grimoire's first officer: the early thirties, spiky-haired man who'd shot us a death glare on his way out of Rocco Thorn's office on our first visit. According to MPD records, Tae-min Lee was a combat sorcerer who'd been with the guild for four of its five years.

"We could try calling him and see if he wants to chat over drinks, but that might put him on his guard. You may not realize this," I added in a deadpan, "but lots of mythics don't trust the MPD."

"I've noticed." She sighed. "This case has been nothing but dead ends, screwups, and misdirection."

No exaggeration there. I agreed all the way down to my still-aching bruises.

"I feel like I have no clue what I'm doing," she finished in a mumble.

Hold up. How strong had that exquisite cocojito *been*? Because I was clearly hearing things. "*I'm* supposed to be the idiot without a clue. I've been wondering this whole time if I'm cut out for fieldwork."

"You kidding? I wouldn't have gotten half this far without your help." She shook her head bemusedly. "We're both in over our heads on this one, aren't we?"

"We've managed to turn an assignment that didn't even include a crime when we started into an actual investigation. That's not bad for two clueless rookies, you've got to admit."

"I guess we make an okay team, huh?"

"We're a goddamn *dream* team, partner."

Lienna rolled her eyes. "We're getting there."

"Hell yeah. We just need Tae-min to spill the beans on his guild master."

She curled her hands over the steering wheel. "Maybe you should handle that part. You have a way of getting people to talk."

I'd always assumed that was because most folks figured the best way to get me to shut up was to interrupt me. "I'll give it my best shot, but if things escalate to another demon battle, I'll be Robin and you be Batman."

"Robin, like, Page?"

"No, I mean I'll follow your lead."

"Oh. Okay."

She smiled slowly, and I grinned back. We could handle this. We'd figure it out. We were the Dynamic Duo, minus the spandex, masks, and cool Kit-mobile.

Her smile softened to a slight curving of her lips, and a slow flush of anticipation rose through me. Her eyes were on mine, and she was looking at me *that way* again—the way that made me want to reach across the console, cup her cheek, and pull her mouth to mine.

Her gaze slipped down to my lips.

She jerked her focus back up, then looked sharply out the windshield. "Oh! Is that him?"

My mind was still lingering elsewhere. "Sorry, what, who now?"

She pointed through the windshield, where a slim man had just exited the Grand Grimoire. He turned up the street, heading away from us. We'd watched several guild members exit, and this was the first one who wasn't roughly the size and weight of a leather-clad buffalo.

I squinted as he passed under a streetlamp. "He's the right build, but—"

Apparently, that was enough for Lienna. Satchel under her arm, she flung her door open and sprinted down the street. Swearing, I jumped out and ran after her.

The man had stopped beside a parked coupe just past the guild, his hand digging in his pocket for keys. At the sound of our running footsteps, he looked at us. Yep, it was Tae-min, a black beanie on his dark hair and his jacket hanging open to reveal a t-shirt with a Glitch Mob logo splashed across it.

As Lienna and I trotted up to him, I noted that his demeanor wasn't any friendlier than our first encounter.

"You two again." He crossed his arms. "Do you have a summons for me?"

I spread my hands in a peaceful gesture. "Nope. We don't need one when we're trying to help you out."

He scoffed. "MagiPol would rather outlaw Demonica and shut us down than help us."

Lienna bristled at the accusation but remained silent, deferring to my alleged conversational skills.

"We want to keep everyone safe, including Demonica mythics," I said placidly. "So when we came across some nasty business that looked like bad news for your guild, we thought we should ask someone who could shed light on the situation. You know, before things got messy."

"Nasty business? Contracting a demon isn't 'nasty business' and it doesn't mean we all want to go on a crime spree. That's a stupid, outdated stereotype."

"As a Psychica mythic, I totally get it." I offered a slight smile, figuring I didn't need to explain that psychics were scorned by all the other mythic classes. "Help us out with this, and maybe you can help dispel that stereotype."

His expression didn't soften. "I don't need to. The Grand Grimoire has a strict code of conduct that our leadership team strongly enforces. If there was any nasty business going on, we'd know."

"What if it was coming from *within* your leadership team?" I asked.

His dark eyes narrowed. "What are you implying?"

"The last thing the Grand Grimoire needs is a scandal where their GM is arrested for using his guild to hide his illegal summoning and connections to Red Rum."

"Red Rum? Rocco is connected to *Red Rum?*"

"Looks like it." I stepped closer. "We don't want his actions to bring down this entire guild, but if we can't intercept him now, that might not be an option."

Tae-min shifted his weight from foot to foot, his gaze darting toward the guild. "No way Rocco is involved with Red Rum. You're trying to trick me into—"

"Don't be an idiot, Tae-min."

I jolted at the deep, rough voice. With the crunch of rock under heavy boots, a man walked around the corner of the guild right behind us. It was Leroy, the gregarious Grand Grimoire mythic we'd met on our last visit. A cigarette stuck out from between his thin lips, and with no sign of his friendly smile, the formerly harmless-looking old contractor seemed even more intimidating than his Koko-esque guildmates.

"If you think these agents are tricking you," he growled at Tae-min, "then you don't know the MPD or Rocco." Pulling his cigarette from his mouth, he swiveled toward me. "What is it you think our honorable leader is doing with Red Rum?"

I hesitated, unsure about involving a random guild member. For all I knew, he could run straight to Rocco and tell him what we were up to. "We're not sure yet."

"You don't even know what he's allegedly guilty of?" Tae-min snapped angrily.

Guess I'd have to play a few more cards, even with our extra witness. "We know he's selling something related to infernuses to Red Rum. And we know he's preying on mythics in desperate straits and using them as soul-fodder for demon contracts they aren't even using."

Tae-min and Leroy exchanged a look I couldn't interpret.

"Do you have proof?" the first officer asked.

"Some," I hedged. "But we need—hey!"

Leroy had just flicked his cigarette away and strode past me, heading for the guild. I was still gawking as he vanished inside.

I rushed after the contractor, waving at Lienna to hurry up. "Get your cat's eye going!"

She slapped her hand against the pendant and whispered its incantation. I dropped an invisi-bomb, erasing us from the perception of everyone in and around the building.

Still standing beside his car, Tae-min let out a surprised gargle at our sudden disappearance. "Agents?"

Adding another warp to hide the opening of the door, I zoomed after Leroy, Lienna right on my heels. He'd already disappeared from among the dusty collection of incomplete board games, and the door to the back was unlocked.

Following the same route as our last visit, we hastened to the stairwell and opened the door. Somewhere above, heavy shoes thudded against the steps. We raced upward to the second level—but I could still hear footsteps. Leroy was heading for the third floor.

He *was* running straight to Rocco to warn him.

I picked up my pace, sprinting for the top floor. As Lienna and I burst into the long hallway, Leroy knocked on Rocco's office door at the other end. The GM's gruff voice called for him to enter.

We reached the office in time to slip in behind Leroy, and I pulled Lienna into the corner as the contractor shut the door.

"What do you need, Leroy?" Rocco demanded, seated behind his desk with irritation and surprise competing in his bearded expression.

"I need a word," the contractor said, pulling back one of the chairs in front of Rocco's desk as though he required twice the usual amount of legroom. He dropped into it.

Rocco glanced impatiently at his monitor. "Make it quick."

"I'll get right to the point, then, Rocco. I don't like being the odd man out."

The GM fixed his full attention on his guilded. "The odd man out of what?"

"I thought you wanted this over with quick. Why are you playing dumb?"

"I'm not playing dumb. Say whatever you came to say."

"Red Rum, Rocco," Leroy said in a low, menacing tone. "Tell me about Red Rum."

The GM stiffened. "What about them?"

"You haven't covered your tracks as well as you think you have." Leroy leaned back and crossed his arms. "I want in."

Rocco's eyes narrowed suspiciously. "You do?"

"Damn right. You screwed us all the moment you crawled into bed with Red Rum. You and your debts and your greed. If you're going to destroy the guild I helped found, I want something out of it."

Whoa, wait. Leroy was *a founding guild member?* Clearly, Lienna and I should've done a better background check on this guy, but he'd seemed like a strangely affable demon contractor, not one of the faces on the Grand Grimoire's version of Mount Rushmore.

"I'm not destroying the guild," Rocco snapped.

"The MPD knows you're involved with Red Rum, and it's only a matter of time before they tear the guild down, and you with it." Leroy arched his eyebrows. "So you can either let me in on the deal you're doing, or I'll hand you over to the MPD myself."

Rocco's blond beard bristled, and it took me a moment to realize he was smiling coldly.

"Leroy, Leroy," he chided patronizingly. "The whole reason you were such a well-liked first officer when this guild formed was because of your ideals. After five years of your do-gooder bullshit, did you really think I'd buy this 'dark side of Leroy' charade? You don't have the stomach to handle the things I've done for this guild."

I goggled at Leroy. When Darius had told us to talk to the idealistic first officer of the Grand Grimoire, had he meant Tae-min, or had he meant this guy, the contractor who was Thomas Jefferson to Rocco's George Washington?

Leroy sat forward in his chair. "The things you've done for this guild, Rocco? Or the things you've done for yourself?"

The GM's cheeks pinched inward, as though Leroy's words had left a sour taste in his mouth. There was a lull as the two men considered what the situation had come to and where it was inevitably about to go.

"Ah, crap," I muttered.

And they both reached for their infernuses.

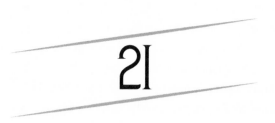

21

IMAGINE one of those cutesy Norman Rockwell paintings—the ones that embody nineteen-fifties America. They have a delightful, everyday-life appeal to them. Everyone is happy and relaxed, the colors exist in a pleasant pastel palette, and the moment seems frozen in perpetual goodwill.

Now erase the very essence of that. No Coca-Cola bottles on a hot summer day. No energetic puppies and enthusiastic young children. No first dates and cherries on top of your vanilla ice cream.

Scrap all that shit.

Take that newly empty canvas utterly devoid of joy or aesthetically diffused lighting and fill it to the brim with chaos, the very spirit of violence, and the eyeball-blistering energy you would normally associate with the climactic battle of a badly CGI-ed alien-robot movie.

That's what it was like standing ten feet away from a demon-on-demon battle.

Leroy and Rocco backed against the walls on opposite sides of the office as their demons beat on each other. Rocco's was tall and protected by scaly armor plates, while Leroy's gargantuan horned pet was only marginally smaller than The Thing and exactly the same build. Their beasts didn't move as fast as the electramage's illegally contracted demon, but each blow met the other demon's flesh with the horrific thud of a concrete block landing on unyielding earth.

I didn't want to imagine how hard they could hit.

Lienna and I pressed into the corner a few feet away from Leroy, and since neither demon had reacted to our presence, both men must have normal, legal contracts. Thank Asmodeus.

Leroy's super-sized hellion flipped Rocco's desk into the other demon, computer gear crashing to the floor. It was hard to tell which demon was winning. They might've both been losing somehow. I had trouble imagining how anyone could come out a winner with so much ruthlessness involved.

Probably time to intervene.

The best warpish distraction I could come up with on the spot was the flashing of blue and red police lights through the Grand Grimoire's windows, which I targeted solely at Thorn. His head whipped toward the lights, and for an instant, his demon froze in place, crouched in preparation to leap at its opponent.

That blip in Thorn's focus was enough for Leroy to send his demon into a flying knee drop on top of Thorn's immobile marionette. The two demons collided—and the floor collapsed.

Not just the floorboards. Turned out that the weight of two full-grown demons bashing themselves into the floor had been too much for the building's old bones. A virtual sinkhole opened up, and the pair of brutes plunged into the guild's communal room on the second floor.

The hole in the floor, almost eight feet in jagged diameter, was laced with broken wires and splintered crossbeams—but that didn't stop Rocco. With no worry for life, limb, or tears in his fancy suit, the guild master leaped into the hole and landed next to the immobile demons.

Leroy, just as fearless, jumped after him. He landed beside Rocco in a crouch, popped back up, and slugged his GM in the face.

And that's when the dozen contractors and champions who'd been lounging in the room burst into the action. Red light flashed as more demons appeared, while the champions rushed forward with magic blazing.

Seizing my hand, Lienna hauled me through the door and into the hall, heading for the stairs. As we ran, I heard Rocco shouting, "Leroy betrayed us! Kill him!"

Uh-oh.

"What's the plan?" I asked breathlessly as we tore down the stairs.

"I'll immobilize them." Digging into her satchel, she pulled out a wooden object with a short handle and an arrow-shaped blade with runes etched into it. "But that won't stop the contractors from moving their demons around. You need to distract them."

"You got it."

She flung the door to the second level open and sprung into the chaos.

The Grand Grimoire mythics had split into two allegiances, half the men siding with Leroy and half fighting for their GM.

Six new demons had emerged from their respective infernuses, making eight total, which was a hell—a literal hell—of a lot of six- to eight-foot demonic beasties to cram together, even in a room this large.

Said demons were beating on other demons, a telekinetic was flinging computers and chairs at his opponents, a pyromage with a flaming mace was attempting to crush the skull of anyone who came near him, and a couple of sorcerers were using their artifacts to enhance the general sense of anarchy and rampage filling the room.

It was a fire-and-brimstone death match.

I braced our invisi-warp as it became harder to maintain. "Hurry, Lienna!"

She pointed her wooden knife at the densest blob of demons and flashing magic. "*Ori consistere!*"

A blue-tinged ripple zoomed out from the blade in a wide, spreading arc. It swept across the room at a slightly downward angle, hitting the mythics somewhere between knee and ankle.

Their legs locked into place, leaving the rest of their bodies to flail around. Every single one of them swung their arms violently, trying in vain to move their feet. It looked like a field of tattooed, temperamental sunflowers swaying angrily in a windstorm.

Before they could realize that their stuck feet didn't stop them from hurling magic or steering demons, shadows rippled across the floor. The roiling darkness solidified into an army of skeletal black arms with long, bony, clawed fingers that reached up through the low haze. The zombie hands wrapped around the legs of each mythic as though the phantom limbs were holding the men in place instead of Lienna's spell.

Bending my concentration, I imagined the press of strong fingers against their legs. The prick of digging claws. The cold, damp aura of the rotting arms leaking into their flesh.

Adding sensation to a warp was always touch and go—pun intended—and doing it for such a complex halluci-bomb was even more difficult than usual, but luckily, precision accuracy wasn't needed for this.

No one tried to continue the battle—not even Rocco. They were all gasping and wrenching at Lienna's spell, trying frantically to escape the slimy black arms coming out of the floor. In desperation, the pyromage lit himself on fire to burn away the phantoms, but all he accomplished was melting his clothes and exposing a cute pair of teddy bear-patterned boxers.

While I panted with the effort of maintaining the creepy arm warp *and* keeping us invisible, Lienna rushed toward Rocco, pulling out a pair of abjuration handcuffs. Unseen by the GM, she grabbed his wrists, yanked his arms behind his back, and cuffed him with precision skill. For good measure, she pulled his infernus over his head and dropped it in her satchel.

The other mythics gawked at their GM, probably wondering why his infernus had floated off him and vanished.

"What—" one of them began.

"Contractors," Lienna announced loudly, "recall your demons and drop your infernuses now!"

Leroy's gaze skimmed the room. He couldn't see her, but he must've recognized her voice. With a meaningful look at his allies, he held his infernus up. His colossal demon dissolved into red light and sucked into the silver pendant. He tossed it on the floor, and his comrades followed suit, recalling their demons, then dropping their infernuses and weapons, leaving only Rocco's supporters still armed.

"Wherever the hell you are," the pyromage shouted furiously, fire igniting over his hand, "you're dead—"

Lienna whipped her hand out, hissing an incantation under her breath. A stun marble flew across the room—and completely missed him.

Fortunately, the Thorn-supporting contractors were somewhat clumped together, so the marble thwacked a sorcerer's arm. He went limp and fell forward, but her leg-binding spell kept him suspended by the shins. His skeleton made an odd crunching sound as his knees locked.

Watching their pal collapse from an unseen attack, the others decided this was a losing fight. They tossed their weapons down too, leaving only Rocco's demon locked in a bizarre mid-punch pose.

Taking that as my signal to drop the dual warps before I passed out, I let them fade, then bent at the waist, hands braced on my knees as I endured a wave of gut-wrenching dizziness.

Lienna cuffed the pyromage, who seemed the likeliest to attack her as soon as she turned her back, then planted herself in front of the GM. "Rocco Thorn, you're under arrest for attempted murder and incitement."

His lips curled in a sneer. "Do you really think those charges will stick, little agent? You're the one coming into my guild and inciting violence. Not only will I be back here by morning, but you'll be out of a job."

"Except that two MPD agents witnessed you attempt to murder one of your own guildeds," Lienna fired back. "Never mind the illegal sale of infernuses to Red Rum, which we'll also be charging you with."

Rocco's disdainful sneer deepened. "You can't prove anything."

"I wouldn't bet on that."

That announcement came from the stairwell, only a few feet behind me. I whirled around to find Tae-min standing there with a heavy-duty protective case. With his stare locked on his GM, the first officer flipped the lid open.

Nestled in black foam were over a dozen silver pendants, along with a packet of paper.

Tae-min's cold glower bored into Rocco. "Maybe *these* will help those charges stick."

ROCCO WAS SEATED on a chair in a dusty, unused room that acted as catch-all storage for extra tables and office furniture. His first officer and ex-first officer towered over him like angry sentinels, but the broad-shouldered, Viking-esque GM maintained his derisive sneer.

Back in the main communal area, the other Grand Grimoire mythics were bound with zip ties from Lienna's satchel. The guild was eerily quiet, except for the odd creaks and patters emanating from Rocco's office, where the floor had been shattered.

Lienna and I stood shoulder to shoulder at a table. Spread across it were the heavy-duty black case Tae-min had uncovered from Rocco's smashed-up office, a stapled packet of paper, and fourteen infernuses. Lienna was poring over the pages, her eyebrows scrunched together in concentration.

"How long have you been using us to hide this underhanded shit?" Tae-min asked Rocco, his voice ice cold.

"All this time, Leroy and I have been trying to build a guild that defies the Demonica stigma, and you—"

Leroy put his hand on Tae-min's shoulder, quieting the younger man, then said to Rocco, "You going to tell us what you've been doing with Red Rum?"

The GM curled his upper lip. Nothing like prideful contempt to keep a man going after complete defeat. "I've never dealt with Red Rum."

"We have evidence right here!" Tae-min snapped, waving at the items spread across the table.

Rocco glanced at them, then smirked. "I've never seen that case before. Where did you find it?"

"In your office!"

"Must've been planted there." His deep-set eyes swung to me and Lienna. "Maybe the MPD planted it. Their agents were sneaking around our guild without a search warrant."

Tae-min made a growling sound so reminiscent of an angry demon that I scanned the room for one, just in case.

"Kit," Lienna said quietly. She tapped the page she held. "Are these names from your spreadsheet?"

I leaned closer to read it, our arms brushing. On the paper was a simple table, with each row containing a name, a number, a date, and a nonsense word. I skimmed the list, recognizing most of the names.

Halfway down, I paused and read aloud, "Harold Atherton, 240,000, October fourteenth, Rash ... sir ... us?"

"Rash'sērus," Leroy said.

"Gesundheit," I replied.

"It's the name of the Eighth House." He circled the table to join us, glanced across the page, then pointed at the column of nonsense words. "These are all demon Houses."

"Ah." I coughed. "I knew that."

Or rather, I'd known that demons came in around a dozen types—or "Houses"—and each had its own name. I might have read a list of those names at one point, but why would I bother to remember a bunch of unpronounceable gibberish? It wasn't like I'd be chillaxing over tea and cookies with a demon anytime soon, so I wasn't going to waste my brain space on memorizing their incoherent nicknames.

Leroy reached for one of the infernuses. "Pretty sure this is Luhh'varis, the Ninth House."

I checked the list. "Two of those. Sofia Rudd, 175,000, August twenty-fifth, Luhh'varis. Dave Gillett, 90,000, September ninth, Luhh'varis."

"What does it all mean?" Tae-min asked, still standing over Rocco, who'd sat back in his chair like a lord at the head of his dining hall, oozing foul smugness into the air. "What are those infernuses for?"

My mind spinning, I stared at Harold's name on that list. I remembered the demonic spirit that had possessed him and taken his soul when he'd died. I recalled that surfer-haired dickwad Gilmore calling out a demon on the Red Rum ship, and how other Red Rummers had claimed to have "tried it."

I looked at Rocco, disgust welling in me. "You bought Harold Atherton's soul for $240,000."

Lienna, Leroy, and Tae-min jerked toward me with equal surprise. The GM didn't react, his expression as unreadable as stone.

"He needed money to save his deli from going under," I continued. "You paid him to offer his soul up for a demon contract he'd never use himself."

"What's the point of a demon contract that won't be used?" Tae-min asked.

"Oh, it was getting used."

Lienna abruptly turned to Leroy. "Call out the demon in that infernus."

He looked down at the pendant he held. "An infernus can only be used by the contractor who—"

"Just try it."

His eyes narrowed, then he said, "*Daimon, anastethi.*"

Crimson light ignited over the infernus. The power streaked down to the floor, then pooled upward as though filling an invisible mold. With a flash, the glow solidified into a tall demon with tusks protruding from its lower jaw, a line of dark hair running down its back, and a lion-like tail. It looked like a mad scientist went on a safari, stole all the freakiest parts of the scariest animals he could find, put them in a blender, then squeezed the contents into a vaguely human-shaped tube.

And it was identical to the demon Gilmore had called out on the Red Rum ship.

Leroy's eyes went wide with shock. He tightened his grip on the infernus, and the demon raised both arms, then lowered them, as though pantomiming flapping bird wings in slow motion.

"I can control it like my own demon," he breathed in disbelief. "But infernuses can't be—"

"—shared," I finished. "But that's what these are. Shareable infernuses. Rocco's been making them, using the souls of whatever broke, desperate mythics he could convince to sell theirs, and Red Rum is buying them from him."

"That's—" Tae-min broke off with a shake of his head. "An infernus that can be passed from person to person and doesn't require a contract or soul to use … with that, Red Rum could arm every mythic in their ranks with a demon."

"They could create a whole goddamn demon army," Leroy growled. "*Daimon, hesychaze!*"

With a flare of red light, the demon dissolved and whooshed back into the infernus. Leroy tossed the pendant down onto the table with the others, and the four of us stared at the fourteen shareable infernuses that had almost ended up in Red Rum's hands.

Unfortunately, that still left us with a trio of chill-inducing questions: How many had Rocco already created? How many had he already sold?

And how big was Red Rum's demon army?

22

WHY WAS I NOT SURPRISED that the Grand Grimoire's furniture was as unpleasant as the majority of its members? The supposed recliner I sat on neither reclined nor offered anything remotely resembling comfort. I could feel every spring through the worn seat cushion. I hoped they'd kept the receipt.

Still, my butt was not moving from that cushion. The waves of dizziness from overusing my abilities had passed, but a headache throbbed in my temples. I needed to recover, and quickly.

I cracked an eye open. The guild's communal area was completely demolished from the brief eight-way demon battle. That was the secondary reason I was keeping my butt parked where it was—mine was the only surviving chair.

Five agents, including Sir Ultimate-Stick-Up-His-Ass Harris, the burly and flannel-loving Jack Cutter, and buff terramage Wolfe, had arrived at the guild to help. The fourteen shareable infernuses were back in their sturdy case, which Agent Harris carried around while he directed his agent underlings to take Rocco and his supporters downstairs.

Lienna zoomed around, giving brusque orders and filling in the responding agents on the prior chaos. Hard to believe it'd been only thirty minutes since we'd figured out Rocco's game.

Closing my eyes again, I left Lienna to it. I wasn't much of an order-giver, so I'd only get in the way, and there was a good chance I'd need to be back to full strength sooner rather than later. Thus, I was sneaking in as much R & R as I could, even if that meant enduring the other agents' looks every time they walked past with another zip-tied suspect in hand.

"Kit!"

I started slightly, disoriented. Had I drifted off for a minute?

Lienna waved at me. "Come on. Captain Blythe just arrived."

Feeling every dent in my torso from every cruel spring, I pulled myself out of the non-recliner and speed-walked to catch up to Lienna's frenetic pace. We headed for the stairs.

"How are you feeling?" she asked.

I opened the stairwell door and held it wide for her. "Better. Ready to rock again."

She went through first. "What did you do to distract everyone? They looked terrified."

I waved away the compliment. "Just something I saw in an old zombie movie."

"Whatever it was, it was effective. I don't think we could've stopped them without it."

"You seemed to have those dudes locked down on your own. How come I've never seen that spell before?"

"It's an experiment I was working on a couple of years ago. I'd actually forgotten about it, but the holding spell the electramage used reminded me of it, so I grabbed it when I was changing earlier." She patted her satchel absently. "The spell tends to fire in a random direction. I gave up on it after immobilizing myself three times in a row."

Thank Lady Luck that hadn't happened this time.

We swept across the main level, through the dusty front shop, and out onto the dark, rainy street. A smart car, a black sedan, and a large, unmarked van were parked at the curb, the latter loaded with Rocco and his cronies in anti-magic cuffs. Agent Cutter guarded the van's rear doors.

Another vehicle was idling in the middle of the street, pointed in the wrong direction—a big black SUV that I immediately knew belonged to our esteemed captain. She'd sooner crush a smart car with her telekinesis than get inside one.

As Lienna and I strode toward it, the driver's door opened and Blythe climbed out. No folders. I peeked inside the vehicle, checking if they were stacked on the passenger seat.

"Report," she barked.

"We recovered fourteen illegal infernuses from Rocco's office that allow anyone to control the demon inside them," Lienna answered promptly.

"Anyone?"

"Yes. They're shareable, with the soul of an unrelated person linked to them. Harold was a soul donor for one."

"*Shareable* infernuses?" Blythe repeated in a tone of disgust that perfectly matched my feelings on the subject. "Rocco intended to sell them to Red Rum?"

"We believe so." Lienna gripped the strap of her satchel. "He's already sold at least two—Harold's and another one. It's impossible to know how many they have. Rocco isn't talking."

Blythe folded her arms. "Then get him to the precinct and into an interrogation room. You got the evidence we needed, and now all the GM privileges he was counting on will work against him."

She smiled as she said the last part, and frankly, it was terrifying.

"That'll take too long," Lienna disagreed, a note of nervousness infecting her voice as she challenged the captain's instructions. "We already know Red Rum has at least one of his infernuses, and they could have more. We need to seize their ship before they realize Rocco has been arrested and make a run for international waters."

Blythe turned her cool gaze on me. "And your opinion, Morris?"

"Rocco will play innocent until the eleventh hour. If we waste time trying to get more information from him, Red Rum will disappear. When we were eavesdropping on them, they mentioned they were ready to get out of the inlet ASAP." I widened my stance, ready to go to verbal bat over this. "Even one of these infernuses is too many. We have to stop them."

The captain assessed us, then swiveled back to Lienna. "The Vancouver precinct will initiate an immediate emergency operation to seize the Red Rum ship, apprehend all mythics aboard, and recover their illegal Demonica artifacts. You may use any resources necessary."

"M-me?" Lienna stammered.

"Agent Harris will lead the operation." Blythe speared her subordinate with a stern stare. "You will be his second-in-command. I don't want any loose ends, Agent Shen."

Lienna nodded vehemently. "Yes, ma'am. I'll inform Agent Harris immediately."

She gave the captain a quick, distracted salute, then pivoted on her heel. As she sprinted back into the guild, she slid to a sudden halt.

"Kit!" She pulled her car keys from her satchel and tossed them to me. "Can you bring up your laptop? We'll need it."

I caught the keys with a grin, then remembered I had an audience. Once Lienna had vanished inside, I cast a sidelong glance at the captain.

"So are you sending her back to LA?" I asked.

Blythe eyed me. "Did she tell you why she's adamant about staying here?"

"Yep." I arched my eyebrows. "If you send her back, her career will be over."

A quiet pause. "Don't you have work to do, Agent Morris?"

"Agent?"

She grunted. "You should've passed your field exam on the first try, Morris. I didn't offer you this job because you fit the mold of an agent. I wanted you because you don't."

On that enigmatic note, she pulled the door of her SUV open, climbed behind the wheel, and slammed the door again. The engine revved, and I stepped back as the tires squealed. The vehicle swerved to the correct side of the road and sped away.

I watched the taillights disappear, then heaved a long, slow breath. I should've passed on my first try, huh? Even though I didn't fit the typical agent mold? Even though she'd stacked the field against me?

I felt like I was missing something.

Shaking my head, I passed the cluster of MPD vehicles and headed up the street. Our lonely smart car waited half a block away beneath a dark streetlamp with a shattered bulb. It seemed like ages ago that we'd been sneakily watching for Tae-min's exit, even though it'd only been an hour.

Man, these last few days had dragged on forever. Did you earn overtime if you squeezed an eternity into forty-eight hours? Or vacation time, at least? All I wanted right now was a beach, an endless supply of cocojitos, and maybe the company of a certain abjuration sorceress.

As I fumbled with Lienna's keys in the dark, silently cursing the broken streetlamp, the back of my neck prickled. I glanced down at the guild and MPD bustle half a block away, then turned to look in the other direction.

And found myself face-to-chest with a broad, bare, reddish-toned torso.

My gaze shot up and met a pair of glowing crimson eyes above a pointed jaw and bared fangs.

I had no chance. The scant instant it took me to recognize the danger was all the demon needed to wrap its huge hand around my throat. It lifted me off my feet, squeezing my windpipe even tighter. The keys fell from my hand. My mouth gaped, lungs instantly screaming for air and hands tearing futilely at the demon's thick fingers.

Movement in my peripheral. A shadowy figure leaning against the wall, sunglasses on despite the darkness, watching as his demon strangled me.

In a panic, I threw every warp I could think of at him and the demon. The Funhouse, the Split Kit, even a copy of the demon's own ugly mug floating around behind me, but the beast kept right on choking me. My head spun. Black spots popped in my vision. The need for air obliterated every other thought in my head.

Agent Cutter was fifty feet down the road, but this useless streetlamp had cloaked us in darkness. Even if he looked this way, he wouldn't see me. No one was coming to save me.

The demon's lips pulled back. Its vicious grin and glowing eyes were the last things I saw as my consciousness plunged into a pitch-black abyss.

23

I CAME AWAKE to deep vibrations rattling my soggy brain and the revolting taste of moldy cilantro, fermenting grass, and rusty brine coating my tongue.

My neck throbbed fiercely, my throat burned even worse, and as I sucked in a shaky breath, I realized the vibrations came from a massive engine, the continuous rumble echoing in a way that suggested a huge space.

None of that explained the inconceivably horrific flavor of—I suppressed a gag—*cilantro* in my mouth. I have a long-held belief that cilantro was planted on Earth by Satan to punish humankind. Which, thinking about it now, made sense for it to be assaulting my taste buds after a demon had strangled me.

I cracked my eyes open.

Well, I'd been both right and wrong about the space. It was large, yes, but about ten times more cavernous than I'd imagined. Eighty feet wide, twice as long, and with walls that rose sixty feet high and were punctuated by giant square holes in the rusting steel, forming a larger-than-life gridwork my brain couldn't figure out. Dull, yellowish strip lights glowed from narrow hallways behind the grid.

And I was lying smack dab in the middle of it on the cold, damp floor.

It wasn't until I painfully twisted my head to look the other way and saw a stack of shipping containers, their ends lined up with the grid—or rather, the docking brackets, each one sporting a large open manhole in its center—that I realized where I'd ended up.

I was inside the cargo hold of a ship. Red Rum's ship, if I were to hazard a guess. Based on the floor's movement, it was likely chugging its way into the Pacific Ocean.

And if that weren't bad enough, I wasn't alone.

Idling nearby was a familiar cast of criminals I'd seen on my first visit to their ship. The good-looking guy with nightmare tattoos from the bridge, the Arnold Schwarzenegger sorcerer, and surfer-boy Gilmore with one of Rocco's shareable demons, along with three more crew members I hadn't seen before. The Psychic Grandmother and the Ugly Guy were conspicuously absent. Up on the bridge, maybe?

The Red Rummers were tense and quiet—and luckily, not looking my way. Probably because I'd been unconscious up until now. That nauseating taste of grassy cilantro still coated my tongue, and when I licked my lips, the taste was even stronger. I'd been dosed with something—probably a potion to keep me unconscious while they'd moved my kidnapped ass to the ship.

I tried to spit the flavor out of my mouth. Red Rum truly was evil to use such an abhorrent herb in their potions. Maybe one of those shipping containers was stuffed with mouthwash.

I could worry about the safety of my palate later. Right now, I needed to figure out how to escape, though the odds of doing so with my head attached to my shoulders seemed downright shit-tastic. Still, I had to assume something was going on here besides a convoluted plot to murder that rookie MPD agent with the annoying hallucination powers. Why drag me out here just to kill me?

My wrists were bound behind my back with duct tape, and a persistent grogginess dulled my thoughts. I swallowed hard, which just made my abused throat ache more.

Disappearing seemed like a good starting point. While no one was looking my way, I attempted to Split Kit myself.

Have you ever pulled an all-nighter that left your eyeballs burning, your spirit begging for a caffeine IV drip, and your ability to focus reduced to two-second blips between an endless stream of "Why do I do this to myself?" and "If I close my eyes now, I'll be a much older individual by the time I wake up" thoughts? That's what it felt like trying to warp with that chloroform-esque potion in my system.

I managed to invisify myself for three whole Mississippis before my concentration broke. Tattooed Guy glanced at me and I hastily shut my eyes, feigning unconsciousness. When nothing happened, I peered through a slit in my eyelids. He'd returned to ignoring me.

Any warp that needed to last for more than a few seconds without stuttering was out. I concentrated on breathing, trying to think through the punch-drunk daze blanketing my brain. Why was I even here? What did Red Rum want with me?

Squinching my eyes, I debated between surfer-boy Gilmore and sorcerer Arnie, wondering which one would be more suggestible. Deciding on the musclebound meathead, I focused on my memory of the goateed, sunglasses-loving electramage and projected a flicker of him in Arnie's peripheral vision.

No reaction. I tried again, holding the warp for a second longer.

Arnie shifted his weight, then swiveled toward the tattooed looker. "How long does Ortega expect us to wait down here?"

A subliminal-messaging success?

"Until that agent shows up," the man replied irritably.

"Why can't we just kill this guy? Don't need 'im alive."

Gilmore rolled his eyes. "Has your brain turned completely to muscle? Because he's our hostage. We can't trade him for the infernuses if he's dead."

"The MPD ain't gonna hand over Demonica magic for one agent," Arnie protested, surprising me and his comrades with his logic.

Tattoo Guy sauntered toward me, and I closed my eyes again. "Ortega left the ransom note for this idiot's partner, not the whole MPD." He punctuated his statement by kicking me in the side. "She'll show. If she doesn't, that's Ortega's problem. He's the one who didn't collect the infernuses on time."

Teeth gritted, I pretended I was unconscious and not internally howling from the aftermath of my left kidney imploding.

His fingers closed over a handful of my hair. He jerked my head up, startling me into opening my eyes. "Figured you were awake. Got any idea why Ortega has a grudge against your partner, eh?"

My jaw flexed. "No idea."

"Too bad." He pulled harder on my hair, bending my neck back like I was a Pez dispenser. "Should we take bets on whether your little girlfriend will walk into a death trap for you? Or is she too stupid to realize you're already dead and she'll be too if she sets foot on this ship?"

"Last I checked," I said, sounding way tougher than I felt, "I wasn't dead."

"You'll wish you were, MagiPol shitbag."

Releasing my hair, he slammed his steel-toed boot into my gut. The others laughed and whooped as he kicked me a third time, and I jerked my knees up to my chest to protect my internal organs as best I could with my arms bound behind my back.

With a barking chuckle, he swung his foot at my face instead. Pain exploded through my left cheekbone, and as my head whipped to the side, I rolled away from him. Warm wetness ran down my skin from the split in my cheek, and the taste of blood filled my mouth. I gagged and spat.

Blood and cilantro were a vile combination.

He planted his boot on my shoulder and shoved me onto my back. Grabbing the front of my jacket, he hauled me onto my feet, but between the potion's aftereffects and the blow to the face, my legs buckled under me. I crumpled back to the floor.

Laughing, he waved at Gilmore. "I don't think our guest is scared enough yet. Show him your large friend."

Grinning, Surfer-Boy tugged an infernus from beneath his coat. Red light flared off it and his demon took form. Its enormous, gangly frame was a near-perfect match to the one from the shareable infernus Leroy had puppeted at the Grand Grimoire.

With stilted movements, the demon reached down. Its claws tore through my jacket and scraped my chest as it grabbed a handful of fabric. The thick muscles in its arm bulged and it lifted me like I was a toddler. Wrists bound, I hung from its grip, nauseous and reeling, barely able to remember my own name, let alone create a warp.

"There's a slight chance we might hand you over to your MPD pals to get those infernuses," the tattooed guy mused. "But we'll make sure that if you make it off this boat alive, it'll be as a cripple."

Grinning viciously, Gilmore squeezed his infernus. Holding me with one hand, his demon drew the other back, its massive fist aimed at my chest for a blow that would shatter my ribs.

"*Kit!*"

That desperate cry hit me harder than the demon's punch would have. It pierced me straight through the heart with horrified dread. No, she wouldn't have come. It was suicide.

Not bothering with a doorway, Lienna sprang through an oversized manhole in the docking framework that formed the walls of the cargo hold. She landed in a crouch thirty feet away, then straightened and faced the violent assembly—me hanging in a demon's grasp, surrounded by six Red Rum bruisers with enough magic between them to give a combat guild trouble.

I held my breath, waiting for a squad of black-clad agents to rappel down from the ceiling and land in a dramatic semi-circle around her, each one with a different epic battle pose, like Black Widow and the rest of the Avengers moments before an ass-kicking commenced.

But no one else appeared; it was just Lienna.

Her battered satchel hung from her shoulder, but that was the only familiar thing about her appearance. Sturdy black clothes fit her like a second skin, a protective combat vest layered over top, and several straps crisscrossed her chest, presumably holding objects she was carrying on her back, but I couldn't see what.

Not that combat gear and an extra weapon or two would make a difference.

"Let him go," she ordered loudly, her voice echoing over the deep throb of the ship's engine.

Let me go *where*? Don't get me wrong, I loved this heroic, piss-and-vinegar version of Lienna. But we were on a Red Rum ship that was on its way to the middle of the ocean. There was nowhere to escape to.

The tattooed leader of the goon gang pulled a dagger from a hidden sheath on his back. "How the hell did you get down here without ... ah." He glanced upward, then refocused on Lienna with a nasty grin. "Looks like you *didn't* slip past Ortega's notice."

As though in answer, a clang of metal reverberated through the hold. I looked up and immediately wished I hadn't, because not only did my nausea triple with the movement, but I caught a terrifying glimpse of the demon crouched on the lip of a manhole in the wall forty feet above. It watched us, its eyes fuming like hot coals and bat-like wings curved around it. Its left wrist ended in a stump, marking it as the same demon we'd fought in the precinct's parking garage.

Lienna took in the winged demon with a quick jerk of her head, then reached into her satchel and pulled out a saucer-sized metal disc.

The Red Rummers instantly shifted into defensive stances, several pulling out weapons. The demon holding me pivoted slowly.

"Make one move and he dies," Gilmore threatened.

Her hard gaze met mine as she turned the disc in her hand enough for it to catch the light. "Kit."

My eyes widened as I realized what she wanted. Pulling my drugged, concussed concentration together, I dropped a halluci-bomb on the six mythics, hiding the real Lienna and showing them a fake version holding the disc aloft but otherwise not moving.

The real Lienna had barely given me enough time to create the warp before she flung the disc. It sailed through the air—and the winged demon arched its wings, undeceived by my warp.

The disc hit the floor with a clang and skidded noisily to a stop almost directly below my feet. I tried to suppress the noise, but the echoey cargo hold amplified every little sound and hiding the sight of the disc was already stretching my current limits.

As the six rogues jerked, searching for the source of the racket, Lienna pulled a second disc from her satchel.

The winged demon launched off its perch, diving like a peregrine falcon straight for her.

"*Ori spatium aperio!*" she shouted as she dropped it on the floor at her feet.

Violent green light erupted from the disc, swirling into a glowing portal. The demon plunged down, claws reaching for her—and she dove headfirst into the spinning radiance.

24

THE RUNE-ENGRAVED DISC at my feet opened into a churning pit of darkness, and Lienna shot up out of it as though fired from a cannon. For an instant, the upper half of her body appeared from the portal exit while the lower half of her body was still going into the entrance thirty feet away.

She cleared the vortex, landed with a slight stumble, and thrust her Rubik's Cube toward the demon holding me. "*Ori te formo cuspides!*"

Instead of her usual watery shield, a barrage of shadowy black spikes erupted from the cube and shot straight through the demon. Its grip on my jacket went slack, and as I dropped to the floor, it staggered backward and sank to one knee, its red eyes darkening as though someone had hit the dimmer switch on its magic glow.

Thirty feet away, the winged demon had slammed into the floor, missing Lienna by a bare second. This time it didn't reach into the magic after her; it launched across the distance between us, closing in with impossible speed.

Lienna swung around and slammed a roundhouse kick into Tattooed Guy's gut, knocking him away, then she seized my arm as she threw down a third disc.

"*Ori spatium aperio!*"

Swirling green erupted in front of us, and Lienna yanked me forward. I pitched headfirst toward the glow.

You know those tower rides at the amusement park where they strap you in, hoist you a hundred feet in the air, then drop you for an adrenaline-inducing free fall? And you know that instant when your body begins to plummet but your organs haven't quite figured that out yet, so it feels like you inhaled your spleen into your nasal cavity?

That's the ultra-diet-soda version of what falling into the portal felt like. Because I wasn't merely *falling*. It was like a black hole-powered vacuum nozzle—or like an actual black hole—sucking me in and squeezing me into an extra-condensed blob of Morris molecules.

The crushed-to-nanoscopic-size feeling lasted for only an instant, then we were shooting out the other end of the portal with all the momentum of the portal's suction force. The reversal of gravity hit my poor brain like a cosmic slap, and I didn't have a chance to think about landing on my feet.

I crumpled to the floor in a heap, wheezing.

"Kit!" Lienna gripped my arm. "Kit, are you okay?"

"That ... was ... *awesome*," I gasped. "Can we do it again?"

She tugged hard on my wrists, tearing away the duct tape. Agony roiled through my bruised body as she jostled me, then my arms came free. I sucked in a relieved breath as I sat up. We'd come out of the portal in a narrow hallway, the wall on one side interrupted by giant manholes that looked out into the empty hold. We were one level up.

"Come on," she panted, dragging me to my feet. "We have to move before—"

With the screech of claws on metal, the winged demon swept through a manhole thirty feet down the long, dimly lit corridor.

"Run!" I yelled.

She didn't need me to tell her twice. She bolted, giving me a clear view of her back and the weapons she was carrying, and I almost forgot to run after her.

Sweet holy hand grenade. That explained how Lienna had gotten here. Or rather, *who* had gotten Lienna here.

We raced for the far end of the corridor, where ladder rungs protruded from the solid wall opposite the cargo hold. The thundering racket behind me warned that the demon was giving chase. We couldn't outrun it but we had to try. As our prior encounter had made painfully obvious, neither Lienna nor I were a match for an illegally contracted demon.

She skidded as she reached the ladder, grabbing for a rung. I launched up it right after her. The square opening in the ceiling was barely wide enough for my shoulders. As I popped through it, Lienna grabbed me and hauled me out.

My feet had scarcely cleared the hatch when the demon's slashing claws whipped across it. Its horned head appeared, its wings catching on the frame.

Lienna ran. I sprinted right behind her. I could see the next ladder, but it was too far. We'd never make it before the demon caught us.

"Please tell me you didn't come alone," I half shouted.

She shot a wide-eyed look back at me. "Uh—"

The winged demon vaulted through another manhole and landed in our path. Its lips peeled back in a vicious grin. A second set of claws screeched over metal as Gilmore's demon heaved itself up through an even closer manhole. Why were the walls full of holes, damn it!

We faced the pair of demons, two dozen very short yards between us. The amount of fan-hitting shit had just doubled.

"Portal?" I asked desperately.

"Used them all." Hopelessness tinged her voice.

We both knew our Screwed-O-Meter had maxed out. But if we were going down, it would be in a blaze of glory—or in a literal blaze of gunpowder and shrapnel.

I grabbed Lienna's arm, pulled Vera's rocket launcher off her, and hefted it onto my shoulder. "Get your shield ready."

Her eyes popped with terror, then she yanked out her wooden cube and frantically rearranged the runes. Gilmore's demon broke into a lumbering gallop toward us, the winged demon right behind it.

I'd never fired an RPG before, but I'd seen enough Bruce Willis movies to know how it worked. Dropping down onto one knee for stability, I gripped the handles and pressed my eye to the scope, centering the charging demons in the crosshairs.

"Ready!" Lienna shouted. "*Ori—*"

"Wait!" My finger jiggled the flaccid trigger. I needed to cock the hammer first. Where—

The demons thundered toward us, the faster winged one snarling with impatience at the tusked beast filling the hallway.

Bruce Willis wouldn't forget about the stupid hammer.

There! My thumb found it on the back of the trigger handle and cocked it. "Now!"

"*Ori te formo—*"

I pulled the trigger, the blast of the grenade drowning out Lienna's final word.

Part of me expected that slow-motion effect in movies where you can actually watch the RPG exit the launcher and blaze dramatically toward its target. But real life doesn't operate in slow motion. The effect was virtually instantaneous.

The second my finger depressed the trigger, the recoil jerked me backward. A blue shield snapped into existence in front of us, and a massive explosion nearly burst my eardrums.

The demons disappeared in the fireball, shards of shattered steel bombarding Lienna's shield.

Before I could channel my innermost John McClane with a witty insult for my vanquished opponents, I realized my miscalculation. The super-charged alchemic explosion hadn't merely wiped the demons from existence, it had also punched a car-sized hole in the corridor's steel wall.

Which, it turned out, was actually the ship's hull.

And unlike the hole Vera had blown in this same ship with this same RPG, *my* hole was below the waterline.

The ocean flooded through the breach in a roaring torrent and engulfed the hallway. The deluge broke against Lienna's barrier for all of two seconds before the magic gave out. A frigid wave slammed into Lienna and me, sweeping us off our feet and straight through an oversized manhole.

Lienna's scream rang out as I scrabbled for something to cling to. My hands caught the steel edge and I jerked to a halt, agony tearing through my palms. The RPG launcher plunged past me, spinning down toward the bottom of the cargo hold.

Squeezing pressure around my middle—Lienna clung to my waist as water poured over us, trying to drag us off. Teeth bared, I clung on for dear life.

Lienna jostled against my back, and I hoped as hard as I'd ever hoped for anything that she was about to climb off me and into the relative safety of the corridor, because my hands were slipping and I had about three more seconds of grip in me.

Instead, she pointed Vera's grappling gun toward the upper docking brackets and fired it. The hook flew upward and didn't come falling back down.

"Kit!" she yelled.

My grip gave out. As I fell, I grabbed for the bulky black gun. I caught it and the rope pulled taut. With both of us hanging precariously, she hit the winch. It vibrated as the motor hoisted us out of the raging flow of water.

Breathing hard, I looked down. The six Red Rummers were fleeing toward an exit as the Niagara-esque torrent flooded the cargo hold. The water level was shallow but rising with terrifying speed.

The winch pulled us to an upper level of the hold, where we swung through a manhole and onto a near-identical corridor to the one I'd blown up. Lienna flipped the grappling hook loose, then pushed the gun into my hands as she bent forward, breathing hard, her limbs shaking.

I slung the gun over my shoulder and inhaled deeply. The roar of water flooding into the ship echoed through the hold.

"Now what?" I asked.

Lienna glanced up, still panting. "We get on deck and signal Vera."

Right. I'd known Vera was helping Lienna, because who else did we know with super RPGs and grappling guns? Actually, it wouldn't have surprised me if our precinct had a few such things in its arsenal. Which made me wonder: "Why not get the MP—"

"Because the team wasn't ready!" Lienna straightened, a strange desperation sharpening her voice. "I didn't even tell Blythe I was going. I just grabbed everything I could think of and—"

And rushed straight into a death trap to save me.

Ignoring my throbbing injuries, the sinking ship, and the general state of catastrophe that was threatening our lives, I swept Lienna against my chest and kissed her.

Her arms clamped around my neck. She crushed her mouth to mine, fierce and desperate and still shaking. I kissed her just as hard, just as urgently. Nothing like thinking I was a goner, then thinking she was a goner, then thinking we were both definitely goners to kick my emotions into high gear.

She pulled back, water—or maybe tears—clinging to her eyelashes. "I was afraid they'd already killed you, and it was my fault."

I reluctantly released her. "But we're still kicking, and now we need to get off this ship."

She nodded. "Do you have one more invisibility warp in you?"

I had no idea. I was drugged, bruised, probably concussed, drenched in icy water, shivering like mad, and running on a fast-diminishing adrenaline rush. We were stranded on a sinking steel tube surrounded by miles of frigid ocean, and every other living thing aboard wanted us dead.

"For you?" I said lightly. "Always."

"Then let's go."

I grabbed her hand, and for a second, we just held on, all too aware that escaping alive was a one-in-a-million chance. Then we ran for the ladder that would take us up to the deck, where the rest of the murderous crew was waiting.

25

THE LIGHTS on the navigation bridge glared down at the shipping containers stacked three high on the deck. Crew members swarmed between them like ants whose hill had been kicked by a sadistic five-year-old—ants that would transform into angry killer bees the moment they noticed us.

These insect analogies weren't helping my shaky focus.

I ducked below the steel hatch and closed it, muffling the crew's shouts. The rumble of the ship's engine competed with the echoing roar of the seawater filling the cargo hold we'd escaped.

Sliding down the ladder, I rejoined Lienna, both of us still breathing hard from our headlong charge up here. In the few minutes it'd taken us to reach the deck, the floor had taken on a distinct tilt. I wasn't sure if the ship would actually sink, but I didn't want to stick around and find out.

"My phone got soaked." Lienna tapped urgently on the device's black screen. "I can't call Vera to get us."

"She probably didn't go far." I bounced on the balls of my feet to ward off the violent shivers racking my body and keep my adrenaline flowing. "If we get up on deck, we can try to signal her. We just need to not die while we're up there. Got any magic to help with that?"

Riffling through her satchel, she produced three stun marbles, two holding spells I recognized from my field test, and a black pistol from the holster on her belt.

"That's it? No more super-holding spells?"

"No, and my cube is recharging. But you can invisi-warp us, right?"

"Not for long." The cilantro poison/head trauma combo wasn't doing me any favors, and the grappling gun slung over my shoulder didn't make much of a weapon. I waved sharply at her hair. "What about all that?"

"These?" She yanked on one of the strings of silver beads in her ponytail, each bauble sporting visible runes. "None of these work! They're all failed prototypes. Why else would I wear them as jewelry?"

"So, what, you just wear your failures everywhere? *Why?*"

Scowling, she shoved the gun at me. "Head for the starboard side and we'll try to spot Vera."

"Lead the way."

She scrambled up the short ladder and shoved the hatch wide open. I followed her, and we darted out onto the deck. The grip of the gun was familiar to my hands—it was the same model of paintball pistol I'd trained with.

Lienna streaked left into a gap between containers. I followed behind her, my equilibrium complaining about the weird slant to the deck.

"Bilge pumps!"

The raspy screech preceded the chain-smoking grandma I'd last seen on the bridge. She ran past the gap in the shipping containers, two men following on her heels.

"The bilge pumps in hold two aren't running!" she brayed. "Where's Ortega?"

They didn't glance our way, and as soon as they were out of sight, Lienna rushed forward again. We cut between two more stacks, heading for the railing. The rogues were far more focused on their ship than watching for intruders, and I started to think we might just make it off this doomed boat alive.

We burst from our shadowy gap—and almost ran straight into a tall, gangly Red Rummer around our age.

"Hey!" he yelled.

I swung my potion gun up.

"What are we supposed to be doing?" he babbled, panic shining in his eyes. "Are we abandoning ship?"

"Uh." I stuck my gun behind my back. "Yeah, man. Get to the lifeboats."

"Right. Yeah, lifeboats." Relieved to have received clear instructions, he hastened away—then stopped. Looking back at us, he frowned. "Who are you?"

Shit.

Lienna was faster than me, whipping a stun marble at him—which flew over his right shoulder. We really needed to work on her aim.

"Intruders!" he bellowed, yanking two long knives from beneath his coat. "MagiPol agents! Here—"

I fired my gun and a burst of yellow potion exploded over his face. He keeled over, but his big mouth had already drawn the attention of a dozen crew members. They swarmed toward us from the port side of the ship, just like my stupid imaginary ant-bees—except these homicidal shit gibbons were more like those murder hornets I'd heard about.

Shouting an incantation, Lienna threw one of her two holding spell artifacts into the oncoming horde, then ducked behind a shipping container.

Right. Life or death battle. Focus, dummy.

I fired a couple of sleep potions at them, then dove behind a container parallel to Lienna's as some telekinetic asshole hurled a small battle-axe at my head. I peeked around the corner of the container and emptied my clip. Men collapsed with each shot. Lienna flung the remainder of her artifacts at them as she retreated toward the railing behind us.

My gun popped uselessly, the magazine empty, and I chucked it away as I prepared to warp, hoping I had enough energy for a halluci-bomb. But before the remaining three rogues could attack again, a metallic groan ran through the vessel. From somewhere on the port side, a reverberating boom shook the hull, and the whole ship shuddered. The already uncomfortable slant to the deck increased by several degrees.

The crew members cast alarmed looks at each other, then turned tail and sprinted for the bridge.

Lienna and I needed to get off this industrial Titanic before we found ourselves in a Jack/Rose situation.

Grasping the railing, I looked out across the rippling water, searching for the silhouette of Vera's boat against the reflection of the cargo ship's lights. My shoes wanted to slide on the slippery deck, and I couldn't pretend the ship's port side list wasn't increasing at a steady and extremely alarming rate.

Beside me, Lienna held the railing as she too scanned the dark ocean surrounding us. "I don't see Vera! We need to signal—"

All the hair on my body stood on end, and it took me a second too long to realize why the air suddenly felt like the world's biggest static shock was coming.

Lightning blasted along the railing, met my hands, and every muscle in my body spasmed, sending me careening backward. I crashed into the deck and slid several feet down the slanted surface.

If getting my ass kicked in the cargo hold had been the bottom slice of bread on the cilantro-flavored shit sandwich that was my kidnapping, the unnecessary defibrillation was the soggy top slice. Groaning, I raised my head to find Lienna a few feet away in a similar state. As she pushed up onto her hands and knees, sudden fear widened her eyes.

Striding toward us was the filling of the aforementioned shit sandwich—the goateed electramage, who had both hands outstretched on either side of him. White ropes of electricity leaped from every nearby surface on the ship supplied with electricity—lights, cables, antennae—and into his palms.

He was sucking power from the ship to build up his internal charge.

With a loud clunking sound, the ship's engines died. The ever-present vibrations stilled, and the glaring lights on the bridge blinked out, leaving only red emergency lights to illuminate the deck in a moody crimson glow. An instant later, a bugle-like alarm blared warningly, and a distant voice shouted, "Abandon ship!"

The power flowing into the mage petered out, but he kept coming.

Lienna shoved to her feet, her back to the railing, and I scrambled up beside her, preparing for the sequel to our parking garage battle—*Maniacal Mage 2: Electric Boogaloo.*

Time to find out how well I could pull off a warp in my current condition.

As though anticipating my next move, the electramage grasped the infernus hanging around his neck. He'd finally ditched his sunglasses, and his sunken eyes narrowed in concentration. An alarm was still blasting every ten seconds.

He halted his approach, then growled, "*Daimon, hesychaze.*"

I recognized that incantation. Leroy had used it to recall a demon into an infernus.

"Watcha doing, Electro?" I called out. "Trying to summon your ugly pet?"

He sneered at my taunt, sparks crackling off his bared teeth.

"Yeah, sorry about that," I said with phony contrition. "I sort of blew it up."

A menacing smile tugged at the corners of the electramage's mouth. "I don't need a demon to kill the both of you."

"I'm well aware of that," I said, raising my hands non-threateningly. "But I also have the sneaking suspicion you didn't drag me all the way out here with my heart still beating merely for delayed gratification. You want a trade. My life for Rocco's infernuses."

I turned to Lienna. "You have the infernuses, don't you, partner? In your satchel?"

Her eyes narrowed, but I gave her a confident nod and her hand slowly reached into her bag. When she pulled it back out, fourteen psycho-warped infernuses dangled from her fist.

Gaze fixing on the pendants, the mage stepped forward.

Lienna swung her arm over the edge of the railing, dangling the demon bling above the water. "Kill me and you'll never get them."

His attention snapped back to her, and white sparks jumped off his hands. This dude was so amped up I half expected him to sprout a head full of bleached blond hair and go Super Saiyan on us. There was no way in hell he wasn't itching for any opportunity to cook Lienna from the inside out.

Just above her head, a flash of light caught my eye. A hundred yards away on the black water, the faint light flashed again, briefly illuminating the silhouette of a small fishing boat.

Vera.

Praise be to Aquaman. Help was on its way—but we were trapped in a tenuous stalemate with our voltaic foe. We had nowhere to go and no weapons, and he couldn't attack Lienna or me without kissing his sweet, shareable infernuses goodbye.

I just needed to stall him until Vera was close enough for us to make a break for it.

"I'm sure you're aware of this, Ortega—that's your name, right? Ortega?"

His eyes shot to me at the mention of his name. I was going to take that as a "yes."

"I'm sure you're aware of the whole capsizing thing going on here. Thanks for killing the engines, by the way. I'm sure that helped the situation. Anyway." I waved around at the deck, now devoid of swarming sailors. "Seeing as your crew has already bailed and none of us is named Molly Brown, this standoff can't last forever."

I glanced out over the water, watching the fishing boat edge closer to us. Come on, Vera, pedal to the metal. Or rudder to the puddle, or whatever the marine equivalent was.

Lienna and Ortega shot silent death glares at each other, the latter seemingly caught in an existential question of "kill girl" or "save loot."

"From what I've seen," I said before he could decide on the former, "these infernuses aren't your only point of interest. I don't know what Lienna did to wind up on your hit list, but judging by the car bomb and that food truck stunt—"

"An eye for an eye," Ortega interrupted, electricity flaring from his fingertips. "Or rather, a daughter for a daughter."

Lienna tensed visibly.

Oh, Papa Shen, what did you do?

Sparks rained from the electramage's hands, splashing and dying on the deck, which was tilted significantly more than before—like, enough that I had to widen my stance to keep my balance. Enough that the stacks of shipping containers were attempting the scariest Leaning Tower of Pisa impersonations I'd ever seen, held together only by the sturdy X-shaped lashing bars fixed to their fronts.

Heedless of the state of the ship, Ortega pierced Lienna with a stare mired in hatred. "Shen killed my little girl."

"You're lying," she fired back. "My dad would nev—"

"He killed her!" Ortega roared. "So I'm going to make him suffer the same way I've suffered for the past thirteen years."

Lienna's hand holding the fake infernuses shook, making me work harder to keep the warp believable. That familiar fogginess of psychic exhaustion crept into my mind, and I darted a glance at the dark water.

"Killing Lienna won't fix anything, Ortega," I said. "It won't bring your daughter back and it sure as hell won't get you those infernuses."

He ignored me, fixated on Lienna with the mindless intensity of a thirteen-year-old grudge.

"But you know that," I muttered. "And you don't care."

The entire ship lurched, knocking all three of us to our knees.

I caught myself and shoved back up, but it was too late. Ortega was already snarling, his face twisted with unfiltered rage as he stared at Lienna.

At her empty fist. I'd lost the fake-infernuses warp.

"Like father," Ortega snarled, lunging to his feet, "like daughter."

He thrust out his hand, and a twisting bolt of lightning as thick as a python flashed straight for us.

26

I DOVE ONE WAY and Lienna leaped the other way.

The white-hot bolt hit the railing and electricity rippled through the steel deck, buzzing against my hands and knees as I shoved back up. Whirling, I spotted Lienna, mentally braced myself, and threw up that one last invisi-warp I'd promised her.

We both vanished, but Ortega's deranged smirk didn't falter. He cast his arm wide, flinging a sheet of lightning in my direction. It caught me in the midriff and I crumpled, muscles convulsing, burning heat searing my innards.

It took my lungs an agonizing ten seconds to unlock enough to breathe. Heart thudding against my ribs as though protesting the beating my body was taking, I dragged my head up.

My invisi-bomb had failed, just as Ortega had intended. Lienna fled down the slanted deck, her feet slipping on the slick surface, leading the electramage away from me.

I shot a frantic glance toward the flash of Vera's light—she was closer, but not close enough—then scrambled after Lienna and Ortega. Running on the deck felt like sprinting down a ramp. The ship's list had become dangerously pronounced and was worsening with ever-increasing speed.

As Ortega raised his hand to unleash another bolt at Lienna, I threw a warp at his mind. I didn't have enough mental juice left for full invisibility, so I blurred Lienna as though Ortega were seeing quadruple.

He hesitated, and she ducked into the gap between two terrifyingly crooked stacks of containers.

Rushing after them, my breath rasping in my throat, I jumped the six-inch-wide gap where the doors of the cargo hatch didn't quite meet. As I landed, the deck shook violently. I staggered, almost falling.

The massive door shuddered, then buckled upward. Another slamming impact, then a deep groan and a sharp crack. The gap tore wide open, and from within the cargo hold, a demon shoved through as though clawing out of hell itself.

I'd read more than once that demons were practically unkillable. That you had to pierce their hearts or chop off their heads to bring them down. But I hadn't believed it until right this moment.

Ortega's demon unfurled its tattered wings. Steel shrapnel peppered its body, and trails of dark blood marked its limbs. Half of its face and part of its left side was blistered with burns, like an unholy Harvey Dent, and its eyes had changed from glowing magma to solid, nightmarish black.

Even a goddamn rocket launcher hadn't stopped it.

The demon panted, though whether from pain, exhaustion, or the effort of battering its way out of the cargo hold, I didn't know. Its lips peeled back from its fangs as it snarled low in its chest.

It sprang at me.

I dove away, unintentionally rolled a few yards down the slanted deck before I could stop myself, then leaped to my feet and sprinted for the nearest stack of containers. The demon charged after me, slower than before but still faster than this psycho warper. I leaped into the narrow space, and the demon slammed into the corner of a container at full speed.

A loud snap. As the demon rebounded from its impact with the container, the shattered pieces of lashing bars that secured the stack of forty-foot-long containers in place scattered across the deck.

I looked up, horror closing my throat.

With a shuddering creak, the stack above me tipped into the one beside it. They collided with a horrific bang, and as metal clanged and cracked, and lashing bars and clamps snapped, I dove back out into the open. I'd rather take my chances with an injured demon than ten tons of falling shipping containers.

Like dominoes, the stack of containers the demon had dislodged fell into the next, which fell into the next, which fell into the next. The ship rocked violently as all that weight collapsed onto the port side, containers plunging into the sea.

I flattened myself to the deck, clinging for dear life.

The ship rolled and heaved, and when it steadied, the deck was tilted at a precarious forty-degree angle, one side of the vessel so low that waves splashed onto the deck. Even the demon, wings flaring and tail lashing, struggled for balance.

A scream rang out.

Appearing on the port side, Lienna slid twenty feet down the sloping deck. Panic shot through me as she hit the rail feet first, but she didn't go overboard.

Ortega appeared from behind a shipping container farther up the angled deck. He had a hand braced on it for balance as his gaze swung toward me—then jerked to his demon.

"There you are!" He pointed at Lienna. "Kill her now!" A manic grin twisted his face. "*Drown her!*"

Snarling, the demon pivoted toward Lienna as she unsteadily pushed to her feet, one foot on the railing for balance. The beast spread its damaged wings—and leaped into the air.

"No!" I yelled.

She didn't have a chance to dodge. The demon swept down the deck and slammed into her, throwing her overboard and plunging into the dark water after her with a violent splash.

"Lienna!"

Her only chance was stopping the demon, which meant stopping the contractor. If I killed Ortega, the Banishment Clause would be invoked, and the demon would be sucked back into hell where it belonged.

Heaving up, I grabbed a three-foot-long rod of inch-thick steel that had broken off a lashing bar. Clutching my makeshift weapon, I charged up the incline toward Ortega, leaping over the gap between the cargo hold doors for a second time.

He laughed like an evil, goateed Thor as he extended his hand toward me, lightning crackling over his arm.

Before he could unleash the thunder, I hit him with a warp of the deck dropping away beneath his feet.

Gasping, he instinctively lurched backward to keep his balance and fell. His ass hit the deck and he slid down it, careening straight for me. I lunged to meet him.

We slammed together, and I drove the steel rod into his lower chest.

His weight and momentum pulled me down too, and we tumbled across the deck—straight toward the gaping hole where the demon had torn out of the cargo hold.

Ortega grabbed the rod protruding from his torso, the other end still in my hands, and sent a bolt of electricity ripping through it. My muscles seized, hands clenching around the steel, and as we pitched over the edge, it tore from his flesh.

The rod caught on the opening, jarring me to a halt—and Ortega plunged into the hole with a strangled cry that echoed through the cavernous, flooded cargo hold.

Gasping at my near death, I stared into the pitch darkness below, then shoved away with shaking limbs. The Banishment Clause. Where was the red flash of the demon's power? Why wasn't it appearing?

Sliding toward the spot where Lienna had vanished, I caught myself on the rail, almost going overboard, and desperately scanned the black ocean. Twenty feet away, huge demonic wings beat at the water. The demon was hovering just above the waves, but I couldn't see Lienna. Where—

Splashing. Something writhing beneath the surface.

The demon was holding her under, drowning her just as Ortega had commanded.

"Lienna!" I cried.

I looked back over my shoulder. Ortega. He wasn't dead yet. He was wounded, probably unconscious, but not dead. And I couldn't reach him to finish it. I couldn't distract the demon; my powers didn't work properly on the semi-autonomous beast. I couldn't do *anything*.

With jerky movements, I grabbed the only weapon I had: the grappling gun. Lifting the strap over my head, I sucked in a deep breath to steady my shaking core and took aim.

I pulled the trigger.

The hook whined as it arced across the water and hit its mark, wrapping around the demon's beating wing.

I pressed the winching button and the line snapped taut, but instead of pulling the demon off Lienna, it yanked me forward. I braced against the railing, hooking my knees through the steel spindles. The motor made a loud, angry grinding sound.

The demon reached up with its good hand, trying to grab the rope around its wing. Lienna's head broke the surface for half a second before the demon shoved her back down with the stump of its amputated forearm.

My exhausted muscles strained as I tried to reel the winged bastard in like a demonic sea bass, but it was too strong. Desperate, helpless tears stung my eyes as I wrenched pointlessly on the gun.

With a hoarse shout, I imagined the grappling hook morphing from a small steel prong into a heavy ship's anchor, four times larger and exponentially heavier. In my mind's eye, tiny hooks thickened and bulged, and I could almost feel its mass crushing me. But the demon's wings kept beating. The warp did nothing, because of course it wouldn't—

The grappling gun tore from my hands. The demon plunged beneath the water, disappearing from sight.

What the hell had happened?

I clutched the railing, staring at the undulating water.

A little splash broke the surface, then Lienna's head burst out of the waves. Her wet, hacking cough barely reached my ears but it was the most wonderful sound I'd ever heard. She was alive. Somehow, impossibly, she was alive. And so was I.

A spotlight hit me in the face, blinding me.

"Kit! Lienna!"

Vera. Shouting. The fishing boat chugged toward us, the light flashing like a frantic, beckoning wave.

Time to jump ship. Literally.

Gulping down air, I threw myself over the railing and dove into the water. Into freedom.

And I immediately sank. The agonizing cold, magical abuse, and bone-deep exhaustion had turned my limbs to rubber and I slipped beneath the waves.

27

"HIS NAME WAS LUIS ORTEGA."

Lienna was perched in a familiar chair beside a familiar hospital bed. A bed I was lying in. Again. This room and I had developed an uncomfortably close relationship after my last near-death experience—the one where I'd been shot in the chest by my former best friend while stopping him from enacting his plans of world domination via empath superpowers.

This harrowing adventure—beaten to a pulp, severely hypothermic, and electrocuted half to death while escaping a sinking ship after blowing a hole in it with a borrowed RPG—seemed more preposterous than the last. They should make a movie about it. Or, even better, a TV show. *Kit Morris: Warp Master Extraordinaire*, starring Tom Hardy. No, wait, he was too broody. Maybe Chris Evans was available.

"Ortega was my father's partner for six years," Lienna continued, studying the information on her shiny new phone. "A talented electramage. Well respected. Definite leadership qualities. No indication that he was a demon contractor, though."

"He probably acquired the demon after joining Red Rum," I mused.

She nodded. "Thirteen years ago, my father found out that Ortega was leaking MPD information to Red Rum. According to the report, Dad suspected Ortega had evidence in his house. They didn't want to risk him destroying it, so the LA captain ordered a raid on his home. There was an accident during the raid and … his daughter was killed."

"An accident? A real one, or an 'accident'?" I added air quotes to the last word.

"Actual accident, I think." Sadness filled her eyes. "There was a standoff between Ortega and the agents, and his daughter got caught in the crossfire. She was only ten."

"Damn," I whispered.

We were both quiet for a minute before Lienna continued. "Ortega was arrested, but he escaped before his trial and vanished."

"So killing you was payback. A daughter for a daughter."

"Yeah." She slid her phone into her satchel. "He must've thought it was too risky to attack me when I was around my dad all the time. But when he learned I was in Vancouver …"

"He made his move." I nodded. "Which is why he tried to kill you with that car bomb before Rocco had a chance to inform Red Rum that we were investigating Harold. Ortega was already stalking you."

"Seems like it." She drew in a deep breath, held it for a second, then let it out in a rush. "How's your eye?"

"My eye?" I leaned back against my pillows. "That's what you're most worried about? Not my cracked cheekbone or internal burns or bruised ribs?"

"None of them look as ugly as your eye," she said with an impish smile.

"I wouldn't even *have* a black eye if Vera hadn't thrown the lifesaver right at my face."

"You're lucky she has good aim. You were barely keeping your head above water."

"I guess it does make me look tougher," I remarked unenthusiastically, wincing as I poked the swelling around my brow. "How did your meeting with Blythe go?"

The healer had released Lienna early this morning, since her worst ailment had been water in her lungs after her demon-assisted drowning. I was stuck in this antiseptic purgatory until tomorrow morning.

"Better than I expected." She shifted uncomfortably. "Agent Harris's team captured the Red Rum rogues in their lifeboat. They're all in custody. The infernuses were delivered to Illicit Magic Storage. They'll euthanize the demons and destroy the infernuses there. All of Rocco's clients' souls will be safe."

All except for Harold's.

"What about Rocco?" I asked, my mind jumping to the man responsible for Harold's damned soul. "Is he talking yet?"

She shook her head. "The bastard pled not guilty. Says we have no proof he was involved with the infernuses. He's blaming everything on Red Rum."

I snorted. "Remember what the Judiciary Council tried to do to me? He can deny it all he wants, but we have more than enough to put him away forever."

"I guess we'll find out," she muttered.

"What about the Grand Grimoire?"

"Tae-min has taken over as acting GM. The guild should be fine." She shrugged in an extra casual way. "So that's all wrapped up nicely, and if there were more shareable infernuses, they went down with Red Rum's ship ... along with any other not strictly legal artifacts."

Such as Lienna's forbidden portals. Logically, I knew it was better that her experimental teleportation devices had vanished in an ocean abyss, but another part of me was painfully disappointed that I wouldn't get to experience vortex travel again until she could make more.

I puffed out a breath. "And your job?"

"Captain Blythe isn't happy with how I handled things at the end, but we got Thorn and I think that's what matters most to her. So I get to stay."

Warm relief settled over me, and I relaxed back into my pillows. It seemed like ages had passed since the most exciting part of my day had been introducing Vinny to his new eight-legged friend, Biscuit, but at least I didn't have to worry anymore about Lienna returning to LA and leaving me alone in the captain's merciless care. Somehow, I couldn't imagine doing this MagiPol agent thing without her.

One worry down—but an even more terrifying problem still weighed on my mind like a black cloud of doom.

"I know we survived and caught the bad guys and all that," I murmured, pushing my anxieties aside before Lienna noticed, "but I still feel like I don't have a single, itty-bitty clue what I'm doing. Like I Mr. Magooed my way through that investigation."

"Same here."

"Do you think we'll ever feel like we know what we're doing?"

"I hope so. Maybe with more experience." She raised an eyebrow. "You could work on those reality-warping skills. Then, if you don't like how something is going, you can warp it out of existence."

Ah, yes. The infamous reality warp.

By our best guess, I'd saved Lienna from her waterlogged demon encounter by warping the small grappling hook into an honest-to-goodness anchor. I wasn't sure if the hook had actually changed shape, or if I'd only changed its mass. Either way, it'd taken the stumpy-armed hellbeast on a one-way ride to the ocean floor.

"Maybe we should do some experiments," she suggested eagerly. "Let's figure out how it works. What you're really capable of!"

That was the last thing I wanted, but I wasn't going to tell her that. "You have enough experimentation on your plate in your evil basement laboratory."

"This is bigger than that. Don't you realize what it means that you can—"

"Of course I do," I replied too sharply, then immediately softened. "But aren't you worried about what might happen? I could create a rip in space-time and end up exploding the planet or jumping forward in time to the heat death of the universe."

She gave me a skeptical look.

"I don't think I could live with that kind of blood on my hands," I added. "I mean, no one could live with it. Because no one would be alive."

"Right." She punctuated the word with a sarcastic eye roll. "You're probably overtired. Speaking of which, do you think you might be back to normal by tomorrow afternoon?"

"I hope so." The healer hadn't given me a recovery timeline, and my pulped innards would probably dictate my release far more than my personal hopes. "Why?"

"Captain Blythe mentioned something during our meeting. About you."

Oh, great. Was being kidnapped a fireable offense now?

Lienna nibbled her lower lip worriedly. "She said an unexplained analyst aboard that Red Rum ship might raise questions about the legitimacy of our investigation."

"It's not like I went willingly."

"The optics are still bad."

Leave it to the MPD to worry about the optics of a situation like this. "So pretend I wasn't there."

"Too many people saw you." She waved around the room, presumably indicating the healer who'd most definitely seen me. Not to mention the dozen Red Rum goons in holding who'd engaged in face-to-face meetings with yours truly. "But she said there's a simple solution. You need to pass your exam so we can put 'field agent' on all our reports."

"Okay," I agreed slowly, unsure what she was getting at. It wasn't like I'd failed my previous attempts on purpose.

She cleared her throat. "So the captain has scheduled your retake of the field exam for Monday afternoon."

"*Monday* afternoon?" I stared at her. "As in *tomorrow?* As in *twenty-four hours from now?*"

My partner offered me an encouraging smile. "I'm sure the healers will have you ready in time."

Sure, I might be physically fine for the exam.

But I had a much bigger and far scarier problem to worry about.

I STOOD on the spray-painted X, feeling like Wile E. Coyote seconds before he inadvertently drops an ACME-stamped anvil on his own head.

My burns, bruises, and electrocuted organs were all healed up, with lingering fatigue as my only remaining health issue. I was fit enough for the exam, as I'd proved by rocking the first two challenges.

But that wasn't what had my gut churning with anxiety worse than anything I'd felt on my previous exams.

Waiting for the foghorn to signal the start of Phase Three, I considered Blythe's words to me outside the Grand Grimoire. She'd told me I didn't fit the mold of a typical MagiPol agent, but that was why she'd hired me.

What the hell did that mean?

Did she want me to revert to my criminal past? Maybe I should rush the observation deck, take the judges hostage, and refuse to release them until I was granted field agent status.

I inhaled, and as the air rushed through my nose, the foghorn blared.

The first assault came instantly.

'Twas brillig, and the slithy toves did gyre and gimble in the wabe.

I scrunched my eyes against Agent Tim's brain-piercing nonsense. Really? Blythe had put me up against a telepath *again*? Her words had indicated she expected me to pass, but her choice of opponents said otherwise.

I memorized this one just for you, Tim informed me, then continued in dramatic iambic, *All mimsy were the borogoves, and the mome raths outgrabe.*

This might be one of the greatest poems in the history of English literature, but Tim's delivery was ruining it for me.

As I held my position on the starting X, Tim's voice dug into my mind, but he wasn't merely distracting me. He was picking at my thoughts, waiting for me to decide on a strategy so he could relay it to his teammates.

With one more slow, calming inhale, I Split Kit myself. Bending all my concentration on it, I then Redecorated the dirt road ahead of me, shifting the left wall of the nearest building out two feet to create a hidden corridor to sneak down, doubling my protection. It was a subtle change that would be difficult for the other mythics to detect.

'Beware the Jabberwock, my son!' Amusement colored Tim's telepathy. *'The jaws that bite, the claws that catch!'*

I stepped off the X, focusing hard on the Split Kit and Redecoration—then burst into a sprint, streaking straight down the road.

My opponents reacted instantly. One sprang out a window on the opposite side of the street to my Redecorated wall, and the other sped out of a gap between buildings and braced his feet, a long spear in his hands.

Agent Wolfe, the terramage I'd cuffed in Phase Two of my previous exam. This time he wasn't empty-handed, but at least he wasn't likely to stab me with that spear. The weapon was his switch, used for directing his elemental magic. You know, creating earthquakes and rifts in the ground beneath your feet. Fun stuff like that.

The second guy was Agent Shephard, a short sorcerer and thin as a rail, who moved like a cat. His rune-inscribed staff packed a lot of ouch-inducing spell-power. He'd used me as a demonstration dummy during a training exercise and I still remembered the sting.

I didn't slow, concentrating as hard as I could through Tim's deafening recitation. All I could or would think about was keeping my warps impenetrable, no matter what the mage and sorcerer threw at me.

Shepard pointed his staff at the fake wall I'd created and muttered an incantation. A stream of silver smoke whooshed across the street and poofed against the wood in a hazy burst. He swept the spell along the wall, searching for an invisible psycho warper.

I held that Redecorated wall for all I was worth, simultaneously adding puffs of silver smoke to make it look like his magic was hitting it.

Tim's poetry reading paused as he relayed info to his team.

"Gotta give you props for realism, Kit," Wolfe called, raising his spear. "Let's see if you can keep it up through a little earthquake."

He smacked the butt of his spear into the ground and a tremor rocked the street. I staggered, then dropped to one knee as the earth trembled.

"Come out, come out, wherever you are," he taunted. "You can't hide forever."

As Agent Tim layered on his poetic assault, I refocused on my Split Kit and Redecorator. Pushing to my feet, I continued down the street in a casual saunter, hands in my pockets.

Shephard fired another spell at the wall. "Did he make it past us?"

"Come on, guys," I called. "You can't find one little rookie psychic?"

They ignored me as I ambled nearer.

"He's really close." Tim jumped off the roof of a low structure and landed beside Wolfe, a paintball gun in one hand, held ready to fire. "He can't hold his warps under pressure. Shake it up!"

Instruction delivered, the telepath resumed his recital with a toothy grin. *He left it dead, and with its head he went galumphing back.*

Was that a threat? Could a nonsense poem be a threat?

Grunting, Wolfe spun his spear, then brought the blade down. It hit the earth, and a quake stronger than the first rocked the arena. The ground cracked, fissures opening beneath the wall of the Redecorated building. The flimsy wood buckled and the roof collapsed, sending a plume of dust shooting into the air.

Adding all that dramatic imagery to my warp, I waited for the ground to still, then hastened forward again. Tim was only a few yards away, hefting his gun impatiently as though itching to give me a few more painful welts.

"We've seen this one before too, Kit!" he called laughingly. "I can sense you nearby. Come out and play."

I honed my focus on the Split Kit, the collapsed building, and roiling dust. "I *am* playing, Timmy, but you're ignoring me."

He looked right past me, searching the dusty haze, discounting the Kit he saw right in front of him. It was an insubstantial distraction, illusory and harmless. It couldn't hurt them. It was a decoy, and they weren't falling for it.

My magic was nothing but a deception, and with Tim reading my mind, I couldn't fool them.

Except I could.

My hand flashed out. I caught Tim's gun, wrenching it from his hand as I jammed my other elbow into his sternum, knocking him back a step. Whirling, I fired a shot into Shephard's chest, then Wolfe's. Letting my spin carry me full circle back to Tim, whose mouth was still gaping with winded shock, I fired a third shot into his chest at point-blank range.

And that's how I passed the third phase of my exam.

Tim looked down at the burst of yellow paint on his vest, then patted me on the head as though checking I was actually real. "But ... you're a fake Kit."

"Nothing was fake, Tim." I smirked. "I didn't use a single warp. I just pretended."

His jaw fell open all over again.

After my second failed exam, Lienna had said something that'd stuck in my mind. She'd said my powers relied on deception. And she was right, but there was a key element I'd missed—one that I'd unwittingly first used when I'd tricked Vinny with a real spider.

I'd thought that once someone knew I was deceiving them, I lost my advantage. But even though my warps required magic, *deception* didn't require any magic at all. Every rookie came into their exam with magic a-blazing. But like Captain Blythe had said, I wasn't like other agents.

Grinning victoriously, I tossed Tim his pistol. "O frabjous day! Callooh! Callay!"

And I chortled in my joy.

His scowl gradually morphed into a wry grin. "Well played, rookie."

"Thanks. Now if you'll excuse me, I need to go find out my score."

An hour later, I walked into the precinct's bullpen. It was after five and everyone had either gone home or taken a dinner break. Everyone except Lienna.

As I headed for my cubicle, she hopped up from my chair and rushed toward me, her brow scrunched with concern. I kept my expression neutral as she halted in front of me, searching my eyes.

"How'd it go?" she asked gently.

My lips twitched but I couldn't prevent the triumphant grin from overtaking my face. "Passed with a perfect score!"

"*What!*" she shrieked, grabbing my shoulders. "No way!"

Her surprise was a lot more gratifying than it'd been last time.

She shook me slightly as though impatient for me to spill the deets. "Was Agent Tim—"

"Oh, he was there. I walked right up to him, took his gun, and shot all three of them."

"What? How?"

"He thought I was a warp," I said with a shrug. "I wasn't."

A loud, beautiful laugh roiled past her lips. "That's amazing! I've only heard of, like, two rookies passing their exam by eliminating all three opponents."

Her hands were still on my shoulders, and I curled my fingers gently around her wrists, hoping to prolong the touch, the connection between us. "I didn't even use magic. Just made them think I was."

"Like the spider, huh?"

She got me. This gorgeous, brilliant, ass-kicking woman truly got me.

Her beaming smile was irresistible, and the innocent press of her palms on my shoulders and the soft skin of her wrists under my hands wasn't enough. The thought must've shown on my face, because a pink flush spread across her cheeks.

But she didn't let go.

I slowly slid my hands along her forearms to her elbows, where they met the pushed-up sleeves of her black shirt. With a slight tug, I invited her closer. Her eyes on mine, she took a small step, putting us mere inches apart.

The last half-week had been hell. A vengeful, megawatt assassin, more than a couple demonic fiends intent on killing us, and one dose of odious cilantro poison. But here I was, alive and well, officially ascended to the rank of field agent, and ready to wrap this amazing woman in my arms.

Maybe I could even forget the cold anxiety I was working hard to keep buried deep enough that Lienna wouldn't notice it.

I lightly touched her cheek, my thumb brushing her jaw, then leaned down toward her nervously expectant, uptilted face. The distance between us vanished as I drew her into me, my mouth dipping to hers.

A stinging whip slashed me across the back.

I jerked straight, belatedly realizing the whip was actually a voice—one that cracked with a dangerous edge.

"Agent Morris. Agent Shen."

We both turned. Captain Blythe was striding across the bullpen toward us, her aura of stern disgruntlement as potent as ever. The stack of folders she carried had somehow gotten larger.

She halted two long steps away, that laser-beam quality back in her eyes as she scanned me. I hastily sidled away from an intensely blushing Lienna so we were standing at a "close buddies" distance instead of a "tango dancing" distance.

"I assume it *is* 'Agent' Morris now?" the captain asked.

"Yes, ma'am."

She grunted. "About time."

Okay, mood killer. Jeez.

Blythe shifted the enormous weight of her folders to her other arm. "Despite your questionable decision-making, you two complement each other's skills well. I'm assigning you as partners on a trial basis."

Wait, was she serious? Were words that I actually wanted to hear coming from the mouth of our very own Captain Blythe?

"But," Lienna stammered, wide-eyed, "rookie agents are normally partnered with an experienced agent—"

"Are you objecting, Agent Shen?"

"No! I believe Kit—Agent Morris and I will work very well together."

Hell *yes*. I started to grin, then froze when the captain's stare speared me.

"I expect you two to have Thorn's case ready for the Judiciary Council by the end of the week." She started to turn away, then glanced back at Lienna. "I've always appreciated your professionalism, Agent Shen. It's one of your best qualities. I hope you'll have a positive influence on Agent Morris."

Lienna nodded jerkily, her face flaming, while I belatedly processed the subtext of the captain's remark. Was she saying what I thought she was saying?

With no further comment, the captain disappeared into the hallway, leaving me and Lienna alone in my cubicle once more.

I forced a grin. "I guess this means I can call you 'partner' for real now."

She smiled weakly. "Yeah. Looks like we're going to spend a lot of time working together."

Was it just me, or had she put an unnecessary amount of emphasis on "working"?

"Lienna," I began hesitantly, reaching for her.

She pulled away, trying to hide the motion by picking up her satchel from my chair and hitching it over her shoulder. "I should go home. Early start tomorrow. We have reports to finish."

"Lienna," I tried again as she turned away, but she didn't stop. If anything, she hurried her steps, her shoulders hunched as though invisible missiles were bombarding her.

Or as though my voice saying her name was an unseen blow.

"See you tomorrow," she called over her shoulder, her voice cracking slightly.

Muted by that resounding rejection, I watched her cross to the door and disappear through it.

Alone in the bullpen, I dropped heavily into my office chair. Talk about going from a cloud-nine high to a ground-zero crash and burn. With my exam success and nearly kissing Lienna for the first time while *not* under extreme duress, I'd almost been able to forget about my biggest problem.

The one I'd been hiding from everyone.

The alarming feeling I'd first noticed while crawling aboard Vera's boat as she and Lienna had hauled me out of the water. The disconcerting absence that'd forced me to use my wits and nothing else to pass my field exam. The terror that was worse than physical injuries, worse than failing exams, worse than Lienna rejecting me.

My magic was gone.

Completely. Gone.

At first, I'd thought it was fatigue. I'd experienced psychic weakness before, but this was different. It was an utter drought of power. The spot in my head that was normally bright and warm with magic had gone dark.

Almost forty-eight hours after reality warping, my powers were still MIA.

Bracing my elbows on my desk, I dropped my face into my hands. It stood to reason that the reality warp had somehow wiped out my abilities—that altering the fabric of existence had this one little aftereffect, which considering the universe-imploding alternatives, didn't seem all that severe.

But it kind of fucked my life up, didn't it?

I'd warped reality once before, and my powers might have died for a period of time afterward—for a week or less, which was how long I'd been in abjuration handcuffs. They'd blocked my powers and my ability to tell if they were working. Could I assume that if my powers had returned after that reality warp, they'd return after this one?

It was a risky assumption, considering I knew nothing about reality warping and its possible side effects—and considering everything that mattered in my life required me to remain a mythic with functioning magic.

I lost track of time as I sat there at my desk, alone in the bullpen I'd spent five months fighting to earn a place in. The distant hum of a janitor's vacuum, the steady whoosh of the heat vents, and the creaking of pipes filled the empty silence. My thoughts, anxieties, and the heavy weight of dread closed around me like an impenetrable cage.

A sudden patter of approaching footsteps made me look up. Lienna? Was she back?

"You look miserable," the mohawked intruder remarked, waltzing into our cubicle. "Did you fail your field exam *again*?"

Ugh. The last person I needed adding more kill to my buzz was Vincent Park. And while I would've loved to rub my perfect score in his face, I didn't have the gumption to banter with him. Slouching back into my chair, I closed my eyes.

His cargo shorts rustled as he sat at his computer and tapped on the keyboard. "In case you were wondering, I'm working late with Agent Harris on processing all those Red Rum rogues. You know, the ones who kidnapped you."

On another day, I would've made him regret that asshat remark. But short of slugging him in the jaw, there was nothing I could do. What I wouldn't give for a warp of my arachnid accomplice. I imagined Biscuit crawling out from behind his monitor and pouncing on his computer mouse. The very notion filled me with a warmth reminiscent of—

Vinny yelped and his chair crashed into the back of mine. My eyes popped open.

"Real mature, Kit," he snapped.

"What?"

"You already did the spider trick once. Find something new."

As he glowered at me with indignant annoyance, I stared back at him, nonplussed. Slowly, it dawned on me what I'd done—and I belatedly registered the bright, warm spot in my mind where minutes ago it'd been dark and empty.

I couldn't help myself; I laughed. I laughed so hard. The crushing bubble of dread that'd been lodged in my chest for two days burst, and giddy laughter boiled up from its remains and overflowed out of my mouth like an unstoppable tsunami. I doubled over, bracing against the arm of my chair as my shoulders shook.

"It's not that funny," Vincent grumbled. "It wasn't even funny the first time."

Regaining my composure, I stood up, grabbed my backpack, and stepped out of the cubicle. "Have fun with that overtime work, Vinny."

He shook his head at me. "You need a new hobby, Morris."

I took two more steps, then pivoted back to give him a crooked grin.

"That's *Agent* Morris to you, pal."

Discover Kit and Lienna's next mystery in

A LITTLE WARPED

A GUILD CODEX STORY

In this prologue to the next installment in
The Guild Codex: Warped, a violent murder has caught
the attention of the MPD …

———— KEEP READING FOR THIS EXCLUSIVE STORY ————

A GUILD CODEX STORY

A LITTLE
WARPED

ROB JACOBSEN
ANNETTE MARIE

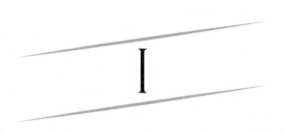

FROM THE ROOFTOP of MPD headquarters, I could see most of downtown Vancouver. Low-hanging clouds shrouded the city in a wet mist, obscuring the tops of the tallest skyscrapers. I had my hood pulled up from under my black denim jacket, but it didn't help much. It was a cold, gloomy day.

Well, the *weather* was gloomy.

I was freaking hyped.

"Finally," I declared. "I can check this off my bucket list."

Huddled in the roof access doorway, Lienna raised an eyebrow. "Your bucket list includes investigating a murder on a farm?"

"Not that part." Of course not. Who got excited about murder? Well, maybe Hannibal Lecter, but the only bright spot for me was the interruption in my normal duties. A homicide investigation sounded significantly safer than our usual—

unmasking criminal masterminds, evading assassins, foiling evil plots, and fining guilds for bureaucratic infractions.

Strangely, that last one often seemed the most perilous.

Playing *Murder She Wrote* in cottage territory was a bit outside our scope, but if the boss needed us there, we'd put on our detective hats and be there. Speaking of which, I needed a proper Sherlock Holmes deerstalker.

"The helicopter," I added matter-of-factly. "I've wanted to ride in a helicopter since I was a wee lad binging *A-Team* reruns in my foster parents' basement. Every action movie ever has an awesome chopper scene. *Apocalypse Now*, *Die Hard 2*, *The Matrix*, James Bond movies across the board, *The Dark Knight*, *Black Hawk Down*, *Rambo III* … I could go on."

Lienna tucked a lock of black hair behind her ear. "Doesn't the helicopter crash or blow up in most of those?"

"Yeah, but the good guy always survives."

"And you're the good guy?"

"We're MPD agents. Aren't we always the good guys?"

"Depends on who you talk to," she scoffed. "What else is on your bucket list?"

"For cool methods of transportation? Let's see. A dragon boat, a tank, a snowmobile, a zeppelin, a double-decker bus, a cruise ship—"

"We were on a ship last month."

"That was a cargo ship—and we almost died on it." I gave her a dubious look. "Are you really comparing that industrial monstrosity to a luxury cruise liner with buffets, gift shops, and Elvis impersonators?"

A black dot appeared on the horizon, growing steadily larger as it flew toward us. Lienna stepped out of the doorway and we waited—me fidgeting impatiently—beside the landing pad that spanned the east end of the rooftop. A low *whump-whump-whump* reached my ears and my heart rate spiked.

"What about a rocket?" Lienna asked. "Or a space shuttle?"

"Huh?"

"For your bucket list. No outer space vehicles?"

"Hell no. Have you seen *Gravity*? Or *Alien*? Or *2001*? Nothing good happens in outer space."

She rolled her eyes.

I got that a lot—the classic Lienna eye roll—and I loved it. You'd think it was an expression of annoyance, but I saw it more as a sign of affection. And Lienna was extraordinarily affectionate.

The unmarked black helicopter plunged downward. It slowed to hover above the landing pad, then settled onto the rooftop. Cold gusts from its thunderous rotors whipped Lienna's long hair all over the place like a maniacal hair dryer. My hood blew off, but since I kept my hair short—I liked to think it gave me that Jake Gyllenhaal appeal—it mostly stayed put.

"Get to the choppa!" I yelled to Lienna in my best Arnold Schwarzenegger impression.

That earned me another eye roll. See? Super affectionate.

Bending at our waists, we ran toward the whirlybird. The large door swung open and the copilot hopped out, waving us over. Lienna climbed inside. Grinning broadly, I jumped in after her. Three jump seats were lined up side by side, and I was surprised to see that a weirdly small man, about forty years old with a perfectly bald head and round, dark-rimmed glasses, already occupied the furthest one.

It was Dr. Bunsen Honeydew! Except, you know, a human and not a Muppet.

Recovering from my surprise, I dropped into the seat beside Lienna and fumbled for my harness. The copilot shut the door and handed us each a bulky headset. As I squashed it on my head, the chopper lifted into the air, vibrating with the power of the rotors. The surrounding rooftops shrank away as we shot skyward, and my stomach flipped.

"This is awesome," I squeaked quietly to myself.

Feminine laughter sounded in my ears, buzzing with distortion. My startled gaze flicked to Lienna.

She tapped her headset. "We can hear you."

Aw, crap. I looked past her to the distinctly unimpressed Honeydew, then cleared my throat and asked in my deepest, most masculine voice, "Do you know where we're headed?"

"A farm," he replied curtly, his voice equally distorted by the mic.

Gee, thanks, Mr. Informative. "Did someone murder a horse?"

Lienna tensed so abruptly she elbowed me in the side. "God, I hope not."

I shifted over a few inches, wincing. Note to self: horses were no joking matter for Lienna Shen.

"I have a second question," I said, turning the conversation away from the glue factory. "Who the hell are you?"

Dr. Honeydew forced a smile and reached across Lienna to offer me his hand. "Shane Davila."

"Did you say de Vil? Like Cruella?" I asked, shaking his hand as I pictured him in a floor-length fur coat. It worked in a vaguely Liberace way.

"Davila," he repeated, with extra emphasis on the last syllable. "And you are?"

"Kit. Agent Kit Morris."

That wasn't me trying to pull off a "Bond, James Bond" thing. I still wasn't used to introducing myself with a job title—especially *that* job title.

"You're an agent?" Shane squinted through his glasses, studying me then Lienna. "Both of you?"

I got that Lienna and I didn't have that "stick up the ass" agent vibe, but we *had* just boarded an MPD-issue helicopter, which had picked us up from an MPD precinct for a secret MPD mission. We didn't look *that* unagenty, did we? I even maintained some manly stubble to offset my big baby blue eyes and general youthfulness. It must not be giving me the badass agent mien I was aiming for.

If possible, Lienna was even more unexpected than I was. Bracelets, necklaces, earrings, hair beads, and more decked her out from head to toe, and she carried a hemp satchel containing her arcane arsenal.

Side note: She was also gorgeous. Way too gorgeous to be a stuffy MPD agent. And no, that wasn't just my she's-my-amazing-and-attractive-partner bias talking.

She coolly offered her hand to Shane. "Agent Lienna Shen."

Surprise washed over his face. Lienna, at the ripe old age of twenty-three, was already a minor legend in the mythic community. Be impressed, non-famous Muppet man.

"Your work on the Scarlet Killer case last year was very impressive," she added. "My entire precinct followed along."

Uh, what?

Shane nodded modestly. "It was a difficult one. I knew I had the right rogue, but I wasn't sure we could make the tag. We almost lost him in the final hour. Di-mythics are tricky."

"I think your only case that got more international attention was TelepathyGate. People talked about that one for months."

Okay … maybe he wasn't non-famous after all. Did that mean I was the only nobody in this helicopter? Who was the pilot? The Pope?

I tapped Lienna on the leg and scrunched my eyebrows meaningfully. Someone please fill in the commoner on how starstruck he should be.

"Shane's a bounty hunter," she revealed. "Well known, particularly among MPD employees."

I looked from her to Shane and back, checking for signs of a prank in the making.

A bounty hunter. *This* guy? This tiny, leather-gloved Muppet with Harry Potter glasses and male pattern baldness? That defied everything I knew about bounty hunting and the tough-as-nails mythics who engaged in it. Almost without fail, they were gritty, vulgar, muscle-bound dickbags with bad attitudes and a penchant for breaking rules.

"What's your class?" I blurted.

He stiffened, but I was too curious to care about decorum.

Lienna elbowed me in the side again. She, apparently, did care. Don't tell me she was a bounty hunter groupie or something.

"What brings you out here?" she asked extra politely. "Is this homicide related to your current bounty?"

"Not precisely. I'm in town on a different matter, and Captain Blythe asked me to join the team to see if I could shed any light on this new case."

"What *is* this case?" I jumped in. "What's so special about this homicide that the MPD is flying us millionaire-style to the crime scene?"

Shane shrugged. "The captain didn't provide any details."

"You're going after a Vancouver bounty?" Lienna asked, leaning forward eagerly. I suppressed a scowl. "I didn't think we had any rogues big enough to merit your interest."

The Muppet smiled mysteriously. "There are a few enticing options, but I have my eye on one in particular. What about you, Agent Shen? I believe you were stationed with the LA precinct before this?"

"I transferred here to fill a staffing gap."

That was a neat way to sum up a long story that started with my dramatic arrest at LAX.

"The Vancouver precinct is lucky to have you," Shane said. "Good abjuration sorcerers are few and far between."

My scowl deepened. Flattery now? If he tried to flirt with her, we'd all get to find out if bounty-hunting Muppet-men bounced.

Shane mentioned a case he'd worked on in LA a couple of years ago, and as they chatted, I looked out the water-streaked window. Snow-blanketed mountains swept by beneath us, wispy white clouds hanging around the peaks like cotton fluff, and a fresh wave of "hell yeah, this is so cool" lightened my gut.

I watched the fog-draped, toy-sized scenery pass until the pilot's voice crackled through our headsets.

"Two minutes to arrival."

Leaning into the window, I craned my neck to see where we were headed. The helicopter began a casual descent, dipping between rolling peaks. Snowy forests clung to rocky slopes all around us. Compared to the urban bustle of the city, it was ruggedly beautiful and welcomingly serene.

That all changed the moment the helicopter flew over a ridge, revealing a hidden valley. Without a doubt, this was our destination, and it wasn't just a murder scene.

It was a goddamn apocalypse.

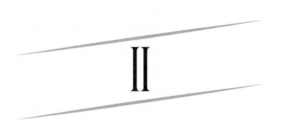

II

I STEPPED OUT of the helicopter, and my shoes crunched against the grass. Or what was left of it. The ground was scorched and crispy, and a whirlwind of ash and dust billowed around us as the helicopter lifted off again. I wished I was still inside it, flying right back home. This place wasn't giving me any "cozy mountain retreat" feels.

Winter lay over the surrounding peaks, and beyond the valley, towering trees bowed under the weight of snow on their branches. But here, there was no snow. Only destruction.

Grass was far from the only victim. The trees had been reduced to skeletons, with bare, stubby branches, and the meadow was black. Charred posts, in neat rows, marked the former fence lines, and fire had consumed most of the buildings. I didn't look too closely at the sad humps scattered across the field. A couple hundred yards down the hill were the remains of a large house, a single plume of gray smoke rising from one corner. Holes marred its walls and one side had crumpled inward, as though a giant had stepped on it. A gigantic giant.

I was starting to understand why the captain had called for backup on this one.

Shane wasted no time in marching toward the scorched house. Lienna cast a long, somber glance at me, then followed. I trailed after them through the desolation. As we drew nearer, I spotted four people gathered out front, talking. One of them peeled away and trudged up to meet us.

Blythe, our sharp-eyed captain with blond hair that hung down to her chin and an aura that screamed, "Bullshit not welcome here," greeted us in rapid succession. "Agent Morris, Agent Shen, Mr. Davila, come with me. The body is this way."

The cap was not one for small talk. Or first names.

"Late last night," she began as she led us to the house, "local law enforcement received multiple reports of a forest fire in the area. As you would expect, a fire in early January was cause for surprise. Emergency responders were dispatched to this property, which they found engulfed in flames, although the fire hadn't spread beyond the property's borders."

"That must have raised suspicions," Shane remarked.

"It did," Blythe confirmed. "By the time these reports reached us, the fire was out. We took over the scene as quickly as possible."

We joined the waiting team. I recognized Nick, our precinct's coroner, from past dead-body experiences. He was an older man who looked more or less like Santa Claus, minus the red outfit, but including the beard, belly, and dimples. His name wasn't actually Nick, but until he corrected me, I'd keep calling him jolly ol' Saint Nicholas.

The other two were strangers: a tall, stick-thin dude with a camera, and a young, gothic woman with dark hair, black eyeliner, and more than a few facial piercings. She held a funky set of potions in test tubes and shiny tweezers. Did I want to know the purpose of the tweezers?

I was so busy analyzing the team that I didn't immediately notice the object of their attention—a blackened and distorted shape at the base of the porch steps. A heavy weight settled in my gut. That was a body. A very, very, very dead human body.

"Who is that?" I asked. "I mean, who *was* that?"

"We don't have an ID yet," Blythe answered brusquely. "Could be the owner of the property or an intruder."

Lienna stepped closer to the body and knelt to get eye level with it. Not that there were eyes to get level with.

"Do we know anything about the victim?" she asked.

Nick consulted his clipboard. "Female. Mid-twenties. Average build. I'll know more once we get her back to the city."

Lienna wiped a finger through the soot near the remains, then skimmed the wreckage of the house. The fire's residue wasn't the normal shade of gray you'd see in your backyard firepit. It was all dark, deep, unforgiving obsidian.

"Black magic," she murmured.

"It appears that way. Agent Goulding"—Blythe indicated the goth woman—"is our forensic alchemist, and she's confirmed that there are signs of black magic present all over the property. Mr. Davila, what are your thoughts?"

The famous bounty hunter, hovering two long steps behind me, cleared his throat. "The location of the body suggests she was either entering or leaving the house. The level of destruction …"

He trailed off. Wow, insightful.

"While we finish here, spread out and search the property," Blythe ordered me and Lienna. "I want every inch of this valley examined. I'll call you when I'm ready for you."

Lienna nodded purposefully, stepped around the body, and ventured into the crumbling house. I watched her vanish, then headed in the opposite direction. I needed fresh air before I gave the house a go.

Yeah, maybe other agents would call me a wuss, but I hadn't been at this long enough to shrug off the charred remains of a young woman.

I wandered across the blackened grass, taking in my surroundings. The mountainous terrain, with its forested slopes and snow-capped peaks, provided a pleasant vista, if you could ignore the line of absolute desolation that cut through the trees and earth. At least the weather was nice—for early January.

After a few minutes ambling in random directions, I approached the ruins of another building—a barn, by the looks of it. Like the house, the framework remained intact but the rest was a mess. The door, twisted and split, lay askew at the entrance, forcing me to climb over it. The ashy crap that coated everything was inescapable, and I was grateful I'd worn mostly black today.

The barn's interior was dark and I struggled to differentiate between soot and shadows. Once my eyes adjusted, the horror of the place came into focus. My gorge rose. I didn't like seeing dead humans, but something about dead animals ripped at the heart—even more so when they'd been trapped inside a burning building with no hope of escape.

I turned away. How dark did your soul have to be to commit this sort of atrocity?

"Kit? You in there?"

Shit! I rushed toward the entrance but not fast enough. Lienna poked her head around the broken door, searching for me. With no time to warn her, and knowing her reaction to the equine bodies would be stronger than mine, I did the only thing I could:

I made them disappear.

Spotting me, Lienna scaled the mangled barn door with remarkable grace. She hastened to my side and peered cautiously into the nearest charred stall. "Anything in here?"

"Doesn't look like it," I answered.

She sighed with relief. "The animals must've escaped. Well, that's one good thing, I guess."

"Totally. Any luck inside the house?"

"I only took a glance around before I realized you hadn't come in with me."

Was she here to check on me? Aw. "Figured I'd start out here. Where did the Muppet go?"

"Who?"

"Shane," I clarified. "Do you think he has a tall, skinny sidekick back at his lab who speaks exclusively in meeps?"

"He's more of a lone wolf, Kit."

"That was a Muppet joke." Maybe I needed to switch up my material. Puppet-based humor could only be stretched so far.

"I know." Another eye roll. "I'm telling you that Shane Davila doesn't have a sidekick. He doesn't even belong to a guild."

"What? How's that possible? Does Blythe know?"

"He's so good at what he does that the MPD awarded him special status, giving him more freedom to take on big cases."

"Like a mysterious countryside murder that reeks of dark magic?"

"It would seem so."

Another voice echoed through the barn. "Agent Shen? Are you here?"

Speak of the devil. Shane climbed over the door, somehow achieving even more awkwardness than I had. Seriously, this guy was a famous bounty hunter with MPD-awarded special status? I didn't get it.

Dusting his gloved hands off, he joined us. "Agent Shen, Captain Blythe would like your opinion on something."

I'd bet my measly MPD paycheck that she hadn't asked that nicely.

"On it," Lienna replied. And she was off, vaulting over the blocked exit with ease while we watched bemusedly. She disappeared outside, and the scorched barn seemed imperceptibly darker and colder without her presence.

Shane observed the dimly lit interior. "Tragic," he remarked. "Why kill the horses?"

"I was wondering that myself."

He tugged off a glove and placed his bare hand on the nearest stall. Ash crumbled beneath his fingers. He hurriedly donned his glove again and peered at me through his dorky round glasses. "What do you think happened here, Agent Morris?"

I almost replied with a flippant comeback about figuring it out himself, but the somber attentiveness in his question quashed my usual smartassery. Mouth thinning, I crossed the barn and scrambled over the door. Out in the chill wind, I let my gaze travel from the scorched fields to the crumpled house.

With a clatter, Shane stumbled to my side and straightened his jacket. He looked at me expectantly.

"You mentioned the level of destruction." I waved a hand at the valley. "A dark arts practitioner squashing some poor, unprepared shmuck would've left one smoking crater and nothing more. What's-her-face, the forensic alchemist, found signs of black magic all over the place. Does that mean this farm belongs to a black-magic user, and another one showed up for an apocalyptic showdown? Is this the result of a no-holds-barred battle?"

"That's what Blythe thinks," Shane murmured, not quite hiding his surprise that I actually had a brain. "Am I wrong to think you aren't sold on that theory?"

My attention slid over to the house. "The woman died near the front porch …"

"And?"

"She was just … there, like she'd walked out the door to see what the ruckus was and got obliterated in an instant." A shiver ran over me. "Where's Lienna?"

He gestured across the field, and I squinted. The rest of the team was gathered around a random patch of burnt ground. They looked busy.

"I suspect you're right," Shane said. "I don't think this was a dark arts showdown either."

With a fussy little nod, he strode away. Curious, I followed him. Bypassing the dirt path that would've led us to the others, he headed to the house. The body was now zipped up in a black bag for transport. Shane moved around it and entered the charred threshold.

I hesitated, then stepped inside. The small vestibule faced a staircase to the second floor that looked moments away from collapsing. Shane removed a glove, placed his hand on the crumbling railing, paused thoughtfully, then turned away from the stairs. I trailed after him into the kitchen, recognizable by the fire-damaged appliances. He scrutinized the room, then cautiously touched the fridge.

I waited again as he stood there, eyes glazed like he'd stubbed his toe and was desperately trying not to openly weep from the pain. Toe-stubbing was the worst.

Weirded out, I crunched past the island to the far end of the kitchen. Judging by the heaps of burnt and broken glass lying against the wall, there had been shelves here. I opened the nearest cupboard and found mostly intact plates. Lots of plates. Enough to serve dinner to Willy Wonka's entire Oompa Loompa workforce.

"How many people lived here?" I muttered. "Or did this gal love entertaining?"

"Many people."

I jumped at Shane's sudden mutter.

He pulled his hand off the fridge. "Many people lived here, but I'm getting a read on only three long-term occupants. Two men and a woman."

"You're getting a what now?"

He tugged his glove back on. "I'm a psychometric."

Cue the lightbulb above my head. "So you can read an object's past by touching it?"

I'd bet that came in handy—pardon the pun—in the world of forensics. You want to know who shot this gun last? Get a psychometric to rub their magical paws on it and they'll tell you. What better dude to invite to a mysterious crime scene?

"Is that why you wear the gloves?" I asked.

He nodded. "I don't need to know every mouth that's drunk from my mug."

"What about every ass that's sat on your toilet?"

He frowned. "My powers only extend to my hands."

"You flush, don't you?"

His frown deepened.

I shrugged. "What did you get from the fridge?"

"Kitchens are the heart of a home," he replied cryptically. "I need to read more of the house."

I followed him as he wandered through the wreckage. Some rooms were burnt beyond recognition, but we found two bedrooms with multiple bunk beds. Shane did his creepy touching thing while I moseyed around uselessly, my brain churning through the facts and a whole lot of nonsensical theorizing.

Maybe if I had one of those Sherlock Holmes hats, I could deduce my way into an "Elementary, dear Watson" breakthrough.

"So…" I prompted Shane as he pawed through a pile of thrift-store clothes that had escaped the fire by means of an indestructible tote. What name brand was that? Because I had about seventeen dollars in a savings account that I was ready to invest. "Figured out anything?"

He tossed aside a jean jacket. "Have you?"

"Maybe. You first."

Shane sat back on his heels and looked up at me. "The woman who died outside lived here, but she didn't own this property."

My eyebrows arched. "How'd you get that?"

"Ownership leaves a different feel." He threw a pair of sweats out of the tote. "What did you figure out?"

"That this wasn't a fight. Even a dark magic battle wouldn't result in *everything* getting torched. Once your opponent is dead, it doesn't make sense to burn the entire property to a crisp—unless that was the whole point."

"What are you saying?"

"I'm saying this was a massacre. Someone was sending a message, but I have no idea what that message is."

Dr. Honeydew pushed his glasses up. "I have suspicions along the same lines. The man who left traces of ownership on everything here hasn't been present in months."

That got my attention. Mr. Dark Arts Farmer had either ditched his homestead or chosen a really bad time for a vacation.

"But the burning question," Shane added, digging into the tote as he spoke, "isn't who he is but who the other people are … and …"

Eyes going out of focus, he lifted a pair of women's runners out of the bin. My nose wrinkled. A disgusting black stain had ruined the shoes, but Shane was clutching them like they'd been autographed by Serena Williams.

"… where they are now," he finished distractedly.

Still clutching the shoes. Weird. Super weird. I waited to see if he'd come back from mentally feeling up the runners, then shook my head and walked away. Shane didn't even notice.

Thoughts spinning, I picked my way back to the front porch. The plastic-wrapped body was gone, and I could see Nick and Photo-man in the distance where a single overgrown road joined the valley. A black van was parked at the edge of the trees. Clearly, not everyone was special enough for a chopper ride.

I gazed at the spot where the woman had died. If I was right, she was the victim of a power play between the mysterious attacker and the equally mysterious owner of the property.

Lienna, Blythe, and the goth alchemist—Agent Goulding— were still clustered in the same spot, and with a mental shrug, I headed toward them. As I drew closer, I spotted more torched fence posts and deduced that the ladies were in the middle of a former garden. Blythe stood off to one side, while Lienna and Goulding were crouched beside a hole in the ground.

"Whatchya digging for?" I asked casually as I stepped between two stubby posts.

"Stop!" Goulding pointed commandingly. "You can't go that way."

I halted and looked down at the sooty earth and crispy stems of overcooked plants in front of my toes. "I might not look it, but I'm more than a match for dirt clods."

"I identified the remains as plants from the Apiaceae family. If you disturb the ashes, we'll all get to enjoy vivid, violent hallucinations for the next hour."

I took a careful step back. "Sounds like this was a fun garden."

"For a practicing alchemist who specializes in poisons, maybe. Do us all a favor and don't touch *anything*."

As I circled around to enter the garden behind Blythe, Goulding bent over the hole. Beside her, Lienna was reaching into the foot-deep pit, her lovely brown eyes scrunched with concentration.

"What's happening?" I whispered dramatically to the captain.

She slashed me with the same look parents give their toddlers when they reappear after a two-minute absence covered head to toe in raspberry jam. "We uncovered a buried container. It's sealed with magic. Agent Shen is nearly finished."

I filled in the rest of that sentence: Agent Shen was nearly finished employing her extra-special, extra-difficult anti-magic abjuration. No sealing spell stood a chance against her.

Leaning closer for a better look into the hole, I spotted a dirty metal surface, upon which Lienna had drawn a double-ringed circle with runes on the inside. The shapes were complex, and she'd added several small objects around the border. Currently, she was chanting in a language I didn't recognize.

She concluded the chant with a bold exclamation of gobbledygook, then pushed to her feet.

"Well?" Blythe demanded.

"I don't know how it was sealed," Lienna replied. "It's probably dark magic, so I'm using a combination of abjuration sorcery to erase the seal and something with more punch to take out the defensive portions, if there are any."

"Wait," Agent Goulding cut in, dripping judgment. "So you don't know if this will work? You're just throwing everything at it and hoping something will stick?"

"You've got a lot of attitude, Wednesday Addams," I shot back at her, feeling more than a little protective of my partner. "Do you have a better plan?"

"Proceed, Agent Shen," Blythe said loudly.

Lienna glanced around. "We should back up a bit."

Blythe and I were out of the garden in a blink; we'd both witnessed the shit Lienna could do. I'd seen her battle demons, roundhouse-kick rogues, and reduce grown men to tears. She'd once threatened to turn all my body hair into catnip and send me to an alternate dimension populated by giant, angry housecats. That might sound outside the realm of possibility, but with Lienna, I never chanced it.

Once we were all clear, Lienna took a deep breath and uttered a final nonsensical phrase.

The runes drawn into the circle glowed so brightly that it hurt to look at them. Even from ten paces away I could feel the heat. I shielded my eyes as the metal hissed and bubbled like a pot of water boiling over.

When the light faded, I peered toward the hole. The case's metal top had melted away, gone without a trace—which didn't seem possible, but then again … magic, so …

The open case was about two feet deep and stacked with strange objects: a Russian doll, a raccoon tail, nunchucks, a crystal orb, and masks that looked like they should either be worn to a Victorian ball or in a Stanley Kubrick film. Curiosity lighting her face, Lienna stepped forward.

A deep, braying laugh interrupted her. It sounded like the cackle of a bad actor portraying a theatrical antagonist. We all glanced uncomfortably at each other as though any one of us could be the source of that villainous jubilation. Where the hell was it coming from? *Who* the hell was it coming from?

The laughter subsided and a low voice echoed from the buried case: "Greetings, purportless mortals! Welcome to the vestiges of mine own hell."

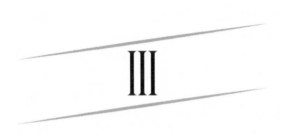

III

LIENNA CAUTIOUSLY APPROACHED the case and peered into its depths. "It's ... a talking skull."

The rest of us followed her back into the ravaged garden. Sure enough, nestled beside the Russian doll was a yellowed human skull with a faint red glow in the empty eye sockets. I hung back with Goulding, letting Lienna and Blythe flank the case.

"I am no mere skull," it retorted, glaring balefully at the two women. "I am power beyond the comprehension of your feeble female minds."

Lienna arched an eyebrow. "A *sexist* talking skull?"

"As I said, mulish heifer, I am not a skull but one of the most feared and formidable Lords of Drangfar. I once ruled—"

"Tell us what you know about this farm," Blythe interrupted, leaning over the hole threateningly.

"Am I to obey a pair of squawking hens?"

Goulding shifted closer to me, her narrowed eyes on the animated noggin. "The Drangfar Lords were mighty darkfae. Thousands of years ago, they terrorized ancient Persia until a druid and a sorceress, both the most powerful of their age, joined forces to defeat them."

"So the skull is lying?" I asked her.

"Not necessarily. The myths suggest some of them were captured, not destroyed."

"Captured ... inside a human skull?" I twisted my mouth skeptically. "How do you know any of that, anyway?"

"Pick up a book once in a while and you might learn something too, Agent Morris," she sneered.

I was thinking of a comeback when the shouting skull recaptured my attention.

"I will waste no more breath on these doltish femmes," it clamored. "Fetch me a man of authority!"

Blythe and Lienna stiffened.

"A *man*?" my partner repeated.

"Are you not familiar with the word?" the skull mocked. "A male of your species, one of the stouter sex, strong-jawed and unburdened by the salacious constitution that plagues shrews such as yourselves."

"I am the one in charge here," Blythe growled at the skull.

The cranium sighed. "The hull of the world has run aground on the beach of emasculated patriarchy."

Lienna stared at the skull in revulsion. Without looking away, she called out, "Kit, get over here."

I obliged, stopping beside her. "What's up?"

"Our bony new friend won't talk unless he's in the presence of a penis."

"I uttered no such statement!"

"Alas, poor Yorick, you pretty much did," I told the skull. "Now, do you need to see the penis or will you take my word for it? Because I'm not sure I'm comfortable with—"

"Putrid bipeds!" the skull spat.

I let out a half-laugh. "I think Skeletor is jealous of our legs."

Beside Lienna, Blythe exhaled sharply in exasperation, then extended her fingers toward the skull. It lifted out of the case and hovered in the air just below eye level.

"I'll only say this one more time," the captain grunted. "Tell us what you know about this place, or—"

"Or what?" the skull interrupted with a condescending chuckle. "Your pathetic psychic energy is but a fitful breeze brushing across a mighty stone peak, hag. This skull is a vessel, a prison for my true form, which, were you to ever lay eyes upon it, would shatter your frangible mind."

"I have a question for you, Crypt Keeper," I began.

"Hold thy ignoble tongue, eunuch."

I guess that answered my "taking my word for it" question. "You're pretty old, right?"

"My history spans millennia."

I nodded seriously. "Okay, then how come you talk like you're stuck in a bad Shakespearean performance from four hundred years ago?"

Blythe huffed, Lienna rolled her eyes, and behind us, Agent Goulding said, "Um, guys?"

"Insolent child," the skull snarled. "You haven't the faintest idea to whom you are speaking."

"Why don't you fill me in, Ghost Rider?" I shot back.

"There is magic deeper, darker, and so delightfully sinister that your tepid spirit could endure not so much as a taste. You are standing on earth which mourns in the wake of such horrific sorcery that even the blood of my keeper, a profoundly potent practitioner in his own right, chills at its name. But I—*I* am capable of far more."

"Guys!" Agent Goulding repeated loudly.

The three of us turned to look at her—and found ourselves staring into a dark shadow solidifying in the middle of the garden. We backpedaled and I almost fell into the hole.

"The hell is that?" Lienna gasped.

"It's him!" Goulding shouted. "It's the skull! You broke the seal with your stupid abjuration magic and now he's escaping!"

As a rolling, gravelly laugh poured out of the skull, Blythe flipped it around with her telekinesis. A crack ran down the back, and a thin trail of dark vapor like smoke from an oil fire, nearly invisible against the backdrop of burnt meadow, leaked out. The smoky line spiraled toward the growing shadow-blob.

Well, shit. If this asshole was, as Goulding had suggested, a genuine Drangfar Lord, we were all oh so screwed.

With a slash of her hand, Blythe tore three blackened fence posts out of the earth and flung them at the shadow. They sailed harmlessly through it and crashed to the ground on the other side, sending up a puff of soot. I hoped that wasn't "violent hallucination" soot.

The skull roared with amusement.

"We have to reseal it," Blythe announced as she sent another post flying at the shadow, eliciting more raucous laughter.

We all knew what that meant: Lienna had to work her magic. She was the only one with any sorcery skill.

Blythe waved her hand again, and the hovering skull flew toward Lienna. She snatched it out of the air—and the massive shadow rushed at her. It knocked her back and she landed on her butt, more surprised than hurt. The shadow whirled on me, and a blast of wind threw me backward. I fell at Goulding's feet.

"It's only going to get stronger," she said, crouching as the shadow spun threateningly, the swirl of darkness obscuring my line of sight to Lienna and Blythe. "The longer it has to regenerate itself, the more powerful it'll get. If it reaches its full form, there's no way we can stop it."

"Seriously, how do you know all th—"

A body flew past us—Blythe, spinning from an unseen blow. She slammed into a fence post and crumpled limply.

As I scrambled to stand, the darkfae shadow swelled to over nine feet tall. From the writhing darkness, six limbs took form, each shaped like a twisted tree trunk and emitting a neon green hue. Knife-like teeth protruded from his lizardy jaw and his spine bulged with horns. Or tusks. Or whatever the horror-monster equivalent of horny tusks were.

Cool.

Time to add some nightmare fuel of my own to this party.

"Hey, Jack Skellington," I called, sauntering along the garden's edge—moving away from the others. "I've got a few more questions for you. First up, do you suffer from arachnophobia?"

The darkfae, his monstrous body growing more solid with each second, twisted to face me—but I was no longer alone. I had my own unsightly ally: a spider the size of a small truck, with multi-jointed legs and a huge, blubbery body. Darkfae prick, meet Shelob, straight out of her hidden Cirith Ungol lair.

His reptilian head tilted as he took in my new fanged friend. Not giving him time to puzzle out what he was facing, I sent Shelob scuttling toward him in a lightning-fast charge. The darkfae lunged sideways, evading the spider's assault. For a "feared and formidable" Lord of Drangfar, he was awfully skittish.

At the other end of the garden, Lienna and Goulding knelt over the cracked skull, the ass end leaking a steady stream of black miasma. Lienna riffled through her satchel as she barked rapid-fire commands at Goulding. The alchemist mashed what looked like pink bubble gum—more likely to corrode your jaw than provide a single moment of cherry-flavored joy—into the crack.

The darkfae began to turn in their direction. Shelob launched into his path and jabbed warningly with the two-foot stinger sticking out of her jiggly ass. The fae came up short, again unsure how to tackle this strange, hideous creature. Toothy jaws snapping, he cast one of his six arms in a wide arc, and a wave of neon green light swept out. Ruptured earth sprayed everywhere as the beam passed.

I clenched my jaw with concentration.

The light hit Shelob and she rolled backward, legs flailing, then popped up again, unharmed. Behold, my invincible spider of Mordor! Nothing could hurt her—not unless I decided she could be hurt.

Which, uh, maybe I should've done.

The darkfae snarled quietly, and the red pinpricks glowing in his shadowy face—his eyes, I was guessing—swung to me. Okay, Plan B.

Shelob dug into the ground like the world's biggest, leggiest gopher and disappeared. From beneath the churning earth, something new rose: a long, bulbous head with bared teeth, three-jointed legs, skeletal body, bony tail, and glistening black skin. A perfect rendition of the Xenomorph opened her terrifying mouth and let out a ghastly shriek.

I couldn't remember the exact pitch of her shrieks in *Alien*, but close enough.

The darkfae froze, quite possibly paralyzed by the realization that he wasn't the ugliest thing ever conceived. His body had grown more solid, with spines jutting from his limbs and his six arms thrashing. The shimmers of green light over him were brightening, and where licks of neon glow touched the earth, the sooty dirt bubbled like molten goo.

The Xenomorph loosed another horrific scream—and the darkfae smiled. Maybe. With that face, it was hard to tell if he was smiling or sneering or just had some bad indigestion.

"You think me fooled, petulant boy-child?" the darkfae hissed, his arrogant laughter gone.

He strode forward, the earth seething in protest under his feet. The Xenomorph leaped at him, but this time, he didn't evade. The slimy alien passed right through his body like she wasn't even there. Which, technically …

And now nothing stood between Skully the Douchebag Darkfae and Lienna.

She had the skull in one hand and a marker in the other as she scribbled frantically across the yellowed bone and chanted in Latin. Goulding hovered helplessly beside her, gripping a silver wand—no doubt from Lienna's satchel—and gawking in terror at the approaching darkfae.

Shit on a stick. Plan C?

I ran forward, stooping to grab one of Blythe's broken fence posts as I went. With loud pops, two dozen knee-high creatures appeared, huge ears flapping and teeth-laden mouths gaping with squeaky cackles. The gremlins leaped at the advancing fae—and these ones were wet, exposed to bright lights, and glutted on a freaking feast after midnight.

308 ◆ MARIE & JACOBSEN

The fae tried to walk through them, but my evil minions weren't mere visions. When Skully McSkullfae felt their clawed hands on his shadowy legs, he lurched to a stop. Roaring, he swiped at the creatures. His toxic green talons passed through them—but he could *feel* them scrambling up his body. Sight, sound, touch—all a little too warped for him to figure out what was real and what wasn't.

With another bellow, he whirled in search for the source of the pests: me.

I was already rushing him, and as he turned, I rammed the fence post into his lizard maw. My gremlins might lack substance, but that three-foot length of splintered wood sure didn't.

The darkfae flung his head back, two of his six hands tearing the post out of his throat—but I'd forgotten about his other four hands.

Twenty clawed digits seized my arms and lifted me effortlessly. The touch of his earth-melting magic felt about as awesome as I'd imagined it would, and my vision went white with pain. Hot breath reeking of dead things bathed my face, and that gaping mouth opened wide to chomp my head off like I was a life-size gingerbread man.

Two fence posts flew out of nowhere and slammed into the fae's head from either side.

His hands opened and I dropped to the ground. As I crumpled, Lienna shouted a final Latin command. Behind the fae, she held a lighter to the pink gum sealing the crack in the skull. The gooey substance came alive in a shower of sparks and flame, and orange light swept over the bony surface.

An unearthly shriek tore from the shadowy darkfae and the green glow that had infused his limbs flared a fiery orange. He launched at Lienna, but before he could impale her on his countless claws, he disintegrated into glowing embers and dust.

A haunting howl, like wind slipping through a window crack in a sixties horror flick, rose from the skull. The beast's ashen remains swirled into a funnel cloud that was sucked into the eye sockets. The bubble gum fire faded and Lienna slumped onto her butt, breathing hard, with the skull balanced on one palm. Its eyes glowed red, but the crack was gone.

"Holy shit," I wheezed. "You did it."

"Agent Morris." Blythe limped into my field of vision. *That's* where the final flying logs had come from. Made more sense now. "How badly are you injured?"

I glanced at my arms. My sleeves had melted away and my skin looked like hot dogs that were roasted in a campfire too long.

Goulding hurried over to me, her brows pinched together. "I can help. I have burn treatments and magical residue neutralizers in my bag. Give me a minute."

As she rushed off, I picked myself up off the ground and pretended I didn't want to whine pathetically from the throbbing agony in my arms. Asshole fae. Speaking of which …

I shot a nasty look at the skull. "No commentary from the newly resealed peanut gallery?"

Silence.

"Nothing?" I asked, peering harder at the glowing eyes.

Nope. Nothing.

Lienna handed the skull to Blythe. "I think my seal is stronger than the original one. The fae can't speak anymore."

Blythe glowered into those red eyes as though she could pry answers out of it with sheer force of will. Considering what else she could do with sheer force of will, I wouldn't be surprised if she succeeded.

Lienna leaned toward me and asked softly, "You okay, Kit?"

I forced a smile, like a proper wounded hero. "I'll be fine."

"Well," Blythe barked, sounding remarkably normal despite the way she was listing to one side. I wasn't the only one in need of healing. "Where are we at?"

"Whoever owned this farm buried a case of dark artifacts in their alchemy garden," Lienna said promptly. "They were from a mixture of magic classes, including Spiritalis, which suggests the owner is a collector of some kind."

"The woman who died on the front steps wasn't the owner," I added. "And whoever killed her did everything they could to destroy this place as viciously as possible, probably as a big ol' FU slap to the farm's real owner."

Lienna and Blythe stared at me. What? Hadn't they figured that out yet?

"I thought we had one dark arts master on the loose," Blythe growled. "Not two."

"Two highly dangerous rogues who are at war with each other." Lienna stared at the scorched valley, the beads in her long hair clinking from the cold wind. "With magic that can inflict damage like this ..."

"We need to uncover what really happened." Blythe looked between us. "Agent Shen, Agent Morris, this is your case now. Find out who owns this farm, where they are, and who killed the woman. Find out everything—and report directly to me. Involve no one else."

Lienna's eyes widened a fraction, and I suspected we were wondering the same thing. Why did Blythe want us to keep this investigation quiet? Was she hiding something from the

MPD or worried someone in the MPD was hiding things from her?

Crunching footsteps approached us. I was desperately hoping it was Goulding with the promised magical pain relief—each gust of wind felt like a thousand bee stings at once—but it was Shane. He carried a brown paper bag that looked about the right size to hold a pair of women's shoes. At least he wasn't stroking them anymore.

Weirdo.

"Mr. Davila," Blythe greeted. "I trust you've made some headway here."

What a nice way to imply that he'd better have made himself useful in the house since his gutless ass hadn't made a single appearance during our life and death battle.

He gave a thin smile. "I think I have everything I need."

Blythe nodded. "I'll call the helicopter. It's time we returned to the city."

She strode away, steadier than before. I allowed one tiny, near-silent whimper as a fresh gust of winter wind stung my burns. Lienna inched closer, her face drawn with concern. Maybe I'd keep the burns for a bit longer. Go back home, let her tenderly bandage my wounds. Maybe she'd shed a heartbroken tear over my suffering, bravely earned in the course of—

Shane's intent stare broke into my happy fantasy. I met his eyes behind those round glasses, wondering what he was thinking—and what "headway" he'd made. Was he investigating this case too, or was he seeking a different prize?

Turning away from the bounty hunter, I asked Lienna, "Do you think there's another way to get back to the city from here?"

Her brows furrowed. "Another way?"

"Yeah, like another mode of transportation? Maybe a hovercraft? Or a hang glider? Crossing two things off my bucket list in one day is also on my bucket list."

Ah, the eye roll. I'd needed that. Flashing her my most charming smile—impressive considering the amount of pain I was in—I invited her to join me with a tilt of my head. Together, we started toward the house and wherever Goulding was dawdling with her alchemic bag of healing potions.

However I got home, I wasn't too worried. This new case promised to be an interesting one, mysterious in a way that made my fingertips tingle with a mixture of anticipation and unfiltered dread. Maybe my travel ambitions would be realized with something crazy like a hot-air balloon or one of those glass balls from *Jurassic World*, but even if I ended up on something lame—like a canoe or, worse, a tandem bicycle—it'd be a new adventure with Lienna.

And I couldn't complain about that.

KIT'S ADVENTURES CONTINUE IN

ROGUE GHOSTS & OTHER MISCREANTS
THE GUILD CODEX: WARPED / THREE

As a former con-artist, I love a convoluted, mind-bending scheme as much as the next guy. But as a recently promoted MagiPol agent, I love it significantly less than that guy.

Especially when the life of a kidnapped teen hangs in the balance.

Between confusing orders and conflicting evidence, this whole investigation has me and my partner, Lienna, spinning in circles. Why is our boss keeping this case off the books? Why is our top suspect, the most notorious rogue in Vancouver, mired in contradictions? And why am I the only one who cares more about the victim than their own ulterior motives?

Everyone wants me to shut up and follow orders, but that's not my style. I'll do whatever it takes to save this kid—even if that means returning to my roguish roots.

www.guildcodex.ca

ABOUT THE AUTHORS

ANNETTE MARIE is the author of YA urban fantasy series *Steel & Stone*, its prequel trilogy *Spell Weaver*, and romantic fantasy trilogy *Red Winter*.

Her first love is fantasy, but fast-paced adventures, bold heroines, and tantalizing forbidden romances are her guilty pleasures. She proudly admits she has a thing for dragons, and her editor has politely inquired as to whether she intends to include them in every book.

Annette lives in the frozen winter wasteland of Alberta, Canada (okay, it's not quite that bad) and shares her life with her husband and their furry minion of darkness—sorry, cat—Caesar. When not writing, she can be found elbow-deep in one art project or another while blissfully ignoring all adult responsibilities.

www.annettemarie.ca

ROB JACOBSEN is a Canadian writer, actor, and director, who has been in a few TV shows you might watch, had a few films in festivals you might have attended, and authored some stories you might have come across. He's hoping to accomplish plenty more by the time he inevitably dies surrounded by cats while watching reruns of Mr. Robot.

Currently, he is the Creative Director of Cave Puppet Films, as well as the co-author of the Guild Codex: Warped series with Annette Marie.

www.robjacobsen.ca

SPECIAL THANKS

Our thanks to Erich Merkel for sharing your exceptional expertise in Latin and Ancient Greek.

Any errors are the authors'.

THE
GUILD CODEX
WARPED

The MPD has three roles: keep magic hidden, keep mythics under control, and don't screw up the first two.

Kit Morris is the wrong guy for the job on all counts—but for better or worse, this mind-warping psychic is the MPD's newest and most unlikely agent.

DISCOVER MORE BOOKS AT
www.guildcodex.ca

THE ──────
GUILD CODEX
SPELLBOUND

Meet Tori. She's feisty. She's broke. She has a bit of an issue with running her mouth off. And she just landed a job at the local magic guild. Problem is, she's also 100% human. Oops.

Welcome to the Crow and Hammer.

DISCOVER MORE BOOKS AT
www.guildcodex.ca

THE
GUILD CODEX
DEMONIZED

Robin Page: outcast sorceress, mythic history buff, unapologetic
bookworm, and the last person you'd expect to command the rarest
demon in the long history of summoning. Though she holds his
leash, this demon can't be controlled.

But can he be tamed?

THE
GUILD CODEX
UNVEILED

Meet Saber Rose: a witch with a switchblade for a best friend, a murder conviction on her rap sheet, and a dangerous lack of restraint.

All she wanted was to be left alone—until *he* showed up.
The Crystal Druid. Together, they might be unstoppable ... if they don't destroy each other first.

DISCOVER MORE BOOKS AT
www.guildcodex.ca

STEEL & STONE

When everyone wants you dead, good help is hard to find.

The first rule for an apprentice Consul is *don't trust daemons*. But when Piper is framed for the theft of the deadly Sahar Stone, she ends up with two troublesome daemons as her only allies: Lyre, a hotter-than-hell incubus who isn't as harmless as he seems, and Ash, a draconian mercenary with a seriously bad reputation. Trusting them might be her biggest mistake yet.

GET THE COMPLETE SERIES
www.annettemarie.ca/steelandstone

The only thing more dangerous than the denizens of the Underworld ... is stealing from them.

As a daemon living in exile among humans, Clio has picked up some unique skills. But pilfering magic from the Underworld's deadliest spell weavers? Not so much. Unfortunately, that's exactly what she has to do to earn a ticket home.

GET THE COMPLETE TRILOGY
www.annettemarie.ca/spellweaver

A destiny written by the gods. A fate forged by lies.

If Emi is sure of anything, it's that *kami*—the gods—are good, and *yokai*—the earth spirits—are evil. But when she saves the life of a fox shapeshifter, the truths of her world start to crumble. And the treachery of the gods runs deep.

This stunning trilogy features 30 full-page illustrations.

GET THE COMPLETE TRILOGY
www.annettemarie.ca/redwinter

Made in United States
Troutdale, OR
08/23/2023

12327309R00213